BRIAN FLYNN

THE EDGE OF TERROR

With an introduction by
Steve Barge

DEAN STREET PRESS

BRIAN FLYNN
THE EDGE OF TERROR

BRIAN FLYNN was born in 1885 in Leyton, Essex. He won a scholarship to the City Of London School, and from there went into the civil service. In World War I he served as Special Constable on the Home Front, also teaching "Accountancy, Languages, Maths and Elocution to men, women, boys and girls" in the evenings, and acting in his spare time.

It was a seaside family holiday that inspired Brian Flynn to turn his hand to writing in the mid-twenties. Finding most mystery novels of the time "mediocre in the extreme", he decided to compose his own. Edith, the author's wife, encouraged its completion, and after a protracted period finding a publisher, it was eventually released in 1927 by John Hamilton in the UK and Macrae Smith in the U.S. as *The Billiard-Room Mystery*.

The author died in 1958. In all, he wrote and published 57 mysteries, the vast majority featuring the super-sleuth Antony Bathurst.

INTRODUCTION

"I believe that the primary function of the mystery story is to entertain; to stimulate the imagination and even, at times, to supply humour. But it pleases the connoisseur most when it presents – and reveals – genuine mystery. To reach its full height, it has to offer an intellectual problem for the reader to consider, measure and solve."

BRIAN Flynn began his writing career with *The Billiard Room Mystery* in 1927, primarily at the prompting of his wife Edith who had grown tired of hearing him say he could write a better mystery novel than the ones he had been reading. Four more books followed under his original publisher, John Hamilton, before he moved to John Long, who would go on to publish the remaining forty-eight of his Anthony Bathurst mysteries, along with his three Sebastian Stole titles, released under the pseudonym Charles Wogan. Some of the early books were released in the US, and there were also a small number of translations of his mysteries into Swedish and German. In the article from which the above quote is taken, Brian also claims that there were French and Danish translations but to date, I have not found a single piece of evidence for their existence. Tracking down all of his books written in the original English has been challenging enough!

Reprints of Brian's books were rare. Four titles were released as paperbacks as part of John Long's Four Square Thriller range in the late 1930s, four more re-appeared during the war from Cherry Tree Books and Mellifont Press, albeit abridged by at least a third, and two others that I am aware of, *Such Bright Disguises* (1941) and *Reverse The Charges* (1943), received a paperback release as part of John Long's Pocket Edition range in the early 1950s – these were also possibly abridged, but only by about 10%. These were the exceptions, rather than the rule, however, and it was not until 2019, when Dean Street Press released his first ten titles, that his work was generally available again.

The question still persists as to why his work disappeared from the awareness of all but the most ardent collectors. As you may expect, when a title was only released once, back in the early 1930s, finding copies of the original text is not a straightforward matter – not even Brian's estate has a copy of every title. We are particularly grateful to one particular collector for providing *The Edge Of Terror*, Brian's first serial killer tale, in order for this next set of ten books to be republished without an obvious gap!

By the time Brian Flynn's eleventh novel, *The Padded Door* (1932), was published, he was producing a steady output of Anthony Bathurst mysteries, averaging about two books a year. While this may seem to be a rapid output, it is actually fairly average for a crime writer of the time. Some writers vastly exceeded this – in the same period of time that it took Brian to have ten books published, John Street, under his pseudonyms John Rhode and Miles Burton published twenty-eight!

In this period, in 1934 to be precise, an additional book was published, *Tragedy At Trinket*. It is a schoolboy mystery, set at Trinket, "one of the two finest schools in England – in the world!" combining the tale of Trinket's attempts to redeem itself in the field of schoolboy cricket alongside the apparently accidental death by drowning of one of the masters. It was published by Thomas Nelson and Sons, rather than John Long, and was the only title published under his own name not to feature Bathurst. It is unlikely, however, that this was an attempt to break away from his sleuth, given that the hero of this tale is Maurice Otho Folliott, a schoolboy who just happens to be Bathurst's nephew and is desperate to emulate his uncle! It is an odd book, with a significant proportion of the tale dedicated to the tribulations of the cricket team, but Brian does an admirable job of weaving an actual death into a genre that was generally concerned with misunderstandings and schoolboy pranks.

Not being in the top tier of writers, at least in terms of public awareness, reviews of Brian's work seem to have been rare, but when they did occur, there were mostly positive. A reviewer in the Sunday Times enthused over *The Edge Of Terror* (1932), describing it as "an enjoyable thriller in Mr. Flynn's best manner" and Torquemada in the *Observer* says that *Fear and Trembling* (1936) "gripped my interest on a sleepless night and held it to the end". Even Dorothy L. Sayers, a fairly unforgiving reviewer at times, had positive things to say in the *Sunday Times* about *The Case For The Purple Calf* (1934) ("contains some ingenuities") and *The Horn* (1934) ("good old-fashioned melodrama . . . not without movement") although she did take exception to Brian's writing style. Milward Kennedy was similarly disdainful, although Kennedy, a crime writer himself, criticising a style of writing might well be considered the pot calling the kettle black. He was impressed, however, with the originality of *Tread Softly* (1937).

It is quite possible that Brian's harshest critic, though, was himself. In *The Crime Book Magazine* he wrote about the current output of detective fiction: "I delight in the dazzling erudition that has come to grace and decorate the craft of the 'roman policier'. He then goes on to say: "At the same time, however, I feel my own comparative unworthiness for the fire and burden of the competition." Such a feeling may well be the reason why he never made significant inroads into the social side of crime-writing, such as the Detection Club or the Crime Writers' Association. Thankfully, he uses this sense of unworthiness as inspiration, concluding: "The stars, though, have always been the most desired of all goals, so I allow exultation and determination to take the place of that but temporary dismay."

Reviews, both external and internal, thankfully had no noticeable effect on Brian's writing. What is noticeable about his work is how he shifts from style to style from each book. While all the books from this period remain classic whodunits, the style shifts from courtroom drama to gothic darkness, from plotting serial killers to events that spiral out of control, with Anthony Bathurst the constant thread tying everything together.

We find some books narrated by a Watson-esque character, although a different character each time. Occasionally Bathurst himself will provide a chapter or two to explain things either that the narrator wasn't present for or just didn't understand. Bathurst doesn't always have a Watson character to tell his stories, however, so other books are in the third person – as some of Bathurst's adventures are not tied to a single location, this is often the case in these tales.

One element that does become more common throughout books eleven to twenty is the presence of Chief Detective Inspector Andrew MacMorran. While MacMorran gets a name check from as early as *The Mystery Of The Peacock's Eye* (1928), his actual appearances in the early books are few and far between, with others such as Inspector Baddeley (*The Billiard Room Mystery* (1927), *The Creeping Jenny Mystery* (1929)) providing the necessary police presence. As the series progresses, the author settled more and more on a regular showing from the police. It still isn't always the case – in some books, Bathurst is investigating undercover and hence by himself, and in a few others, various police Inspectors appear, notably the return of the aforementioned Baddeley in *The Fortescue Candle* (1936). As the series progresses from *The Padded Door* (1932), Inspector MacMorran becomes more and more of a fixture at Scotland Yard for Bathurst.

One particular trait of the Bathurst series is the continuity therein. While the series can be read out of order, there is a sense of what has gone before. While not to the extent of, say, E.R. Punshon's Bobby Owen books, or Christopher Bush's Ludovic Travers mysteries, there is a clear sense of what has gone before. Side characters from books reappear, either by name or in physical appearances – Bathurst is often engaged on a case by people he has helped previously. Bathurst's friendship with MacMorran develops over the books from a respectful partnership to the point where MacMorran can express his exasperation with Bathurst's annoying habits rather vocally. Other characters appear and develop too, for example Helen Repton, but she is, alas, a story for another day.

The other sign of continuity is Bathurst's habit of name-dropping previous cases, names that were given to them by Bathurst's "chronicler". *Fear and Trembling* mentions no less than five separate cases, with one, *The Sussex Cuckoo* (1935), getting two mentions. These may seem like little more than adverts for those titles, old-time product placement if you will – "you've handled this affair about as brainily as I handled 'The Fortescue Candle'", for example – but they do actually make sense in regard to what has gone before, given how long it took Bathurst to see the light in each particular case. Contrast this to the reference to Christie's *Murder On The Orient Express* in *Cards On The Table*, which not only gives away the ending but contradicts Poirot's actions at the dénouement.

> "For my own detective, Anthony Lotherington Bathurst, I have endeavoured to place him in the true Holmes tradition. It is not for me to say whether my efforts have failed or whether I have been successful."

Brian Flynn seemed determined to keep Bathurst's background devoid of detail – I set out in the last set of introductions the minimal facts that we are provided with: primarily that he went to public school and Oxford University, can play virtually every sport under the sun and had a bad first relationship and has seemingly sworn off women since. Of course, the detective's history is something not often bothered with by crime fiction writers, but this usually occurs with older sleuths who have lived life, so to speak. *Cold Evil* (1938), the twenty-first Bathurst mystery, finally pins down Bathurst's age, and we find that in *The Billiard Room Mystery*, his first outing, he was a fresh-faced Bright Young Thing of twenty-two. So how he can survive with his own rooms, at least two servants, and no noticeable source of income remains a mystery. One can also ask at what point in his life he travelled the world, as he has, at least, been to Bangkok at some point. It is, perhaps, best not to analyse Bathurst's past too carefully . . .

> "Judging from the correspondence my books have excited it seems I have managed to achieve some measure of success for my faithful readers comprise a circle in

which high dignitaries of the Church rub shoulders with their brothers and sisters of the common touch."

For someone who wrote to entertain, such correspondence would have delighted Brian, and I wish he were around to see how many people enjoyed the first set of reprints of his work. His family are delighted with the reactions that people have passed on, and I hope that this set of books will delight just as much.

The Edge of Terror (1932)

"Within the next six months from to-day, that is to say by the 31st day of August next, I shall have removed from your midst one of the most prominent citizens of your most atrocious town."

IT SEEMS today that serial killers are ten-a-penny, in crime fiction at least, but this isn't a modern innovation – classic detective fiction has its fair share of multiple murderers as well, although the term "serial killer" was yet to enter common usage. While the German "Serienmörder" – serial murderer – was coined by Ernst Gennat in 1930, it was not, according to the *Oxford English Dictionary*, until the 1960s that the phrase appeared in English. It was probably not a coincidence that the article it appeared in was written by a German writer about the German film, *M*, but it was not until the 1980s that the phrase entered common usage.

Lack of the phrase did not, however, prevent such characters entering classic detective fiction, but it posed a problem for the writer of the pure mystery, in that it was particularly hard to ascribe a motive to such crimes. The author is left with two primary options – either the victims are linked or they are picked at random.* If the victims are picked for a reason, it is often the case that the reason should have been discovered well before

---

* There is one notable other option for an author, but I hesitate to describe it as, if the reader has not encountered it before, it can catch them completely off-guard and I would hate to spoil that experience.

the dénouement of the tale. If the victims are truly chosen at random, it is hard to create a convincing procedural detective story. Many writers have, however, tried. I feel duty bound not to cite examples, as that could spoil the reader's enjoyment of the tales, and there are a number of highly enjoyable specimens of each type. I will just recommend a few titles at random that the curious reader could investigate without saying which is which. These are *The Murders in Praed Street* (1928) by John Rhode, *Death Walks In Eastrepps* (1931) by Francis Beeding, *The ABC Murders* by Agatha Christie and both *X v Rex* (1933) and *Murder Gone Mad* (1931) by Philip MacDonald, the latter being named by John Dickson Carr as one of his top ten mysteries of all time.

Brian Flynn took on the serial killer tale at least twice, in *The Seventh Sign* (1952) and here, in *The Edge Of Terror* (1932), with Anthony Bathurst pitting his wits against "The Eagle". Flynn does a good job of avoiding the common traps in the genre by revealing a reasonable chunk of the killer's motivation sooner rather than later, and making it one applicable to more than one character in the tale, hence keeping the story as a proper mystery.

It's also a story in which a small hole is filled regarding Anthony Bathurst's past. In *The Orange Axe* (1931), we learned that Bathurst didn't pursue romantic relationships due to his first ending badly. Here we meet the lady in question, one Mrs Rosemary Coterill, and we gain a little more insight into our hero. As far as I am aware, we never meet Rosemary again, but it does mean that Bathurst from hereon will occasionally – very occasionally – have a romantic subplot, most notably in *Fear and Trembling* (1936).

For a while, it did look as if *The Edge Of Terror* would be the book that got away – not even Brian's estate had a copy of it, and the one copy that could be found for sale had a stratospheric price tag. We are therefore very thankful to a generous collector of Brian's work who allowed us to use his copy in order to prepare this new edition. It is one of my favourite Bathurst tales and I hope that you enjoy it too.

Steve Barge

Chapter I
THE FIRST MURDER

LET me admit, first of all, that I'm a perfectly rotten hand at telling a story. I may as well confess that before the umpire gives me "two leg". More than that, I never entertained the wildest dream that I should be called upon to do the job. But everybody connected with the show seems to think that it's up to me—so here goes. Just a shade more? Thanks, umpire.

There are various reasons advanced in support of this opinion that I have just mentioned, and I've never heard two given alike. . . . One person argues that I was on the spot, as it were, from the time when the first murder occurred; another says that I was well in at the death (which, come to think of it, might mean exactly the same thing—but doesn't); and a third will flutter round and wax flattering, start chucking bouquets and gurgle more or less incoherently about the help I was to the authorities and so on—all of which is blithering tripe and beautifully dressed at that. The best reason of the lot, they glide peacefully over, and it's in obedience to that last reason that I'm going to pitch the yarn after all.

I'm going right back to the beginning of everything, because it's essential that you should have the facts in some sort of chronological order. I'm going to tell you how the evening of the 31st of August brought back to me by one of those strange shafts of coincidence that are continually being projected, the first incident of the whole ghastly business; an incident, too, which I had at that time almost completely forgotten. It had been a blazing day, that last day in August, and although I'm as keen as the next man on hot summery weather, I had come home from my day's round pretty well all in. I'd had a gruelling time since first thing in the morning, and things had reached a staggering climax when the Resident M.O. sent for me to run over to the Isolation Hospital at Chelmersley for a special tracheotomy "op." on a nipper there, who was about as bad with laryngeal diph. as the poor little devil pretty well could be.

Holmes, the M.O. in question, had a septic finger which turned out afterwards to be tubercular dactylitis, and his deputy was on holiday leave. All the way there, I cursed like hell. I knew the kid. Third boy of one of my own patients in Great Steeping—a Mrs. Barron. (My God, the perversity of names!) Let me tell you, too, that there were more reasons than one why I cursed. Oh—infinitely! For one thing I was most messily and stickily hot; for another, I knew I wasn't carrying any too much petrol—I was on the reserve tank; and for a third I was excessively annoyed at the mother's blasted pig-headedness. All her brood, from Reuben and Simeon, to Asher, Joseph, and Benjamin, were throaty subjects. Tonsilitis positively thrived in 'em—and septic throats held red-hot revel. Two boys had already had diph. and for months now I had been urging upon her to send the whole dozen up to me for immunization. All the darned old fool had done in response to my suggestion had been to shake her muddy-brained head at me and revile Jenner (of all people); and now here was I on the way to slit another windpipe. . . . Curse the woman! Net result of it all was that when I ran the bus into my own little place, the hour-hand was well past seven and my temper most distinctly frayed and ragged.

Dear old Mrs. Ramage met me as soon as I had put away the bus and was crawling into my little dining-room.

"I know you're tired, sir, and hungry as well. . . . What a long day you've had to be sure. . . . how long shall I give you before I serve dinner, sir?" She wrinkled her face at me.

I'm afraid that I was horribly ungracious. "Don't bother about dinner, Mrs. Ramage," I returned savagely. "I've gone past my time. I'm hot, tired, and—er—vindictive. Too hot to eat, too tired to talk, but not too vindictive to murder people who behave like blasted fools."

I slouched to the sideboard and helped myself to a healthy "spot" of Scotch. As I pressed the siphon I noticed that the old girl was shaking her head at me. "I'm going to fall in the bath, Mrs. Ramage," I added rather lamely, "and thank, the Creator for cold water—er—that is for external application."

As I was necking my third "spot" of Scotch, Mrs. Ramage addressed me again. She smiled at me with the full radiance of the maternal instinct.

"You'll feel much better, sir, when you've had a bit of rest. I'll have something ready for you in about half an hour's time. Something you'll like."

She commenced to retreat before me in the pukka Ramage manner to the place in my modest dwelling-house where she belonged.

"No, I shan't," I said snappily. "I know quite well how I feel. Nobody else does. And God alone knows why I ever came down to a wretched, miserable, hell-blistered hole like—" Mrs. Ramage shook her venerable head again and shut the door behind her. She didn't see the ultimate grin that I favoured her fat back with. I took good care that she didn't, and it hadn't quite flitted from my face by the time that I reached the top of the stairs.

A perfectly pleasing bath, a nice cool shave, and I slid gratefully into my glad-rags with a sigh of semi-contentment. As I looked at my image in the mirror, and flicked a fragment of fluff from the lapel of my dinner-jacket, I muttered to myself my most appreciative approval of the idea of dressing for dinner, and drank an imaginary toast in honour of the wise guy who first thought of it. I called to mind the many thousands of times when I had reviled it as a poisonous practice and marvelled at the everlasting wisdom and eternal truth underlined by the old "tag" of "tempora" and "mores".

When I blew downstairs again, newly tubbed and freshly razored, Mrs. Ramage's efforts on my behalf, from the cuisine, took on an added commendableness. The dear old soul had a most positive and uncanny flair for doing the right thing. She had cut out the soup and the joint, and had served me up the most delicious lobster salad. It would have gratified the Angelic host and brought tears of joy to the eyes of Cherubim and Seraphim. Shellfish has always been a weakness of mine and I never remember an occasion when a lobster has tasted better— or even as well. How damnably lucky I was, I argued to myself, to have got hold of a housekeeper of the Ramage calibre. Twenty minutes later the door opened and she brought me in one of her famous loganberry souffles.

Nobody—since the asp bit Cleopatra and Charmian—ever made a better soufflé than the Ramage. A little less of cornflour and a little more of cream were, I think, her two especial secrets.

I sat back in my chair eventually, at peace with my whole world. I thought of them one by one. There was old Bligh, the Chief Constable over at Chelmersley; Jack Tabernacle, my nearest neighbour, who spent a good portion of each year in Rome when he might have stayed in Great Steeping and played billiards with me; and even the before-mentioned Mrs. Barron, the lugubrious mother of the throaty dozen.

I remember that I had just lit a cigar and poured out another "spot" of "Lochinvar", when my eye strayed a bit and caught the ivory tablet calendar that stood on my desk in the corner of the room. Mrs. Ramage looked after its indications each morning— ides, nones and kalends. The date that it showed now, and at which I found myself looking, was, of course, the 31st of August. As I looked at it, I puzzled for just a second or so as to what was familiar about it. Then it all buzzed back to me. You know how this sort of thing will happen to almost anybody. One moment you're dithering about, saying to yourself what the hell, and the next, a flash of light gets loose somewhere and floods across the brain, and there, in front of you, is the very thread for which you've been almost hopelessly groping.

That is what happened to me on this particular occasion. The connection for which I had been seeking, came, when it did come, quite suddenly.

It was so insistent that it made me cross over to my desk and rummage therein for the paper that I wanted. I had shoved it in there some months previously, I knew, and I was forced to go some way down the pile of documents (mostly bills and receipts for the same darned things) before I came to the paper I wanted.

Found, I smoothed it out religiously, and yanked it over to my armchair to read it again. What I looked at was a copy which I had made, out of interest and for convenience, of a letter which had been sent six months previously to Goodaker, the Inspector of Police over at Chelmersley.

The bright effort was worded as follows:

London, Feb. 28th.

To Inspector Goodaker, Police Station, Chelmersley, Essex. Sir,

The town of Chelmersley and its environs are far from pleasing to me. On each occasion when an unkind Fate has decreed that I should be in its vicinity, insult and annoyance have been accorded me. Which is unfortunate, for I never forget! Kindly note therefore, that I have decided to take matters into my own hands. Within the next six months from to-day, that is to say by the 31st day of August next, I shall have removed from your midst one of the most prominent citizens of your most atrocious town. I have not yet made up my mind which one I shall honour in this way, or the exact day upon which the removal will take place. Circumstances will guide me. Moreover, the matter may not end there! Of that, however, more anon. Sufficient for the period ending the 31st August will be the evil thereof.

I remain,
Sincerely yours,
"The Eagle."

God knows why I should have looked at the calendar and remembered the date because the whole thing, months old as it was, had almost passed from my mind.

Goodaker himself had received it on the third of March and one day soon after that, when I had been in the police station professionally, had called me over and shown it to me. Like him, I had treated the matter as a hoax, and had grinned at him cheerfully and fatuously when I had handed it back to him.

"Somebody taking a fat and juicy mike at you, Goodaker," I suggested.

"Just my idea, Doctor. London postmark and typed, on an oldish typewriter. All the same, though, I'm getting on to the 'Yard' to see if this strange bird who calls himself 'The Eagle' is known to them up there at all."

I nodded. "Let me take a copy of it, will you?" He nodded back and I had dashed off the copy of the letter at which I now found myself looking. A day or so later—somewhere about the twelfth of March—when I had been passing, he had chirruped to me and told me that the "Yard" had had his message but couldn't help him.

"No 'Eagle' known up there, Doctor. It's a mare's nest all right. No action."

When I had got home after the first talk about it, I had poked my copy into my desk and hadn't handled it again until now. The date, I suggest, had burnt itself into my memory—hence these tears. I tossed it on to the desk and drew luxuriously at my cigar. There was one thing—the fact that nothing startling had happened, and to-day being the 31st ... at that moment my telephone rang. Cursing volubly and audibly, I leant over to it and unhooked the receiver.

"Hallo, yes, yes ... that you, Doctor Bannerman?"

"Yes," I answered again, "Bannerman speaking. Who is it? Who? Goodaker? Well, what the hell do you want of me at this time? I've been at work for God knows how long, looking after your beastly ... What? The date? Now, that's damned funny, Goodaker. It is really. I was thinking of that when this wretched telephone buzzed in my ear. I was slow. Ought to have guessed there was a blithering fool at the other end of it. What?"

I stopped assing about abruptly, and set myself seriously to listen to what Goodaker had to say.

"What I'm telling you, Doctor Bannerman, is a solemn fact. Been received this evening. Posted in Chelmersley this morning. Made up my mind to tell you about it because you know of the other." I marvelled.

"What's it got to say this time, Goodaker, and how?"

"I can't do better than read it to you, Doctor. Quite short, but far from sweet. Listen. *Sir, I have at length arrived in Chelmersley. You are already acquainted with the purpose that has brought me. You alone—unless you have betrayed a confidence. Fuller details, however, will be yours by the morning.*

Apologising for having misspelt your name in my previous communication, I remain, sincerely yours, Aquila."

"What's that?" I interrogated. "That last word?"

"Aquila. A-q-u-i-l-a." The Inspector spelt it to me over the 'phone, letter by letter.

I nodded acceptance rather ridiculously—as one does, I think, when speaking on the 'phone in this way—and immediately asked him a further question.

"This second business—is it typed again?"

"No, Doctor. Not this time."

I caught what sounded suspiciously like a chuckle.

"Good Lord—you don't mean that it's written, do you?" There was an undoubted grunt now.

"No such luck as that. Listen carefully, Doctor. 'The message is on a postcard which is itself enclosed within an ordinary plain envelope.'"

"Yes, yes," I exclaimed in impatient interruption, "that's all right; but what about—"

"Wait, Doctor, please. All in good time. Give me just a moment for explanation and you'll see. The words of the message have been cut from a newspaper (or newspapers) and stuck or gummed on to the card. Get me?"

I reflected. "H'm. Pretty cute, that. What about the address itself?"

"Same method exactly," returned Goodaker laconically. "My own name's been cut, no doubt, from a recent issue of one of the local papers."

"From one of the police-court reports, you mean, I suppose?"

"You've hit it, Doctor. I reckon it's the same man, you know, that sent the other letter, despite the difference in the signature—apart from what he says himself about my name."

"You can be sure of that. There's no difference really, Goodaker," I called down the 'phone. "Aquila's only another name for the Eagle. It's the Latin form, that's all. I still remember half a dozen words or so. Don't worry your muddy old brain against that."

This time there was no doubt of the chuckle that came to me down the instrument. "Worry! You don't say! I said it was a hoax before and I say the same thing again now." He paused for a moment as though inviting my opinion. I said nothing, however. I waited. The pause was broken.

"Don't you think so yourself, Doctor?" he asked. Again I waited before replying. Unless I were very greatly mistaken there was just the slightest shade of anxiety in his voice.

"Some ass playing a practical joke," I said. "That's my opinion. Don't lose your usual dose of 'shut-eye' over it, Goodaker."

"I can't *do* anything, Doctor, can I?"

"Don't see that you can, within reason. You tried the 'Yard' before and they weren't able to help you. What more can you do? Oh, chuck it, Goodaker. You're a confounded nuisance. Go and fold your fat face round a pot of good beer. The wine of the country, Goodaker. As dispensed by the fair Hebes at the 'White Lion' and the 'Cat and Coffee-pot'. If I were in Chelmersley, I'm hanged if I wouldn't join you. I've a perfectly marvellous thirst. My grandfather would have given quids for it and he included brown herrings in his diet, too. Cheero!" I rang off.

The rest of the evening, I messed about generally. Went down to my little billiard-table, knocked the balls about a bit and then tried to bowl the "Bosey" ball in the way that B.J.T. himself had spun it all those years before. When I had perpetrated a couple of topping "Chinamen", I turned to other things. I cursed Jack Tabernacle, my nearest neighbour (as I think I have already told you), for not being handy so that he could be playing "snooker" with me and, eventually, after two or three more "spots" of Scotch toddled off to Uncle Ned for the "shut-eye" that I had recommended to Goodaker. I slept well, albeit it was devilishly hot and sticky throughout the whole of the night, in spite of a drizzling rain that began to fall about eleven o'clock.

Morning came, and I had just donned my dressing-gown and was bowling along to the bathroom, when I heard that confounded 'phone start ringing again downstairs. I flew down, wondering who it was that could want me so early in the morning. I couldn't reasonably hope that it was Rosemary. Also,

I could think of no lady—prospective mother of a male or female child—whom I could rationally expect to be . . .

"Yes, yes, Bannerman speaking. Who? Goodaker again? What is it this time? More letters?" Directly he started to speak the tone of his voice sobered and steadied me.

"No, Doctor. Not letters this time. Walter Fredericks has been found by a milk-boy this morning in Taggarts Way—the lane that runs between Chelmersley and Cressing. You know that piece of waste ground there. Dead. Murdered."

"Good God!" I gasped. "How?"

"His throat has been cut, Doctor. From ear to ear." He paused for a second and then added something in what was almost a whisper, "What about the 'Eagle' now?"

CHAPTER II

I AM FLATTERED

I LET go a low and unintelligent whistle.

"I'll be down to you right now, Goodaker," I said, "as quickly as I can possibly do it, man. Say in forty minutes. That suit you?" I rushed my fences, both bath and razor, took a piece out of my ear, got the car out and blazed away down to the Chelmersley police station. On the way I mused thus. Walter Fredericks! Walter Fredericks of all people in Chelmersley! That death is no respecter of persons, I am well aware. None better. Any doctor is almost daily aware of that fact. All the same, the murder of Walter Fredericks (accepting Goodaker's version of the business as authentic for the time being) had partly stunned me.

Hereabouts, let me say something about Fredericks himself. In the first place, he was a comparatively wealthy man. Certainly one of the richest men in the town and adjoining district of Chelmersley. He had come there years before (many years before me, for instance), taken a big house just off the road between Chelmersley and the hamlet of Great Steeping, where I lived, and had continued to make money in more than one direction. The two big cinemas in Chelmersley, for example, were his property—the "Mortimer" and the "Beaufoy"—and their joint interests served to take him into Chelmersley, I should say, two or three times a week. He was, in addition, an active and healthy man for his age, and, beyond once or twice for an ordinary winter cold or so, hadn't been under my treatment the whole time I had practised there. A widower, he had two children living, a boy, Donald, in the early twenties, and a daughter Iris, a year or so the boy's senior. Incidentally, she was engaged to my friend and neighbour, Jack Tabernacle, so that I knew her pretty well.

Certainly, if our friend the "Eagle" had wished to create a first-class sensation in Chelmersley, he couldn't have made a better selection for his initial victim. When I blew into the station, Goodaker almost walked into me. His dark, heavy face was grim and set.

"Morning, Doctor, for the second time to-day. Oh, yes—a hoax all right. A mare's nest. Everything else you like. I don't think!"

The last sentence was bitter. I let him alone. The man was raw. The wound was far too fresh for probing.

"Where's the body, Inspector?" I barked this briskly and deliberately, to sting him into action. He jerked his thumb—direction vague.

"In the back room—you know the room I mean. On the table."

"Let's have a look. Come in with me. I may want to know something."

"May," he muttered cynically. "There's a hell of a lot I'd like to know. Always did have a name for greediness."

"How did you get it up here?"

"Motor ambulance. I took the thing down with me to Taggarts Way when they first sent for me. Come on in."

Goodaker followed me into the room at the back. The body of Fredericks lay on the table. A great gash across the throat was a plain and terrible indication of the route that he had travelled. There was a complete severance of the carotid artery. Without a doubt, Fredericks must have lost a considerable quantity of blood. He was fully dressed, however, even to collar and tie, white scarf and light raincoat. The tie and collar were stained with blood. The coat and scarf, however, were comparatively free from stain.

"Suicide a possibility, Doctor Bannerman?" queried the Inspector.

I considered the question for a moment. "Yes," I conceded. "Although, if so, he must have used tremendous force on himself. Any weapon found near at hand?"

Goodaker shook his head. "Not a sign of any. That's the point. That's why I yelled blue murder. What else could it be?"

I was busy now and said nothing. After a matter of minutes, I asked a question. "In touch with his people?"

"You bet. Expect young Donald Fredericks along any moment now. Also the Chief Constable. I 'phoned him as soon as I could."

I sat on a corner of the table by the body, thinking of Jack Tabernacle. He was engaged to Iris Fredericks—only daughter of what lay on the table.

"Who found it?" I tossed my head backwards.

"Young Willie Pope, the milk-boy who works for the Boreham Dairy people, as I told you. On that piece of waste ground up Taggarts Way. About ten minutes past five this morning."

I rubbed my chin contemplatively. "Lots of things about this case puzzle me, Goodaker."

"You don't say, Doctor." The Inspector approximated rudeness. We knew each other—he and I. I grinned at him, ready and willing to make allowances. He saw my attitude and relented somewhat. Walking towards me with a kind of conscious deliberation, he leant over and stuck out an aggressive jaw.

"How long has Fredericks been dead, Doctor Bannerman? Tell me that, will you? It interests me."

I moved over to examine the body again. "Put it at roughly twelve hours, Goodaker. You won't be far out."

He nodded. "So that my little postal communication from Mr. Aquila was fairly accurate after all, wasn't it?" He thrust his hands into his trouser pockets. "Too damned accurate," he supplemented.

"That's one of the things that puzzles me, good Goodaker, as I babbled to you just now. How in the world could any man, chuck him in a spot of the master criminal at that—the pukka Moriarty stuff—post a letter to you this morning—knowing for a certainty that—" The door opened before I could get any farther, to admit two men. The last, I knew only too well—Sir George Bligh, the Chief Constable of the county.

Externally, he presented a picture of the authentic country squire: Christmas carols, waits, snapdragon, blankets for the poor, Athanasian creed, a hunting we will go—all the genuine bag of tricks.

His red cheeks were a shade paler, perhaps, than usual, but he puffed them out and exuded most of his normal boisterous jauntiness.

The man who came in behind him was a stranger to me. Certainly I had never seen him before that I could recall. He was tall and lithe. Although he appeared to move lazily, nothing was farther from the truth than this idea, for there were balance and easy poise in every one of his movements. He was clean-shaven, with sensitive mouth and very arresting eyes. The top lip of the mouth was most distinctive, being a trifle longer than the average, but the mouth itself had a semi-humorous twist to it that commended its owner to me as soon as I clapped eyes on him.

I have said that his eyes were arresting; they were more than that. They were grey. You became aware of this immediately you looked at him, which is not always the case with people. I know many men well, but I couldn't tell you with certainty the colour of their eyes if you offered me a tenner for the information. There was a quality about these eyes, too, that attracted you to them and made you watch them even though the man to whom they belonged was not addressing you or even looking in your direction. It was very soon apparent to me also, that this man was by way of being a big noise, for even so peppery an old blighter as Bligh (sorry) was quite deferential towards him and his opinions. Although it's my ordinary habit to neglect shrines that draw other people, I will candidly admit that I took to this particular bloke very quickly. You know what I mean. You can't explain this kind of thing—there it is, it simply happens—spontaneously or almost so.

There was a quiet, but keen and incisive, efficiency about him, which as a projection of personality made an irresistible appeal. I heard Bligh address him as Bathurst, and even then I failed to grasp the significance of the name.

"Taken by car, you think, Bathurst, eh?"

"Not a doubt about it, I should say, sir. The motor-car has revolutionized crime. Its wheels revolve on the lubricant of lawlessness. The legacy of the gangsters. 'Last rides' are as common in the States as a wet summer's day over here."

Sir George had tried to look important. He always has been a damned old fool and I wondered how long it would be before he condescended to notice Goodaker and me.

"You couldn't, I suppose, Bathurst, er—deduce anything from what you saw up there, as we drove by?"

"How do you mean, sir?"

"Well—er—I mustn't expect too much from you at this stage of the case, I know, but I was thinking perhaps that the tyre impressions, left by the wheels of the car—"

"Good Lord—no, sir. There have, I should say without the slightest exaggeration, been dozens of cars on that road between Chelmersley and Cressing since the murderer chucked the body of Fredericks out there. Not an earthly, Sir George—believe me. That was why I didn't stop." He grinned across at me cheerily.

"Morning, Doctor. Morning, Inspector. Dr. Bannerman, isn't it?"

"Guilty," I replied equally cordially. "How did you know?" He grinned again.

"You can usually bank on a doctor and an inspector of police being present when the scent's fresh and the hunt's just up; besides that, you're the Michael Bannerman, I fancy, who hooked for the 'Quins a season or so ago. Last season was it? Yes?"

I nodded with a gleam of pleasure in my eyes. "I won't deny it. You're right." He went on again before I could say anything more.

"Let me see if I can tell you anything more about yourself." He closed his eyes for a second. "You went over for an unconverted try against the Springboks, a minute before the whistle. You were playing for a 'London' fifteen. Pierre De Villiers at scrum-half, got the ball from a scrum in your twenty-five. He whipped it out to Bennie Osier but you came round and intercepted the pass; sold a most luscious and toothsome dummy to one of the threes, Zimmerman I fancy it was; galloped right through the South African lines; jumped a despairing sort of tackle from Brand, the full-back; and crossed the line near the corner flag. The wind and rain spoiled the place-kick. Let me see—Barry Cumberlege refereed. The date was November twenty-eighth. The Springboks won, fourteen-three. Am I right?"

"Absolutely," I said fervently, and such is the vanity of man, that his memory of my humble effort attracted me to him to an even greater degree than before.

"That's all right then, Doctor," he returned whimsically; "and now that we know all about each other, tell me of this 'spot' of murder to which Sir George here has introduced me—on a holiday too; I never seem able to miss 'em—these affairs, wherever they happen to be."

Before I could get going, Sir George, who had been fermenting fussily during Bathurst's "Rugger" reminiscence, embarked upon a certain amount of explanation.

"I must introduce you people. This is Anthony Bathurst, Bannerman, the celebrated—"

Bathurst waved a protesting hand.

"Now, now, Sir George, please. You promised me, you know. You remember the terms upon which I consented to come. Doctor Bannerman will be prejudiced against me before I arrest him. Give me a dog's chance."

Before I could recover from the shock of surprise that his words gave me, old Bligh was in again.

"You must have heard of Bathurst, Bannerman? I had him on the spot with me; so when the 'phone message came, I brought him along. Scotland Yard has—"

Bathurst's right eyelid drooped in my direction. "Ask Doctor Bannerman to take us to have a look at the body, Sir George. If I weren't able to see it where it was found, I must make do with the next best thing. *We* must make do, eh, Inspector?"

Goodaker shook his head with some emphasis.

"No, sir. I was called to the spot early this morning, did the necessary—everything that was necessary, I think—and brought the body back here on the ambulance. It was found by a milk-boy, you see, on his early round." Bathurst approved.

"Good. That's better news. You saw all there was to be seen, eh? I was very much afraid that . . ." he paused for a moment in reflection before swinging round again on to Goodaker. "Never mind that now. Lead the way, Inspector, will you please. Come, Sir George." I followed them.

"Tell me, Inspector," said Bathurst, as he stood beside the body, "all that you know about this. Every little verse, please. I can bear to hear quite a lot."

Goodaker was soon into his stride. It pleased him to get there. It must be remembered that he had waited some time for the opportunity. Bathurst listened intently but patiently. Not a single interruption came from him. Sir George opened his mouth as though to intervene once or twice, I thought, but Bathurst's acquiescence, as it were, in the Inspecting narrative, choked the old boy off. I was watching him closely, and the strange look in his eyes rather startled me. Then it came home to me how much he liked his own way.

When Goodaker had finished, Bathurst commenced a sort of rapid fire.

"No weapon—you say?"

"None. The ground all round has been most thoroughly searched."

"Not been robbed?"

"No loose money on him. Gold watch, pocket-book and note-wallet each intact. Nothing taken from him at all as far as we can tell."

"Last seen by whom?"

"Can't say yet, Mr. Bathurst. Expecting information along any minute now. I'm in touch with the dead man's family—the house is about three miles from here, on the way towards Great Steeping. I've sent a man up. Would have gone myself only I stayed to see the Chief Constable here."

"Quite right," growled Sir George.

"Popular in the district?"

"Who? Fredericks?"

Bathurst nodded.

"Know of nothing to suggest otherwise."

"H'm. Give me as many facts as you know about him—*everything* that you know about him. I'm thirsting for information."

Goodaker, prompted by me, told the tale. On the whole, I suppose, it must be called a joint effort. Bathurst pulled at that long upper lip of his and I saw the grey eyes become very grave and very steady.

"Have a look at him, Sir George, will you please? You too, Bannerman. You, Inspector. What strikes you about that wound? What *must* strike you?"

I was in like a shot. "The strength of it—the force behind it, if you like that idea better."

He nodded. "Must have been well acquainted with the murderer to let him get as close as that, don't you think? And friendly with him, too."

He shot a shrewd look in my direction as though testing my mental capabilities. "Hasn't been drugged in any way, Doctor, has he?"

I pulled up a dead eyelid, although to tell the truth, in doing so I was merely repeating a performance.

"Before he was killed you mean? No—unhesitatingly, no."

He rubbed his chin thoughtfully and bent closer to the body. "Clothes deuced wet, at that. What time did it start raining, Sir George? Any idea?"

Old Bligh hummed and hawed; Goodaker went to his assistance. "Shortly before midnight, sir. My wife was lying awake, as a matter of fact. She heard it on the windows. Told me so at breakfast-time this morning. Wonder she didn't wake me to tell me at the time. It's happened before."

I pounced on him. "Your wife heard it?" I exclaimed incredulously. "At its heaviest, it was never more than a drizzle."

Before Goodaker could pass comment upon my interrogation, Anthony Bathurst intervened. "Very wetting, these drizzles are, though. Any old how, this poor beggar's wet through. Come and feel his clothes."

I saw Goodaker frown. Sir George Bligh stared. "Let me get this right, Inspector," proceeded Bathurst. "You said just now 'fully dressed', didn't you? Even to white muffler, light raincoat, collar, tie and soft hat? You did say all that, didn't you?"

To my surprise, Goodaker seemed a little uncertain. "I'm not quite sure about the last," he replied slowly, almost weighing his words.

"But here it is," returned Bathurst, pointing to the grey Homburg.

"Yes—I know. But I thought you wanted exact evidence. What I'm not sure about is whether the dead man was wearing the hat when the body was found—or whether it was lying . . ."

Bathurst's eyes caught his and held them. There was a brief interval of silence. When he spoke, it was with incredible softness.

"Which may turn out to be important—don't you think so, Inspector?"

Goodaker seemed to throw off his nimbus of uncertainty. "Let me look at young Pope's statement. I have it here. Just a moment." He was out and back again in a second, scratching his head.

"The boy said 'hat on' according to what I have here, but my memory is that the hat was off, lying just at the side of the man's head."

Bathurst's face seemed to clear suddenly. "Doesn't matter, Inspector. The photographs will show us."

"Yes," said a staring Goodaker, "the photographs will show us all right."

Bathurst's next move rather astonished me. After examining the various blood-stains on muffler, collar and tie, he ran his hand over the coat and waistcoat.

"I can help you there, I think," volunteered Goodaker. "The raincoat was not properly fastened round the body; it wasn't buttoned up. The result was that parts were well exposed to the drizzle."

Bathurst nodded understanding. "Thanks, Inspector. I thought something of the sort must have happened. Still, what I don't altogether . . ." He stopped abruptly and went to Fredericks' head. He stooped towards it.

"Unless of course . . ." He felt the hair carefully. Then he put his own head down close to it—only to shake it—rather despondently, I thought. The dead man's ears, neck, chest and back, particularly the first-named, then occupied his attention—also apparently without any tangible result or satisfaction. Standing away from the body, he suddenly seemed to come to a decision and swung round to me.

"Get me a towel, Doctor, please. A white towel. Clean, if you can manage it."

I knew I had my case in the car and I usually carry a small hand towel with me—so I flew out to get it for him. When I got back, Bathurst took the towel from me without a word.

"Put the muffler round the throat, Doctor, please. Yes—to cover the wound. You'll find it will do so effectively. Fold it just loosely. That's it. Thanks. Now, stand away, will you?" I did as instructed.

Bathurst took the towel and carefully wiped the dead man's face, ears, and as much of the neck as he was able to reach. Having done so, he folded the towel into a square and placed it in his pocket.

"I'll return it to you later, Doctor. May have found something—may not; you never know." He grinned at me cordially.

"Got something?" jerked old Bligh.

"Yes, I think so, Sir George. I may be wrong of course—especially at so early a stage of the case—but I think I know how Fredericks was murdered. That towel may make it into a certainty." As he spoke, Goodaker cocked his ear and held up a finger. I listened and heard the wheels of a car drawing up in the yard outside.

"That's Sergeant Berry," declared Goodaker, "back from the house. I sent him up there, as I told you. I expect young Donald Fredericks has come along with him. Wonder what we shall hear now."

"I'm inclined to share your wonder, Inspector," said Anthony Bathurst.

Chapter III
I AM HONOURED

DONALD Fredericks had a pale face and quick dark eyes. A clever face, with signs of character weakness. His hands were trembling and his lips moved tremulously when he came into the room to us. I knew him pretty well, mainly through Jack Tabernacle's association with his sister, so that I was pleased to make him as comfortable as I could.

He had always seemed to me to be a very decent boy indeed. As was natural, he kept his face averted from the gruesome sight that he knew was on the table and asked but one question of me.

"Is my father dead?"

It seemed strange, I thought, that he should ask it in the circumstances, but I suppose, looking back at everything, that it was the normal question that any ordinary boy would have asked. I nodded. His voice shook and he made a big effort to pull himself together. Then another question came from him.

"Have you any idea who murdered him?" His eyes wandered from me to Goodaker.

"None, Mr. Fredericks," answered the Inspector.

Sir George Bligh thought it was high time that he asserted himself.

"Do you think that you could answer a few questions? Or would you rather wait a little while?"

The boy smiled rather wistfully. "I think I could. You see, the first shock's an hour old now. Sergeant Berry was very kind. He prepared me, very gradually, for something pretty terrible. What is it you want to know—that you want to ask me?"

Sir George turned an eye towards Bathurst who nodded his acceptance of the implied offer.

"When did you last see your father alive, Mr. Fredericks?"

"Yesterday afternoon. Just after lunch. He had lunch at home and motored back into Chelmersley. I had some business in the afternoon, I believe, at one of the cinemas."

"Which one, do you know?"

"I think it was the 'Beaufoy'. But I couldn't be sure."

"When was your father expected back home again?"

"Well—in the ordinary way the car would have gone back to Chelmersley for him and he would have come home to dinner. My father was a man of very methodical habits."

"About seven o'clock to half past, I suppose, that would be?"

"Yes."

"You said the car would have gone back for him. Do you mean that . . . ?"

"My father used to 'phone home from Chelmersley from either of the cinemas, for instance—and inform the chauffeur what time he wanted him to call for him."

Bathurst looked intensely interested. "Did he 'phone yesterday evening?"

Donald Fredericks shook his head. "I have made inquiries this morning. From what I can gather, nobody at home received any message."

Bathurst regarded him queerly. "What about yourself, though? Aren't you in a position to say whether—"

"No. As it happens, I'm not. I was in London last evening. I did not return home till past one o'clock. I went to bed. I did not know that my father was not in the house. Had I known . . ." His voice broke a little, trailed off.

"Surely somebody at home must have been a little worried at your father's non-appearance? Your sister?"

The young man was a little hesitant. "Not altogether. I will try to explain. There were occasions when my father did not dine at home. They weren't frequent, but they did occur, occasionally. My sister says that when no message came from him about sending the car, she wasn't in any way alarmed. She imagined that he was dining in town as he sometimes did. He would go to town by train, you see, and then 'phone for the car to meet the last train at Chelmersley."

"Was any late message sent yesterday?"

"I understand not."

"The first news then, that you had—"

"Came this morning." Donald Fredericks completed the sentence. Bathurst turned to me.

"How long would you say Mr. Fredericks has been dead, Doctor?"

"In my opinion he was killed some time between seven o'clock and nine o'clock last evening."

He was on me again like a flash. "Not later, Doctor? It's tremendously important."

"It's difficult to gauge as closely as you want me to. But not a great deal later. I'll stick to that."

I saw Bathurst rub his hands. "Mr. Fredericks," he said, addressing young Donald, "when your father came home to dine in the ordinary way, what would be the usual time, say, that he would 'phone home for the car?"

"We usually dine at half past seven. My father would 'phone through about seven o'clock or perhaps a little later. The time would vary, of course, but not a great deal."

Bathurst shook his head at Sir George Bligh and me. "Not much help there, is there? The fact that no message was received yesterday means nothing, you see. I was hoping that it might."

I saw what he meant, though I doubt if old Bligh did. If Fredericks were dead at seven o'clock, I explained to myself—but Bathurst was off again, speaking to Goodaker this time.

"What's your theory of the crime, Inspector? It would help me to hear it."

Goodaker brightened up. He had been very quiet for some little time. Here was a certain encouragement.

"The murder took place in a car. The deceased" (his natural instinct asserted itself) "was travelling with somebody whom he knew and trusted. He was off his guard. Result was, he was led into a certain position and—the murder itself became a matter of comparative ease." Goodaker flicked his fingers.

Bathurst rubbed his chin caressingly. "You almost suggest a woman. It's all right—as far as it goes, Inspector—your theory. There's one thing, however, that I'd like to point out to you. If what you surmise is the real goods, there's a car knocking about somewhere with more than a spot of blood in it. Shouldn't take you fellows long to get on to it. And a suit of clothes, too. Unless it's a woman, of course, which for the moment . . ." He fell into deep thought.

Sir George Bligh, all hot and bothered, broke into his reverie. "I'll get that car matter attended to at once, if you think it will help at all."

"Thank you, sir. That's most kind of you." He swept round again on to young Fredericks.

"Forgive me if I distress you unduly. Try to remember that I'm here to help. Can you tell me if your father had any enemies? Known enemies? A prominent local man, such as he was, very often, you know, doesn't pass entirely unscathed through . . ."

He broke off summarily, waiting for the boy's reply. When it came it held a touch of doggedness. At any rate, I can't think of a better word to convey to you the tone in which his answer was couched.

"Everybody has enemies, I think. Of a kind, that is. In this respect my father, probably, was no different from anybody else. But I know of nobody whose enmity was likely to reach the limits that we know have been reached."

Bathurst eyed him shrewdly. It seemed to me that young Donald had somebody in mind, but didn't care about being too explicit. Goodaker chose this moment to jump in. Of course, I knew what he was going to say. I had been expecting the business for some little time. He was diplomatic enough to address the Chief Constable.

"Sir George," he opened, "it's an opportune moment for me to contribute a bit of information. Would you mind taking a glance at that?"

I knew, too, without looking, what it was that he had handed over to Bligh. The Chief Constable adjusted his glasses and put his head back to read it.

This accomplished, he contented himself at first with one comment.

"Good gracious!" Then he beckoned to Bathurst.

"Come and look at this, Bathurst. Good gracious! Most extraordinary! February, too. Six months ago."

Bathurst read the letter through carefully; then turned it over and examined the envelope.

"You connect the correspondence with the crime, inspector?"

Goodaker exhibited eagerness. "The date, sir, the date."

"Exactly." Bathurst flicked a speck of dust from his sleeve. Then came a protest.

"Why wasn't I consulted about this, Goodaker?" fumed Sir George.

"I put a 'chit' through to the 'Yard', sir. They were inclined, I think, to regard the whole thing as eyewash. For instance, they've nothing on any 'Eagle'. So I decided that I wouldn't worry you with it."

For the moment, young Fredericks seemed to be forgotten by everybody. He came down quietly to the group of men in front of him.

"May I look at it, please?"

Sir George Bligh handed him the paper. He read it through, without remark. Bathurst prompted him.

"Well, Mr. Fredericks? Can you throw any light on that?"

"None," he replied, shaking his head. "Seems to me to be the letter of a man with an unbalanced mind."

"That's quite possible, I should say," returned Bathurst drily.

Goodaker seized the moment and produced his master stroke. "Now read that one, Sir George, if you please. Delivered here last night about a quarter past eight. Last post, it would be."

Bligh repeated his previous performance, save that his comment was much more torrid. "Good God! And you, Goodaker, you let this butcher, this hell-deserving fiend, carry out his threats under your very nose. . . ."

The inspector flushed under the stinging reproof and bit his lip. Wisely, he remained silent. Bathurst took the postcard and envelope from Sir George. Suddenly he addressed a question to me.

"How long have *you* known of these communications, Doctor?" he asked with casual nonchalance.

I started almost guiltily, as I realized what the question held in meaning. However, there was no help for it.

"Almost as long as the Inspector himself. I was in his confidence. But how the blazes did you know that?"

He shrugged his shoulders, rather coldly, I thought. "My dear Bannerman. You have made no attempt to look at either. The reason for this unusual disinterestedness on your part was very obvious."

He was now intent on the second message, and I saw him begin to rub his hands again as he surveyed the envelope in which it had been enclosed. "Aquila—an eagle, eh?"

He jerked his head back towards Goodaker. "Local paper been used here, Inspector?"

"The address on the envelope, sir, d'you mean?"

"Yes."

"That's the conclusion to which I've come, sir. Looks to me like the *Chelmersley Weekly News*."

Donald Fredericks went down a pace or two and bent over Bathurst's shoulder. Bathurst showed him the precise manner of the communication. Sir George Bligh considered it was high time to spread himself.

"Let me help you. As it happens, I'm in a position to do so. The words that have been used for the message itself haven't been taken from the *Weekly News*. They have been cut from the *Daily Express*. I'm certain of that. I know the *Express* type too well to mistake it."

"I agree, Sir George. It is the *Daily Express* that has suffered mutilation. I question, though, whether *one* of the words came from the *Express*."

He held up the postcard meaningly—for general inspection. I knew what he meant at once. The word "Aquila" of the signature was much smaller and of altogether different character.

"Obviously, Bathurst," I urged rather hastily, "one would hardly find an 'Aquila' in an ordinary daily issue. The murderer was forced to go elsewhere. To a natural history book, for example."

Bathurst came to the verge of a grin. "Excellent, Doctor. You're a man after my own heart. Yet I have known names appear in the daily Press that gave the bookmakers an immense amount of trouble. Don't you remember 'Abscess on the Jaw'? And the *Express* racing programme is moderately reliable, I believe, on most days. More so perhaps than the safety bet."

"In my opinion," announced Sir George, ignoring Bathurst's last remark, "the word 'Aquila' was in all probability cut from either a Latin grammar or from a Latin dictionary. Looks to me very much like the type of the old *Via Latina* that we used to use. The eminent Dr. Abbott's book."

"It's on the cards," said Bathurst, "of course. At the same time, I'm of the opinion myself that you're both wrong. I would suggest a third possibility."

He looked up at us as though he were inviting our criticisms of his statement. I filled the bill. "Which is . . . ?"

"That the word has been cut from the popular version of one of the finest adventure stories of all time. The world's best seller. The adventures of Paul and Barnabas. Throughout Pisidia to Pamphylia. In Perga and down into Attalia. And in the parts of Libya about Cyrene."

Sir George's hand went to the ends of his white moustache. "I'm not a lover of Rider Haggard," he said pompously. "Never have been. Give me Elinor Glyn every time."

CHAPTER IV

I AM AMAZED

AVOIDING adroitly the glance with which I favoured him, Anthony Bathurst tapped the disputed postcard with an authoritative finger-nail.

"Very remarkable, you know, Sir George, this. Consider all that it means. When you come to think clearly about it, it becomes even more amazing than ever. Which is saying quite a lot."

"You mean—er—the—er—astonishing *certainty* of the writer?"

"Of course. Let's look at the position. Here's a person who is so certain of his crime that he writes to warn the local police inspector, twelve hours we'll say, before the vaticinated crime is actually committed. Look here. This envelope is post-marked eight-ten a.m., August thirty-first. His arrangements either with, or with regard to, Fredericks, therefore, must have been already made—presumably, that is. You've heard nothing, I suppose, Mr. Fredericks, from your father concerning any particular or even unusual appointment, that he had pending?"

Donald Fredericks denied the question without a trace of hesitation.

"Nothing."

"No letter has come recently, to your knowledge, that might have . . . ?"

"No. None."

Goodaker made a contribution. "The appointment that you suggest, *might* have been made by telephone. In that case, Mr. Fredericks junior would possibly . . ."

"That is true, Inspector," agreed the young man. I spotted Bathurst looking up rather queerly.

"How does the post come to you at the station, Inspector? Tell me the exact *manner* of its coming." For a brief shade of a second, Goodaker looked blank. Then he recovered. "Oh, I see what you mean. The postman usually leaves the letters with the sergeant who happens to be on duty in the outer office. Sergeant Berry, it was, last evening. Then he brings whatever there is to me."

"I see. Is the post usually heavy? Much of it?"

"Varies, of course. Fairish though, on the whole."

"Average?"

"In number, you mean?"

"Yes."

Goodaker pursed his lips. "Couple of dozen communications, I should say, of sorts."

"Sergeant Berry about now?"

"Yes. He came along with young Mr. Fredericks here. Would you care to speak to him?"

"I could endure a moment of weighty conversation, Inspector." Bathurst favoured me with a grin of cynicism.

The sergeant was big and ungainly; he would have graced an Aquarium; a moustache, that he affected rather heroically, would have been quite a creditable performance on the part of a hirsute sea-lion. Goodaker brought him in to us. When he saw our number, in solemn conclave as it were, and realized again the burden of the table, he looked a bit scared. Sergeant Berry was a little out of his normal course.

"Good morning, sir." He touched his forehead to Sir George Bligh. A frigid nod was his reward. Old Bligh was as good a man as I've known for dispensing the frozen mitten.

"Morning, Sergeant."

Bathurst was on to Berry at once. "Last night's post, Sergeant—the letters that you took in to Inspector Goodaker. Remember?"

"Yes, sir. Quite well, sir."

"Did the postman bring them into the office?"

"Yes, sir."

"How do you know that?"

"I was there, sir. On duty, sir, at the time the post came in."

"Good. That clears the air a bit for all of us. What did he do with, it when he brought it in?"

"Why—handed it over, sir."

"To you? Into your hands?"

"No, sir. He usually unloads his stuff on to the desk. I go and gather it up from there to carry it in to Inspector Goodaker. At least, that's my usual procedure, sir, when the post is anything like—"

"Thank you, Sergeant Berry," closured Bathurst. "That's all I want to know now, thank you."

"It occurs to me," I said brightly, as Berry made a prolonged exit, "that if anybody wanted to get a . . ." I caught at that moment a look in Bathurst's eye that I was not, I hope, too slow to interpret. I tacked adroitly and Bathurst's eyelid again drooped in my direction. I finished in a frenzy of futility.

"Line through to the dead man—a message that is—it was sent through to him when he was at one of the two cinemas—either the 'Beaufoy' or the 'Mortimer'. Don't you agree?" I asked with asinine ecstasy.

"Undoubtedly, Doctor," said Bathurst, profoundly and impressively, "undoubtedly."

I breathed freely again. The tension was over—temporarily, at least. Bathurst rose.

"We'll drive up again to the place where the body was found, Sir George, if you don't mind. Goodaker can show it to us. You come along too, Doctor, if you've nothing else pressing at the moment. We won't trouble Mr. Fredericks to come." He nodded kindly to Donald.

I assented eagerly and followed on his heels rapidly. He said good-bye to Donald Fredericks and then suddenly turned. The result was that we were in the doorway together. He put his lips close to my ear.

"Don't feel too bright about anything, Doctor, even if you feel inclined, until we're alone. Do you mind? Be as thick-headed as you please. If you feel that you simply must scintillate, try being dumb. It's a marvellous prophylactic."

I nodded acquiescence. I could see what he meant, though I couldn't tell who it was of whom he was scared. But I knew that he knew what I had been on the point of saying a minute or so previously. "Although that he knew that her father was dead," I half muttered to myself under my breath, "and she knew that he knew . . ." then I cursed myself for being half-baked.

"Jump in, Sir George," he said, "and you, Doctor—you direct me. Come in front."

The primrose-wheeled Crossley flew along the main street of Chelmersley at a pace that was definitely vicious. I prompted Bathurst as he drove concerning turnings and ways.

"Don't want to be up here too long, Bannerman," he confided in me as he waved a reproving hand to a cascade of literary invective directed towards him by the driver of a coal-cart. It was no mean effort either, in respect of both fluency and wealth of image. I found myself listening to the adjectival torrent with a certain amount of fascination. Bathurst grinned as he noticed me.

"Keats to Fanny Brawne! As I was saying," he said, "before that somewhat lurid interruption disturbed us, I don't want to be here too long. If you'll come, I'll take you with me to the postal sorting office that serves Chelmersley and its vicinity. I've an idea that I need a spot of exercise. What do you say? Will you come, Bannerman?"

"Only too pleased, old son," I said carelessly, secretly delighted a moment afterwards when I realized that he bore no resentment at the familiarity. "Here we are," I exclaimed a moment or so later, turning round to speak to Sir George Bligh. "We're just entering Taggarts Way."

It was not too wide for motor traffic, but many cars there were that used it. There was just enough space for one to pass another. It was, I suppose, about fourteen feet wide and its hedges were shorn right back to their roots, so that the best could be made, and the fullest advantages gained, of the strait and narrow way.

We had scarcely gone a quarter of a mile along it, when I spotted a car approaching us. It was a Humber landaulette and I felt my heart respond to it. For I thought I knew who would be driving. Bathurst pulled the Crossley in and carried on. His wings just brushed the wild flowers and ferns that nestled in the base of the hedgerow. But the landaulette pulled up sharp and turned so far into the middle of the way that Bathurst was forced to pull up the Crossley as well.

"Ten to one it's a woman driving. Taking me, Bannerman?"

I wasn't accepting that bet, thanks very much. I knew by now—curse him. A proud, lovely and gloriously disdainful face was visible. I heard the voice that I expected. Through the window of the landaulette there came words of frigid politeness.

"I'm sorry. I'm afraid one of us will have to back. Of course, if you won't . . ."

"Not the slightest need, you know, dear lady," returned Anthony Bathurst in nonchalant retort, "unless you simply must have three feet between your near wing and the hedge. If you insist, of course." He commenced to back the Crossley—far enough—and the lovely face, flushed now with a furious anger that heightened the disdain that it had held before, streaked by as the landaulette passed us.

I was amazed to see the look that had suddenly come on Bathurst's face.

"My stars," I heard him whisper. "Of all the perfectly astonishing things; of all the cursed . . ."

"That lady," I said with a strange tranquillity, "was Rosemary Cotterill. The one driving, I mean."

There was a thin tight line round his lips now, and the grey eyes had grown cold. "When I knew her, my dear Bannerman," he said, "she was Rosemary Marquis. I had no idea that she had arrived . . ." He paused.

"She's a friend of mine," I remarked with atrocious lameness. He seemed to pay no heed. I was ignored completely.

"Rosemary," he quoted, "rosemary—for remembrance. Appropriate, as always." His tone changed to address Goodaker but I knew that the alteration had cost him an effort.

"Is this the waste ground, Inspector? Yes? Show Sir George and me then, if you don't mind, where the body of Fredericks was found." He turned to me again. "Who was that with Mrs. Cotterill?" His tone was hard.

"Iris Fredericks," I answered. "Daughter of the man who's been murdered."

His eyes caught mine and held them. But he said nothing; and I waited.

Chapter V

MOVING IN THE DARK

COMPLETE recovery came to him quickly and by the time we were out of the car he was in full control of himself again. I deemed it prudent to hold my tongue. Goodaker took us quickly over to the spot where the body of Fredericks had lain for Willie Pope to find it a few hours previously.

Bathurst glanced back over his shoulder at the lane that we had just left. "Pretty lonely round here of a night, Inspector?"

"Fairish. No turnings, you know, sir. Not a turning off Taggarts Way for miles. Anybody in a car can easily see what's coming, either way."

Bathurst measured the distance between the road and the place where we were now standing. Sir George interrupted him.

"About a dozen yards, Bathurst, I should say. Under, rather than over."

Bathurst turned to me for corroboration or disagreement. I gave the former promptly. "I agree with Sir George." I'd have loved to have said otherwise and then argued with the old blighter, but I hadn't the glimmer of a case to put up against him.

"You won't find anything here, sir," submitted Goodaker. "Nothing tangible, I mean."

Bathurst nodded as though he knew that and bent down to examine the ground. But as far as I could see, the short, coarse, tussocky grass that grew here told him nothing. For a time he circled round, reminding me of a dog that has struck a scent and then suddenly lost it.

"Grass, you see, Bannerman," he said to me eventually, "and coarse at that. Half a dozen quick steps, no more, and the job would be done." He pointed to the hedgerow a few yards from us. "You can see why this spot was chosen, can't you? Notice the break in the hedge there? Just comfortable enough for a man to get through. The first break of its kind, too, I fancy."

Old Bligh made as though to walk towards it.

"That's an idea, sir," said Bathurst. "Let's see if that hedge can tell us anything. Come on, Goodaker."

We went over, more or less in single file. The break in the hedge was, as Bathurst had pointed out, just wide enough for a man's passage. Bathurst and the Inspector peered carefully all round it. Bligh and I joined forces at the side of them. I shall always be proud to think (and say) that on one occasion at least, my eyes were as sharp as the grey eyes of Anthony Lotherington Bathurst.

For, on this occasion, we saw the same thing almost simultaneously. Clinging to one of the sharper hedge-points was a tiny thread of white silk. We saw that it was silk directly Bathurst pulled it away from where it had been caught.

"Doesn't help us overmuch, Inspector," he declared.

"Confirms what we thought, sir," said Goodaker.

"That's something," added Sir George firmly. "Shows us we're on the right track."

"Where did this come from then, Inspector, in your opinion?" Bathurst held up the white wisp.

"From the white scarf round the dead man's neck."

"Full points, Inspector. One hundred per cent. I have no further comment to offer on your answer." Bathurst grinned genially at Sir George Bligh and me. Bligh, however, by this time, was approximating impatience.

"Well, Bathurst," he said rather fussily, "is there any point, do you think, in us staying here? Not likely to pick up anything more, are we?"

"No, sir. I've seen all I want to see. I think we'll move, as you suggest."

Bligh glanced impatiently at his watch. "I must get into Chelmersley before midday. It's absolutely imperative. There are one or two things requiring my urgent attention. If you should want me again, 'phone through to Goodaker. I'll leave word with him so that he'll be able to get into touch with me at once."

We parted at Chelmersley police station. That is to say, Bligh and the Inspector went in and stayed in. Bathurst, after a word with Goodaker, prodded me in the ribs as I was on the point of getting out of the Crossley.

"Your place far from here, Bannerman," he asked me quietly.

"Three miles or so," I answered. "Over at Great Steeping."

"Care to run me over?" he asked.

"What about your car?" I asked in return.

"I'll leave it here. No I won't. I may want it afterwards. I forgot. I've got that sorting-office inquiry to do. It's merely post-poned. We'll take both cars up. Shan't be in the way, shall I?"

"Good God, no," I replied. "Precious glad to have you. I could bear to hear a lot more than I've heard up to now. So let's. I'll get my car out of the yard."

The two cars got away together and we made "The Rowfants" in double quick time. I shooshed Mrs. Ramage away as soon as I got in and made straight for the decanter.

"Good work, Bannerman," said Bathurst; "just the suspicion of a 'splash' for me. When! Thank you, Doctor."

He drained the glass with a gesture of appreciation. "Sit down, Bannerman," he said rather pointedly. "I want to talk to you. Forgive me taking charge, as it were. I know it's your show and all that. That's just my way of talking. I expect you'll get pretty well used to it before long. But I've something here that I want you to have a look at. With me."

From his pocket he pulled the towel that he had used to wipe the dead man's face and neck.

"Let's spread this out somewhere." He looked round ques-tioningly.

I wasn't quite sure, I admit, what it was that he desired to do, but I motioned to the table.

"The inside of the towel is on the top, Doctor. I mean the part that I used to wipe Fredericks with. Here we are."

Taking infinite pains, he opened out the towel on the table. I went and stood at his side.

"Notice anything, Bannerman? *Anything*, mind you!"

I looked hard. Once—and then again. The towel, of course, was slightly soiled as any towel will be that has been used as this one had been. It is bound to be. I'll try to explain. The sudoriparous glands are tubular. The tube is coiled up into a sort of ball in the fatty tissue that lies beneath the substance of the dermis; that is to say, the true skin. There was evidence, to my trained eyes, of the passage of this towel over the sweat glands, in the dullish soiling that showed on the thready surface of the towelling. It had picked up a certain amount of sensible perspiration, apart from ordinary dirt.

I told Bathurst what I saw. He nodded in complete understanding, no doubt, of my point. But I could tell at once that he wasn't entirely satisfied with what I had told him.

"Nothing else, Bannerman?"

I searched his face. I knew that he had seen something which, so far, had eluded my observation.

"There *is* something, you know," he urged, almost coaxingly; "very tiny, I admit, but there all the same. I found it the more quickly because, you see, I happened to have looked for it. I *expected* to find it there. Have another look."

I looked again—my third inspection. This time I was more successful. There were two short hairs on the towel. One was almost lost to sight in a corner, right against the towel's very edge. The other lay on the opposite side, a long way away from its fellow. I found words and announced my discovery. Anthony Bathurst rubbed his hands and the grey eyes of him now reflected a more adequate satisfaction.

"Thank you, Bannerman. And these short hairs are what I was looking for. Despite the fact that our murderer had been so damned careful. But hairs are decidedly awkward things and I banked on one or two at least having escaped his notice—and predatory hands." He chuckled. "Having found those hairs, Bannerman, we'll turn our united attention to the other little matter. In re this."

He produced the envelope that had contained the postcard of the second message to Goodaker.

"Game for a jaunt to the Chelmersley sorting-office? Now?"

"Every time. Your car this time, or both?"

"Mine, I think, if you don't mind. It's faster. Come on."

"It's by the big flour-mill," I explained as I got in, "just by the little bridge that crosses the river."

"Far?"

"Quarter of an hour's run from here. Not more." He grinned. "We'll see if we can make that fifteen minutes into ten. Hold tight, Bannerman. I'm going to step on the juice."

The car with the primrose wheels passed into the Great Steeping road and swept eagerly and hungrily into the distance. It was soon obvious to me that those fifteen minutes, mentioned by me so carelessly, would diminish to ten and very probably to eight. Suddenly, without the hint of a warning, Bathurst shifted his body towards me. For a space that was infinitesimal—he was in the driving-seat, remember.

"Mrs. Cotterill." His tone was short and I sensed atmosphere. "You said she was a friend of yours, didn't you?"

I decided to take my cue from him and be aloof myself.

"Yes." I waited for more. Not long, though. "I presume then that she lives round here?"

"Yes. Next place but one to mine. Tabernacle's between the two of us."

Again I saw the lines tighten round his mouth. He jammed his brake on as a hay-cart wandered aimlessly into our orbit. The danger averted, he came back to me.

"Return-ticket to our mutual mutton, Bannerman. What's Cotterill doing now?"

"Cotterill?" I echoed, semi-foolishly.

"Her husband, man. Whom else could I mean?"

The sky cleared for me when he became explicit. I replied slowly. *"Non est."*

He screwed his face round at me again.

"What on earth do you mean, man?"

"I have never presumed on my friendship to make exhaustive inquiries about him—I have always accepted the fact that Captain Cotterill was dead." The grey eyes gleamed at my reply—and then, to my relief, softened somewhat.

"I'm sorry, Bannerman. Please forgive my abruptness. What you have told me is—er—news to me."

He said no more and I purposely refrained from looking at him. But I knew, of a dead certainty, that he was watching me closely. It chafed me a little, I think, and when we came to Wedlock's mill I was bucked because I welcomed the activity that lay just in front of us.

The sorting-office was a building that stood on the corner just beyond the bridge. As we drew up alongside, I was a little surprised to see Inspector Goodaker waiting on the pavement outside.

"There's Goodaker," I said to Bathurst somewhat asininely, I suppose. "That's extraordinary. He must be on the same lay as—"

"I asked him to meet me here as we left the station. So it's not quite so extraordinary as you imagine, Doctor. Bounce out." My companion seemed to have regained his spirits because he grinned at me. "Here we are, Goodaker," he declared as we alighted; "sorry if I've kept you waiting. But the doctor here is inclined to loiter."

I looked at him sharply, but the grin was still on his face. I said nothing therefore, but walked with him and the Inspector into the sorting-office.

Goodaker was at once in touch with the overseer in charge. He produced the envelope that had contained the postcard from "Aquila". "This is the communication in question, Mr. Sadler," I heard him say. "Reached me at the station yesterday evening. Take a good look at it, will you?"

Bathurst watched the official with great care.

"What is it exactly that you wish to know about it?" queried Sadler.

"Whether you've ever seen it before."

"Here, do you mean?"

"Yes. In other words, did that envelope pass through your official hands in here?"

Sadler held the envelope up for a closer inspection. "Undoubtedly, Inspector. That's our official timing-stamp on it, all right."

Bathurst entered the arena. "Absolutely sure of that, Mr. Sadler?"

"Certain, sir. I know it so well, you see. Can't tell you exactly why, or even how. I just do—from seeing it so often, I suppose."

"That's conclusive, then, I think, Mr. Bathurst?" put in Goodaker.

It seemed to me that the Inspector was right, any old how, but Anthony Bathurst caressed his chin and for a time remained silent. "Mr. Sadler," he said, after an appreciable period of waiting, "there's one little point on which I should like some information if you can give it to me. How many sorting-officers have you here? I don't mean so much the actual number on the staff—but the number of those who would be working, say, at the same time?"

"We work on a staff of twenty-four at a time, sir. Two dozen to a shift. If you look round the room, you'll see them at work now."

Bathurst took him at his word and glanced at the tables. The two dozen merchants at whom he looked were toiling merrily, unaware, of course, that they were the centre of attraction.

"Same staff as you had working this time yesterday morning?" he asked laconically.

"Identical, sir. They're on till four o'clock this afternoon."

"Do me a favour, then," said Bathurst. "Run that envelope round the gallant two dozen, or at any rate, round those among them that might have had it through their hands, and ask them if any of 'em have seen it before. Watch their eyes leave their heads." He rubbed his hands again.

Sadler looked at Goodaker with a touch of dubiety. He seemed to be at a loss to understand. "There are thousands of letters in envelopes, you know, sir," he urged, addressing Bathurst. "To nail a man down to one would be—"

"Good Lord, man," said Bathurst, "this particular example that we're fussing after is surely distinctive enough to notch a niche in a man's noddle if he ever spotted it!" He tapped the envelope with its manufactured words of cut-out type.

Sadler, realizing the position better, rubbed his nose with the back of his finger. "H'm, yes. I suppose it is. But we get a good many queer things, you know, sir, through our hands here—far more than you'd imagine, and one more or less . . ."

He took the envelope and walked over to the goodly fellowship of the sorters gathered round the various sorting tables. I watched him. Bathurst watched him. We watched him all three. Perhaps there was good news to be brought to us.

He went from table to table slowly, but methodically. One by one, the pairs of men to whom he addressed his query, shook their heads in denial of what he asked them. I expected to find Bathurst flying flags of disappointment. But I didn't yet know my man. A quick glance at him told me that the reverse was the case.

Sadler eventually reached the penultimate pair. From them he passed to the last table of all. We watched the usual exchange of words. Negatively! We saw him turn away, the envelope in his hand, and come towards us again. On his face there was a look of bewilderment. Goodaker questioned him.

"It's a bit of a puzzle, Inspector," he submitted to Goodaker in reply, "but none of my men can remember handling this letter. I admit now, having had it in my hands, that I certainly *should* have expected them to—there it is, though, they *don't*, and we can't alter the fact." He scratched his head— the old boy was getting out of his depth a bit and, realizing the fact, Bathurst nodded sympathetically.

I could swear now, from carefully watching him, that the situation, as it had developed, pleased him.

"A funny sort of question, Mr. Sadler, but bear with me, as hard as you can. Put me down as an honest 'trier'—not brilliant but painstaking. What percentage of the letters that pass through your hands here would have the address on the envelope written in pencil? Give me just a rough estimate."

Sadler stared. More head scratching. Then a spot of head shaking. "Bit difficult to say, sir. About five, I should think, answering the question on the spur of the moment as you might say. Yes—five. Five in a hundred. That would be about it. Put it at that and you won't be far out."

Once again, Anthony Bathurst fingered the sensational envelope. "It's a comparatively long shot, but I think it's worth trying. Mr. Sadler, see if there's a genius amongst your squad of assortment who remembers by any strange flickering gleam of reminiscence, envelopes of this shape, size and shade that have been in the post here and borne the same address *written in pencil*."

"Same address as what, sir?" returned the startled Sadler.

"I'm sorry. I expressed myself loosely. The same address each time he has seen them."

"Flying a bit high aren't you, sir? Seems to me it's hardly—"

"Try it, Sadler, for the love of Mike. It's the long shot, you know, that comes off sometimes. If it weren't . . ." He shrugged his shoulders and smiled at me cheerfully.

The overseer returned, somewhat reluctantly, I thought, to the tables. He went through the same process as previously. It seemed, too, for a considerable time to us watching, that the result would be similar to that of the previous arrangement. Suddenly, however, a change came over the scene. One of the sorters left the state of denial and appeared to be explaining something to old Sadler, who then began to behave like an exhilarated elephant. The little group broke up and the sorter came away from it with Sadler. The overseer presented him to Bathurst and the Inspector. Sadler spoke directly to Bathurst.

"There's a man here who fancies he can help, sir. Perhaps you'd like to have a word with him and see what he has to say?"

He turned to his subordinate. "Come, Bell, tell this gentleman what you were telling me." The man stepped forward. He was both intelligent and observant, if I'm any judge.

"Just a minute, Bell," said Bathurst.

The man obeyed. Bathurst came round, close to Goodaker and me. "I'm banking in this case on the power of mental visualization. This man we have here handles hundreds of letters. He sees and reads the address on each of the envelopes. It is possible that the power of mental visualization, that art of reviving in the mind by a process of mental photography, the actual words themselves that have been previously seen by the eye, will give us something tangible upon which we shall be able to work.

Now, Bell, try as hard as you can to help us. It's clear to me that you think you can, which certainly goes part of the way."

The judgment that I had formed of the sorter proved to be sound and accurate. He spoke lucidly and intelligently.

"I haven't a lot to say, sir. In reply to the first question that Mr. Sadler came round and asked us all just now, I can honestly assure you that I have no recollection whatever of sorting that particular envelope that he showed us. I'm pretty certain in my own mind that I should have remembered it if I had. I could hardly help it. But I'm going to say this. During the last six months or so, I have sorted a number of letters in envelopes like that one, where the address on them has been written in pencil. That is to say the same name and address have recurred on letters such as I have described, fairly constantly."

"*Always* written in pencil?" interrupted Bathurst keenly. "That's what you mean, isn't it?"

"Always, sir. And there was one here yesterday morning. That's the real point that I'm coming to, sir. I sorted the envelope myself and remember it well because of that. Attempting to be more accurate, I have had, I should say, at a rough guess, a dozen through my hands during the six months that I spoke about."

"And the pencilled name and address were?" said Bathurst softly.

"Otto Kreutz, Nine, West Street, Chelmersley."

Bell's reply was ready and emphatic. I knew that the man, as far as one can be sure of things like this, believed that he was telling the truth. His promptness left little room for doubt.

"Nine, West Street," echoed Goodaker. "It's a shop—that is. Must be. Let me think a minute," he went on. "I'll tell you what kind of a shop it is." He closed his eyes and put his hand across them.

"I'm a stranger to Chelmersley," interposed Bathurst, with a kind of ominous quietness, "but let me have a shot at telling you what that shop is before you spring it on me. Will you?"

The Inspector gazed at him wonderingly. "I don't quite see—"

"Listen, Inspector, and then you will. I'll venture to say that it's a hairdresser's. Am I right?"

"You are!" I cried in my turn, rather wildly, I'm afraid. "It's Melsheimer's—the barber's. A lock-up shop. I know the place well."

"Very satisfactory indeed," purred A.L.B. "It simply had to be something like that. Bell, you're a treasure! Let me have your address and I'll remember you on all the feasts of the Christian year. There may even be a chance of you and me meeting again."

CHAPTER VI
OTTO KREUTZ

"WEST Street, Chelmersley," repeated Goodaker hopefully, "is no more than a matter of five or six minutes' run from here." He looked eagerly at Bathurst. We were back again in the station.

Anthony Lotherington Bathurst, however, seemed—like Ambrose Applejack—in a mood for dalliance. But not with wenches from brigantines. All the same—surprising and unusual. I ransacked my remnant of brain for a satisfying reason. He knew too, the devil, what it was that I was doing. In a flash it came to me and I came up for air.

"Lord," I declared with annoyance, "the snag is at last visible to me. It's Wednesday—early closing day. The place will be closed until to-morrow morning. It would be a lock-up shop of course. Just our cursed luck!"

"Brightly gleams our Bannerman," he said quietly. There was no resentment on my part, for there was no trace of sarcasm in his tone. There's one thing, I will always say that for A.L.B. All the time that I worked with him on the "Otto Kreutz" case, as it afterwards became generally known, I could never once justifiably lay a charge of sarcasm at his door. A disciple of genial satire—yes. An apostle of mordant sarcasm—no.

Nobody ever realized the tremendous gulf that lies between the two better than he did. I thought often when I was with him, of the old Greek word *sarkazo*, and its etymological meaning of "tearing flesh like a dog", and I always knew that A.L.B. was never essentially cruel, and very, very seldom spoke with the slightest intention of wounding. He was a good scout through and through. After all, *un coup de langue est pire qu'un coup de lance.*

I heard the eagerness of Goodaker blow itself out in a muttered imprecation.

"Who's this man Kreutz?" demanded Bathurst. "That's the most interesting feature at the moment. Know anything about him?"

I wasn't sure whom he was asking—Goodaker or me. We looked at each other. And we each, I think, shook a head. Goodaker embarked upon certain explanations. "I know Melsheimer—that's the proprietor of the business—I don't know anybody named Kreutz."

"Tell me, Goodaker, all that you know. First verse and last verse. I resign myself."

"Well, I suppose Melsheimer's been in the shop in West Street about a couple of years. Pretty well established there by now. He bought the business from a man named Littlehales, the old boy who was Socialist Mayor of Chelmersley about nineteen twenty-seven or nineteen twenty-eight."

"German?"

"German extraction, no doubt. German in that sense. Don't know, of course, where he was born."

"Tell me of the man himself. Describe him."

"Big, tall, blonde man—say between thirty-five and forty years of age. Thick, tawny, curly hair. Plenty of it. Stout, but not ugly fat, by any means. Speaks English moderately well. You can tell he's a foreigner, naturally."

"Married?"

Goodaker shook his head. "Can't answer that. Don't know. Never seen his wife, if he has one. Can't say."

"Ever had any trouble with him?"

"Never. As far as I know he's a perfectly honest and law-abiding citizen. Like most Jerrys who settle here."

Bathurst cocked an eye at me. "One of the original herald-angels, eh? Gabriel's *fidus Achates.* Tell me more, best of Goodakers. Tell me the geographical position of Herr Melsheimer's hairdressing saloon in relation to *(a)* 'The Beaufoy Super Cinema', and *(b)* 'The Mortimer Super Cinema.' I feel that I am right in awarding to each the normal picture palace adjective, even without definite knowledge on the point. Relativity, you know, covers a multitude of inexactitudes."

He paused for the Inspector's reply. I let him do the answering, as Bathurst had asked him.

"Melsheimer's saloon is about twenty yards from the 'Beaufoy', which is actually in West Street itself. Two minutes only from the railway station. From the other cinema, the 'Mortimer', which is in Ashdown Street, it's a quarter of a mile, at least."

"Thank you, Goodaker. Do you think we shall be far wrong if we put Otto Kreutz down as a Melsheimer assistant? Next gentleman, please? Short on the neck and sides?"

Goodaker smiled. "No, I agree with you. I think that's the probable explanation, Mr. Bathurst."

"Interesting bloke, you know, Bannerman," said Bathurst, turning to me, "this comrade Kreutz, of ours."

I played up to the best of my ability. "Yes, I suppose he is. To you that is. I confess that I'm just a little . . ."

Once again Goodaker and I exchanged glances. But Bathurst stroked his chin and watched us. The imp of mischief danced in the grey eyes.

"Interesting from one or two points of view, you know. For instance, why the furtivity, shall we say—concerning domiciliary matters, as the rate-book might have it. H'm?"

I thought it over. "You mean, that, according to Bell, his letters were always addressed to the lockup shop?"

He nodded.

"Do you know, I never thought of that." Goodaker's face took on a far-away look as he made the admission.

"Think of it now, Goodaker. I suppose he has an address somewhere, eh? Must sleep somewhere, I suggest, mustn't he?"

"Just a minute, Mr. Bathurst." Goodaker slipped out of the room and it is significant, I think, of Bathurst's concentration, to remark that neither he nor I spoke to each other during the brief period of the Inspector's absence.

He was away for a few minutes only. "I can trace no person of the name of Otto Kreutz as living in Chelmersley itself or in the adjoining district."

Bathurst nodded. "Inquiries of the Registration Officer will settle the question definitely. Because you can't find him on the register, it doesn't prove that he hasn't an address somewhere about. Probably an alien too. Don't forget that."

He looked at his wrist-watch. "Food and drink, I think, are strongly indicated. Kreutz and Co. can and shall wait till the morrow, and prudence may come with the light. Ten o'clock to-morrow morning then, Goodaker. Here. Also, there may be developments from other directions. You never know at this game."

I had just finished Mrs. Ramage's morning offering of bacon and kidneys when I heard the honk of a car outside "The Rowfants". I rose from the table and went into the garden to cast an inquiring eye round. As I surmised, Bathurst was there in the road, in the Crossley.

"Started badly, Bannerman," he sang out. "I had intended to be along earlier than this. But the old bus chose to misbehave itself."

"Engine trouble?"

"No—played a new one on me this time. Petrol-feed dried up all of a sudden. Engine was so hot that the petrol vaporized in the pipe. Result, my dear chap, was an air 'lock'."

This was a new one on me, too, and I said so.

"What made the petrol-feed dry up like that?"

He grinned amiably. "Ah—there's the rub, as the divine William would have said. I imagine it arose from a combination of circumstances. A rather weak mixture, let us say, of cheap petrol that I filled up with yesterday at a small filling-station on the Finchbury cross-roads and half an hour's run with the wind well behind me. Still—all's well that ends thus. A hefty blow down the tank-filler roused the recumbent spirit, set it on the flow and the old bus was itself again. Fit for Goodaker, and after that, Melsheimer's?"

I nodded in affirmation.

"What about your own work, Doctor? Not taking you away from it, am I?"

"Well, to come to that, I've had to make arrangements, of course. I'll tell you what I've done. I 'phoned Langley before breakfast to do my urgent stuff. We've a sort of mutual understanding with regard to matters like that. It's quite O.K. The rest, the more ordinary cases, I shall have to fill in myself later—I'm missing nothing important."

"That's all right, then. I'm pleased. Go and make yourself decent and we'll hop along."

Goodaker had a companion when we picked him up—old Bligh again. Bathurst did the journey in eight minutes. It usually takes me about fifteen. I could tell that Bligh had been posted with details of what had occurred since he had parted from us. As usual, he was for immediate action. Impatient of anything in the nature of delay.

"Every avenue," he said pompously, "should be used for exploration. Not a single one that offers should be neglected. To me, there seems no reason why a German barber shouldn't have his correspondence addressed to him in pencil, if it's convenient to him. But there, I may be regarded as old-fashioned. Mr. Bathurst, however, attaches an importance to it which he is desirous of investigating. Therefore, it must be investigated. I will accompany you to this hair-dressing saloon, Goodaker."

Bathurst rallied the old fellow. "I *do* attach an importance to it, Sir George. A *tremendous* importance. It's like this, you see: I want to find out *why* Fredericks was murdered. Until I know that . . . Come on, you chaps. The car will hold the lot of us."

"Do you mind, Goodaker," said Bathurst, as we ran past the railway station and turned into West Street, "if I do the 'chin-wagging'?"

"Not at all, sir," returned Goodaker primly.

"I'd rather you did, as a matter of fact. It's your pigeon, this morning. I'm looking on."

"Thanks. You'll get a cue from me, when I want you to spout anything, so be on the *qui vive* and pick it up on the beat. Here we are, Sir George." We entered Melsheimer's, a body of four—two pairs. Bathurst and old Bligh in front. Goodaker and I together—just behind them.

The saloon was comparatively small, but Chelmersley itself is not huge, and I've no doubt the size of the show would be considered average. There were but two chairs there. Melsheimer himself, whom I recognized from Goodaker's excellent description of him, was seated in one of the chairs reading a newspaper. Another white-habited figure, the assistant evidently, was washing the farther basin. This second man was of middle height and stoutish, a little bent across the shoulders. He had dark black hair and a little foreign-looking black moustache. Each man wore spectacles—Melsheimer horn-rimmed, and the other man the ordinary big, round glasses so favoured by his countrymen.

Melsheimer, I took to be about forty, and his assistant about ten years younger. But he was a difficult chap to size up, this second fellow, and I wouldn't have wagered a fortune on the accuracy of my opinion. Bathurst approached the proprietor with something like cordiality.

"Mr. Melsheimer," he opened, "may we have a few moments' conversation with you?"

The big fair German seemed a little taken aback at the request.

"Why, yes." His accent was unmistakable. The "w" had a half "v" sound. "Here?"

"It is as good as anywhere. Why not?"

The stout assistant-chap perked up at this, and he looked us over carefully. Particularly me. Some seconds elapsed before he took his short-sighted eyes off me. Then he turned his head towards Bathurst again, and as he did so the thought came over me that he and I had met before somewhere. Where the hell was it? I slashed at my brain savagely, but the real reminiscence continued to elude me and I felt as though I were flapping futile wings against the bars of an implacable cage.

"Confound it all!" I muttered to my soul. Then it began to come to me; it was somewhere where I had been with young Jack Tabernacle. Then the damned will-o'-the-wisp floated away once more, and, unable to follow it, I was helpless and hopeless again. Further pursuit of it was impossible. A.L.B. had launched his campaign and I found myself listening.

"We are investigating a case of theft, Mr. Melsheimer. A series of thefts, to be more explicit. From the local post office. Here is my authority, if you would care to see it."

The German made a grimace as he looked at Bathurst's card. He was a genial bloke on the whole and I rather fell for him. On the other hand, Kreutz, if it were he, impressed me as a nasty messy piece of work. I don't know why. He just did.

"So."

Bathurst cut in again. "Yes. The position is this. The day before yesterday, several letters for delivery in this part of Chelmersley, went through the hands of a particular sorter. There was one, so it is believed, on the evidence of another sorter, that was addressed here. To a Mr. Otto Kreutz. Was it ever delivered here, do you know? Could you tell me?"

"So." Melsheimer nodded. "It is true that my assistant has the name that you say—Otto Kreutz. He can no doubt what you come to know tell you. Otto—tell the gentleman what you have hear him ask."

The Kreutz merchant came forward and I saw Bathurst more or less size him up.

"It is all right," said Kreutz, "about the letter you inquire for. Here I have him."

He spoke with a strong German accent, much more apparent than his governor's, and curled his face up when he glanced in my direction in a way that made him look predatory. That is the word I want. It came to me immediately, and I've always retained the idea, although more than once I've mentally challenged it. As it's resisted the challenge every time I'm cocksure that I'm right.

When the chap spoke, he tapped the breast pocket of his white coat. Bathurst extended his hand towards him.

"May I see it? Just to make sure that . . ."

"I have no great objection. Although to me the contents private are—and nobody else concern."

Bathurst attempted to wave the objection aside. "Be easy, man, on that account. I have no right to read the letter and I shouldn't dream of doing so. Also, there is no need for such a thing. All I wish to see is the envelope."

Otto Kreutz leered up at him and fumbled in the pocket that I had seen him touch. He pushed an envelope into Bathurst's hands. From where I was standing, I could see the pencilled address. Then I noticed something else. As his finger and thumb came away from the corner of the envelope and released it for Bathurst's acceptance, I saw that the portion where the stamp had been, had been either torn from the envelope or cut away. Also across the man's thumbnail was a purple bruise as though the thumb had been hit with something or badly pinched somewhere.

I saw, too, the muscles of A.L.B.'s jaw tighten suddenly and then relax, just as quickly, into a smile.

"I'm sorry, Mr. Kreutz," he said affably, "but this proves nothing, does it? You see what I mean. How do I know that this is the envelope in question? The date has gone—with the stamp. Naturally."

"I am sorry," returned Kreutz stonily. "That is my fault—yes. I have it removed. But my cousin—he is a lad in Cologne; he is what you call a phil . . ."

He stumbled over the word, but found his feet eventually. "Philatelist. All the stamps off all the letters that I get, I tear—collect them—and send them to him."

Bathurst answered sternly: "Where's this particular stamp, then? You've scarcely had time yet to send that to him."

Kreutz was unruffled. "At my lodgings. A room in Little Chelmersley I have—Ninety-four Thatch Road—my landlady's name Mrs. Rhodes is. A lot of stamps in a drawer in my bedroom I have."

I could hear old Bligh snorting hard in his attempts to achieve restraint. But Bathurst had impressed upon him the necessity of being moderately passive, and I'll give the old lad his due and admit that he played up to his instructions very sportingly.

Otto Kreutz and Bathurst faced each other—eye to eye, toe to toe; almost challengingly. Otto emerged first and spoke.

"It is the truth that I tell. Here is proof." He plunged his fingers again into the pocket that had held the envelope that he had handed to Bathurst. From it, he took four or five envelopes. It was exactly as he had foreshadowed to us. Each one had its address written in pencil and each one had the stamp torn from the top right-hand corner.

"See? So? The stamps from the envelopes I have torn. For my cousin, young Karl Heinrich."

"Yes—you told me that, Kreutz. I can see now that you were telling the truth. Here's your letter of yesterday. Take it."

He held it out for Kreutz to take. But either the man was clumsy, or Bathurst himself maladroit, for the envelope, on the interchange, fell from the meeting fingers and fluttered to the floor. The paper that it had held, slipped out and lay at its side. Anthony Bathurst instantly became all apologies, gallantly retrieved the contents and handed the whole bag of tricks back to its owner.

Then he turned to Melsheimer with a smile. As he smiled, a man shuffled into the shop.

"I'm afraid that we're taking up your time, Mr. Melsheimer. You'll be glad, no doubt, both you and Mr. Kreutz, to see the back of us. I'm glad, though, that everything's all right as far as is concerned here, and that we have been able to trace the envelope that we wanted. Good morning, Mr. Melsheimer."

I saw him motion to Goodaker. Melsheimer expanded profusely.

"A very sad thing, this murder of Mr. Fredericks, sir. I am very sorry. A nice gentleman. Have the police any clue, Inspector?"

Goodaker seemed on the horns of a dilemma. "Well—in a way."

"So! I hope you catch the man that did it. I hope it very much. Mr. Fredericks was one of my customers here. Wasn't he, Otto?"

Kreutz, lathering a stubbled chin, nodded stolidly. "Yes. Fairly regular. I his hair for him cut, I think, a week ago; perhaps ten days."

Melsheimer nodded approvingly. "Yes. He come in here once nearly every week."

The proprietor paused; it seemed that an idea had come to him. "Otto," he said at length, "has Mr. Fredericks not been in during my absence?" The assistant stropped a razor imperturbably. "No, sir. Not all the time away you have been." Melsheimer blew his fat cheeks out and embarked upon an explanation. "It is that I have been away for a week. My summer holiday. Therefore I ask Otto the question. You heard, gentlemen, how he answer."

He beamed effulgently at us as we made our exit. My last impression of Kreutz was that he was holding his injured thumb with his other hand. It was evidently paining him considerably as he started upon his task of shaving the man whom he had lathered.

We entered the "Crossley". Silent—each one of us.

"Bannerman," declared Bathurst, as we took the first corner, "I've a job of work for you, if you'll be good enough to take it on. Man goeth forth to his work and to his labour—until the evening. Come down here this evening in your bus. Hang about in the vicinity till closing time. When Kreutz leaves off work, I want you to follow him. Sleuth him till his funny-bones shrivel. See where he gets to, whom he meets, and so on. Don't on any account let him spot you. How you do it all, I'll leave to your own ingenuity. But I'll see that the police don't interfere with you. If you see me knocking about in the Crossley, don't take any notice of me. Shun me as the spots of the Black Death. I'm going to take a line on that genial old soul, Herr Melsheimer. He interests me almost as much as Comrade Kreutz." He leant back and spoke in an undertone to Bligh and Goodaker. The Chief Constable whistled and, after a moment or so, nodded.

"That's just how it strikes me, sir," said A.L.B.

CHAPTER VII

I PICK UP REINFORCEMENTS

TEN minutes to seven that evening saw me driving slowly by the Melsheimer premises in West Street. I crawled a little way down the street and then turned at a convenient side-road, so that, as I came towards it, the interior of the saloon was partly visible to me.

I went by at a moderate pace and I was enabled to spot both Kreutz and Melsheimer at work inside. There were two or three customers waiting, so that I knew it would be a good deal more than ten minutes before my quarry would appear.

I spun down the road, therefore, that led to Wedlock's flour-mill, knowing that there was but little risk in what I was doing. In a way I was forced to do something of the kind. You can't dawdle very well in a car in a moderately busy street, and I didn't want to be pinched for kerb-crawling, despite what Bathurst had said about squaring the powers that be.

But at seven sharp, I turned the old bus and blew off again towards Melsheimer's. Things now began to move a bit. A man came out, hands stuffed into pockets—a customer without doubt. Melsheimer followed him to the door and called a salutation to him of some kind. I couldn't catch what it was as I rolled past, but I saw Melsheimer turn back into the shop and start to pull off his white jacket.

This looked like business that concerned me, so I sped down the street for a few more yards, turned again, and came back again, this time at a much slower pace. Just as I slithered by the door, Melsheimer himself came out in ordinary clothes, hat on head. He was travelling in the same direction as I was, but he wasn't my red-hot quarry, and I knew it.

For the moment, I was just a wee bit undecided as to when and where to do my Dick Whittington stuff, and just as I was making up my scrappy mind, I had a vision in the driving-mirror of a car coming up to me from behind. I beckoned it on and recognized, with a kind of catch in the throat, the pale primrose wheels that flashed by.

So old Bathurst was after his man and I still had my own particular job of work to do. He had left me my own pigeon. This decided me. I determined to run up a little way farther before I turned this time. When I had executed this last manoeuvre, I was overjoyed to see Kreutz standing at the door, still in his professional outfit.

I resolved to take a chance, so I pulled the car into the kerb and dashed into a tobacco-shop. I didn't mean to wait more than a moment or so; my idea was to avoid this monotonous business of turning back again. When I had thrust the packet of tobacco that I had purchased into my pocket,, I loitered on the step of the shop for a little while and pretended to look round, as though a trifle uncertain as to which way to go.

All this of course to gain time! Kreutz was now on the pavement, engaged in the business of closing up for the night, but he didn't see me. He pushed the blind back and then went inside again. I heard him shut the door too, so I cleared off the step of my tobacco-shop and pretended to have a glance at my car. There was one thing, I concluded: he couldn't, in reasonable circumstances, be long now. I was unutterably wrong, however and a policeman approaching, I was forced into the car again. I took little risk however, and was soon back, covering more than the distance in the reverse direction, that Kreutz could possibly have done in the time, had he come out during the tiny period when I had had my back turned.

There was no sign of him. The pavement had now cleared considerably of passers-by and I could see clearly for a long way in front of me. As I passed the shop itself, I saw the shadow of the man I hunted, flit across the window. There was no mistaking it. Whereat I took heart. Foolishly, and like the utter ass that I was, for that was the last glimmer that I was destined to have of the man Otto Kreutz for many days to come.

The minutes of my wrist-watch ticked relentlessly by. Fifteen, thirty, forty-five—one hour. Fifteen . . .

I couldn't by any stretch of imagination keep up this present game of mine and I anathematized Bathurst for telling me to come and do my sleuthing in the bus. With a last appallingly comprehensive curse that consigned Kreutz into the hottest of Gehennas, I gave the affair up as a bad egg—an egg not even up to the curate's.

Going home, I stepped on the juice, I can tell you, and by the time I reached "The Rowfants", I was in a mood of such savagery and obstinate stubbornness that it would have forced me to argue with the prisoner of the Vatican on auricular confession, transubstantiation, or even with regard to the immaculate conception of the B.V.M.

I had hopped out of the car and was on the point of putting my hoof against my garden gate to open it, when I saw the headlights of an approaching car. I had seen the way it had come and I was pretty sure that I knew whom it held. I was right. It was Jack Tabernacle, and directly he got abreast of me he pulled up.

I was downright pleased to see the boy, although I realized with a heavy heart the reason that had brought him home posthaste. He stuck his fin out to me and we shook hands.

"Put your car away, Bannerman," he said, "and, if you can, come with me. I want news badly—at present I've only the bare facts that Iris has sent me. The barest of the bare," he concluded bitterly.

I needed no second bidding, as I was fed to the teeth with my own pestiferous company. "Where are you off to?" I asked him first of all.

"To Mrs. Cotterill's. Iris is there with her. She arranged to meet me there to-night. Thundering good idea too. Wasn't keen on going up to her own place. Who would be?"

I nodded my understanding.

"Tell me all about it," he said curtly.

I obeyed. I needed no encouragement to do that either. When I mentioned Bathurst's name he pricked up his keen young ears and muttered an enthusiasm.

"Oh, good egg! What luck to have him on the job. How was it managed? Iris never let on about that. Go on. Tell me."

"She doesn't know," I returned. And went on. Right from the beginning, until I came to Otto Kreutz. To the letters, the missing corners from the envelopes, and the unholy mess I had made of things that evening.

He essayed explanation and excuse.

"There are only two things that could have happened, you silly old mutt: *(a)* He's still there in the shop somewhere, or *(b)* there's a back exit and the swine used it. Don't want to be a glittering sleuth to get thus far."

I nodded ruefully as I realized the truth of what he said to me. "I suppose you're right. If only I'd had the—"

"Don't reproach yourself, Mike. It's easy to be wise after the event. Sorry and all that. Tell me the rest. Go on."

Again I went on. Told him of the strange sort of suspicion that had come to me with regard to Kreutz.

Jack Tabernacle seized on this with avidity.

"Can't you *think* where you've seen him before? It's so tremendously important, man. Think! If you could get the connection, Mike, it would mean such a hell of a lot to us."

I responded feebly. "Can't—at the moment. It may come I suppose. It's no good chasing it. That's the way to lose it for ever."

Jack accepted the inevitable. "So Bathurst's after Melsheimer—eh? Guess he'll have something to tell you in the morning."

Then I had a really brainy one. One from the vintage basket. I clutched his arm just as we turned down to Rosemary's. "Jack," I cried, "where I have failed, it's on the cards that you may remember. Two heads are proverbially better than one. Go to Melsheimer's to-morrow and have a squint at Otto Kreutz, will you?"

"I will—like a shot. I'll be early bird's 'nap' selection—come in and see the girls, won't you?"

Iris was a dear little dark thing, ordinarily pretty and vivacious, but it was a weary-eyed kid that came to meet us now. Rosemary was seated on the pouffe in the lounge. Her hands were clasped in front of her. She looked delightfully cool and charming and was wearing a simple black evening-frock. As she gave me her hand, her eyes told me a lot and I would have will-ingly walked on my hands and knees if she had commanded. Oh yes—I had it pretty badly!

"Michael," she said, as I reached her side, "er—Doctor Bannerman"—with more than a touch of her normal imperi-ousness—"who brought Anthony Bathurst, of all people, into this case?"

Now this was the identical opening that I desired more than any other, for there were one or two things that I was itching to have properly explained. But that glorious mouth of hers that asked the question was just a little tremulous too, so I decided to walk with wariness for a time at least and watch my step. I had seen my lady in this mood before and I knew that it had to be treated with infinite tenderness.

"I believe," I reassured her, "that it was Sir George Bligh, the Chief Constable. The fountain-head, as it were."

She seemed a bit relieved at this, although wasting no time in shooting another question at me.

"Are you absolutely sure of that?" The eagerness and anxiety in the voice were there for all to hear.

I glanced round towards Jack to see whether he had noticed it, but he was talking in an undertone to Iris and quite oblivious, for the time being, of Rosemary and me. It seemed to me, as I listened, that he was insisting on something with which Iris was in disagreement.

"Near enough," I answered almost cheerfully. "How I know is through this. When old Bligh came down to the station first thing this morning, Anthony Bathurst came with him—I fancy he'd been glad-ragging it somewhere with the old boy and was ready to hand, so to speak, when he was wanted. Marvellous chap," I concluded.

"Oh, perfectly," she countered. "I'm well aware of that." There was a high spot of colour in each of her cheeks. My enthusiasm for A.L.B. militated against the prudence with which I ought to have invested myself.

"Only known him a few hours," I went on blunderingly, "but it's easy to see how he's established his reputation. Wonderful memory for one thing—knew quite a heap of things about me."

She flashed a quick look at me as though endeavouring to appreciate all that had occurred.

"Yes—too wonderful, sometimes." Her eyes took on that starry look under their long lashes that always made me forget nearly everything else that the world contained.

"You've met before, haven't you," I said asininely, "you and he?"

My reward for this effort was a look of scorn. My lady was pleased to mock. "You have grown intimate with Mr. Bathurst extraordinarily quickly, haven't you? Fancy an exchange of confidences so soon! I thought that we women possessed the privilege in that particular direction?"

"Not quite that, Rosemary," I returned doggedly. "Bathurst told me one thing about you—and one thing only. That was just after your car passed us up in Taggarts Way."

"How interesting! What did he tell you?"

"That when he knew you, you were Rosemary Marquis."

"That friendship, at any rate, didn't prevent him being rude to me, did it?"

"Hold on just a little," I said. "He had no idea it was you, until you had passed us. I'm positive of that."

She softened a bit when she understood, and twisted her handkerchief between her fingers. "Of course, you told him of me—of my marriage." She looked away from me as she put the question.

"He knew. At least, I think so. He asked after your late husband—Cotterill, I told him."

"Didn't he know that my husband was dead?"

"No."

She looked up at this, and seemed to slip her mood off her as a woman, with a quick movement, will release a cloak from her shoulders. Her next question surprised me.

"And whom does the great Anthony suspect? Has he got as far as that yet?"

Jack heard it and answered the question for me. "Yes, Mrs. Cotterill. From what Michael tells me, there's a man named Otto Kreutz well in the limelight of suspicion. A chap in a barber's shop down in Chelmersley, in West Street. One of the assistants there, I believe. I've just been telling Iris about it. But she can't help us, Michael. Can you, Iris?"

He turned and appealed to her. The girl shook her head. Tears weren't far away. The damned shame of the whole thing hit me hard.

"I've thought and thought, and I can't possibly imagine what such a man as that could have to do with Daddy."

"It's close to the 'Beaufoy', Iris," said Rosemary; "there's that to be said about it."

It seemed to me that she rather welcomed the entrance of Otto Kreutz into the arena of suspicion and was desperately anxious that he should remain there.

"No more do I, Iris. Although I believe . . ." It was Jack replying—he didn't appear to have heard Rosemary's intervention, and was apparently attempting to follow a train of thought that had suggested itself to him. Perhaps through what Iris had said. Suddenly he turned to me.

"Tell you what, Mike Bannerman. I'll pop into Melsheimer's first thing to-morrow morning and report to you later. It's just on the cards, I suppose, that I may run across Bathurst knocking round somewhere. What do you think, old man?"

"Can't say for certain, of course. But there's a good chance of it, no doubt."

You could see that Jack was thinking hard. "If I don't—you'll have to do the needful. Still, we'll let it wait temporarily. I've an idea that I'd very much like to put to him. The sooner the better." Rosemary brought us liquid refreshment and we talked, the four of us, long into the night. I was amazed at the time my watch showed when I rose to go. Jack came along with me.

"Iris is staying here for the night, so there's no need for us to worry about her getting home." There was a look on his face that I didn't remember having seen before, and I wondered what it was that had come along to trouble him.

I felt certain in my own mind now that an idea had come to him out of something that had been said by one of us and that it wouldn't allow him to rest until he had shoved it under A.L.B.'s nose for him to have a look at it. I knew, of experience, how tenaciously Jack Tabernacle stuck to anything when he had once pushed his claws into it.

He was silent as he walked round to the front of the car. On the point of getting in, a voice called me back. Rosemary Cotterill had come right down to her front gate, the prettiest of pictures in the moonlight. She called me back from the car. Curtly, almost.

"Michael! May I speak to you again, before you go?"

I turned quickly. "Of course."

She looked straight at me. "I think I had better tell you," she said, "before anybody else does, that when I was Rosemary Marquis I was engaged to Anthony Bathurst. There was no public announcement of the fact; but there was a definite understanding between the two of us that existed for nearly two years."

Before I could reply to her, she slipped away from the patch of darkness into the gleam of light that was coming from the house. To say that I was staggered is completely beside the point.

CHAPTER VIII
THE SECOND MURDER

THE following morning, I expected Bathurst to put in an appearance fairly early, but my expectations were not realized. The result was that I hung about indoors for some little time—irresolute and undecided; it seemed that it was impossible for me to settle down to work again. After a time, however, when I realized that Bathurst didn't look like coming, I managed to pull myself together and went out to see three or four patients whom I'm afraid had been rather neglected of late.

One of these cases took me almost into Chelmersley itself, and I found myself bowling along the main road from Great

Steeping with a strange eagerness which, being interpreted, meant, I think, that I might run into fresh news of some kind affecting the murder of Walter Fredericks.

Nothing happened to me, however, beyond the completion of the trivial round that had brought me out, and I turned towards home, the Ramage, and lunch, shortly after two o'clock, my last consultation having taken me considerably longer than I had anticipated in the first consideration of things.

As events turned out, it was lucky for me that I had been delayed; about a quarter of a mile's distance from "The Rowfants", on the way back, I ran into Jack Tabernacle. He had evidently lunched and left his own place just afterwards. His car was going at a good bat, but when he spotted me in the road he slowed down, and waved a paw for me to follow suit. I could see from his manner that he had news for me, and I got all snappy and teed up, and welcomed it eagerly. He stopped his own car, got out and came round to the front of me.

"Listen, O King! I went into Melsheimer's this morning, Mike, as I promised you that I would. Candidly, I can't make the place out."

He paused, to proceed almost immediately. "There's something deuced funny going on there, in my opinion. Something that I haven't yet been able to place or fathom. But which I shall before very long, my lad! Also, which is more to the point perhaps, I saw your friend Kreutz."

Again the pause.

"Well?" I queried.

"Don't know," returned Jack with a shake of the head. "In a quandary. Much the same as you were. I had a shave there." He grinned at the recollection. "Kreutz shaved me. By the way, old son, did you spot that bruised thumb of his? The thumb on the right hand."

I nodded. "Yes."

"I watched him the whole time, Mike, during the varied processes of his shaving me. Every now and then, an action, usually a sudden involuntary action, gave me the idea that I had seen him before somewhere—just as you yourself thought. But place the beggar accurately, I can't, try as I will."

He grinned at me again. "Towards the end of the old *'spoliam barbam'* job, I'm rather afraid I gave myself away, for the general tactics got reversed. Instead of me watching *him*, I twigged the Kreutz bird watching *me*. I'll swear the beggar was suspicious of me before he'd finished."

"A queer business," I remarked. "A damned queer business altogether. What possible connection could there have been between Fredericks and these people at that shop? The whole thing seems to me to be pretty sickening."

"I agree, Mike. When we find what that connection was, we shall know a lot more than we know now. Perhaps we may even know everything."

An ugly look crept into his eyes as he finished what he was saying, and I knew that the thing had touched him on the raw.

"And then I'll avenge the death of a real good fellow. A man whose goodness of heart was unknown to ninety-five per cent of ordinary people. I'll promise you that much, Mike."

He swung back into the car and called out to me as he drove away. "When you see Bathurst again, don't forget I want a word with him. And as I said before, the sooner the better, too. Cheero."

I had lunch, decided after a lengthy communion with myself that I wouldn't 'phone Rosemary, toured round during the late afternoon picking up four outlying cases that needed attention now and then and blew back home again. Time—about seven-thirty! Had a bath—it was infernally hot still; umpteen "spots" of Scotch and "Polly"; did justice to several of the Ramage's best efforts, including a top-hole scalloped lobster; and sat down in an excessively easy chair somewhere about twenty past ten for half an hour's rest. Which was, however, doomed to be of much shorter duration.

I had, in fact, scarcely elevated my hind legs when I heard a ring at the bell, the voice of the Ramage rising a little querulously, and then the rather cold, incisive tones of A.L.B.

I went to the door of my room and bellowed to him to "come along in".

"You're nice and cosy here, Doctor," he said, stretching his length on my settee. "I've come to the conclusion that there are worse jobs than yours. Nice stretch of country, too, round here. Up there by Saxbury is definitely charming."

This surprised me. I pushed the Scotch towards him. "You've been round a bit then, since I saw you?"

"Just a little. Needs must when the devil handles the reins." He pressed his little finger into the tobacco that he had packed into the bowl of his pipe. "Wanted to think, Bannerman. Think hard. Ever realized how devilishly hard it is to think, sometimes? I mean, to do effectively a job of real thinking—nothing of the contiguous variety. That sort cuts little ice in an affair of this kind. Thought-power can be terrific, you know—comparable with horsepower and candle-power as units of strength and light as a term of measurement of mental concentration. See what I mean? Look at it for yourself. When we think we *evolve* power. When we reflect we do infinitely more than save ideas from being lost. We lay them up in the repository of memory to be revived at some future time by the impulse of will. And the process of reflection means that we are left with impressions that are *permanent*. Which leads to the possession of matter. You're following me, Bannerman, aren't you?"

"I think I am."

"Good. I've expressed myself badly, I'm afraid. Anyhow, I've motored miles, and most of the way I've thought damned hard."

"Got anywhere?"

He tapped his teeth with the pipe-stem. "Don't know. Not quite sure. I've dug a word out of the mess that attracts me."

He stopped rather abruptly. "I've been up, by the way, to the dead man's house. Extended my acquaintance with Donald, the son, and met a rather charming little girl, his sister—the lady I passed in a car a day or so ago—Miss Iris Fredericks. You know her fairly well, I understand?"

"Pretty well. She's a friend of Mrs. Cotterill. And she's engaged to Tabernacle. He lives just up the road here. He's home. Came home yesterday. Did you know?"

"They told me so up there. I'm always sorry for a bloke that gets his holiday messed up by a spot of bother like this. It's happened to me in the past and made me monstrously sympathetic. Roughish luck."

He fell into a reverie, and I was wise enough to offer no disturbance. I contented myself with watching him.

"Tell me, Bannerman," he said at length. "Ever heard the dead man, Fredericks, connected with South America?"

"Never," I replied. "Why?"

"Merely this. There were two South American associations up at his house. For example, to quote one of them. A photograph of the tennis club connected with the Antofagasta and Bolivian Railway hangs on one of the walls. May be nothing in it, of course. Can't tell till we make the definite inquiry. May have a link with somebody else, not Fredericks. Still, I thought I'd ask you."

He puffed steadily at the pipe. "I'm lucky in having you as a Watson, you know. You're in the pukka lineal descent. True Apostolic succession. How did Duncan Fredericks die?"

He shot the question at me with a quickness that almost took me off my feet. What on earth was he trailing? Before I could frame an answer he was at me again.

"You're the family doctor, aren't you?"

"Oh, yes. You rather startled me, though. I wasn't expecting the question, you see. I don't think anything could have been farther from my thoughts than the point you asked about. It wasn't as though Duncan died yesterday. Still, you're barking up the wrong tree. Duncan Fredericks died of acute nephritis."

"Positive? Absolutely? Tell me all you know. Symptoms, etc."

"Lord, yes. Dead certain. The trouble ran on perfectly normal lines. The uriniferous tubules were attacked most severely. There was urine suppression, then, of course, the resultant conditions of uraemia, coma, and death. I prescribed the usual remedies, acetate of ammonia, nitrous ether spirit, and, finally, we were forced to use the hot 'packs'. No good at all. There wasn't an earthly! Nothing doing. The poor chap had been doomed for some time."

"No possibility of poison, by any chance, Bannerman? Just the tiniest chance, say? H'm?"

"None whatever. Dismiss the idea."

"Young for Bright's disease, wasn't he?"

"In a way, yes. But he'd had a nasty diph. turn a year or so previously and this was the poor devil's legacy from it. Not an unusual legacy, either. Diph's a funny customer. Vindictive."

"H'm. You're disappointing, my dear Watson. Do you know, I could have borne to have heard an entirely different story. Still . . ."

He broke off and knocked out the dottle from his pipe. Moments of silence. Then Bathurst darted off at a tangent.

"Kreutz—Doctor. Let's get back to him. He's definite, at any rate. What happened last evening?"

I explained to him. Shamefacedly, I'm afraid. Bathurst regarded me curiously. "Stayed behind on the premises, do you mean?"

"He never came out for a couple of hours at least. After closing time, that is. I'd swear it on the bones of my mother."

He scratched his chin thoughtfully. "Curiouser and curiouser, in the words of Alice. All of a-piece, though. Melsheimer was a wash-out too. He went straight home and, as far as I know, stayed there for the rest of the evening. I got no more than you did, Bannerman, so don't nurse a 'peeve'."

Another idea seemed to strike him all of a sudden. "Those envelopes, Doctor. That little matter of torn corners that we came up against. 'The torn corners of Kreutz.' I'd like to have a look at some ordinary postmarks, while I think of it. From this district and also from other districts. Got any recent correspondence handy?"

I rose from the armchair to supply him. I usually toss recent stuff on to the corner of my table, where it accumulates until I have a periodic clearance.

You can guess that it was a mixed bag that I handed to him. Circulars, letters (several) and postcards (four). He tossed the circulars on one side and set himself to examine the postmarks on the letters and the postcards. Two of the latter were from

Jack while he had been in Rome, one from Rosemary Cotterill from a corner of South Devon, and the other from a man named Sheepshanks who had been at Charing Cross with me years ago. He had kept in touch, corresponding very occasionally.

So much for the postcards. The letters that Bathurst handled, included personal, professional and official specimens. Amongst the correspondents whose handwriting I could identify, as Bathurst sorted the envelopes over, were Torrelli, the proprietor of the restaurant next to the 'Beaufoy' cinema, Montague Corbett, one of the local bigwigs, George Ramage, a nephew of the dear old girl who "did" for me and old Bligh, the Chief Constable.

Bathurst inspected the postmarks on the various envelopes with the most meticulous care. I'm perfectly aware of the cliché. I'm just trying to tell you what he did. I saw him scan dates and times more than once, as though he had a doubt or anxiety about something. Eventually he placed the envelopes in a neat little pile and handed them back to me, Rosemary's card from Ottery St. Mary positioned last of all. His eyes, I thought, held a look that suggested to me that he was still troubled about something. He gave me, however, no hint of an invitation to tax him as to details.

The next thing he put up to me was entirely unexpected. "Care to put me up for the night, Bannerman?" he asked. "Any old place will suit me. Don't mind a shake-down anywhere that's convenient to you."

"No trouble at all, old man," I responded, feeling more bucked than anything else. "There's, a spare room up top with a bed in it. I'll go up in a minute and make it ship-shape for you."

"That's very decent of you. Thanks awfully, Doctor. Later on will do. Don't trouble for half an hour or so. Don't mind if I help myself to another 'spot', do you?"

I nodded assent. "Of course not."

He filled his glass deliberately. "It's motive that's puzzling me in this case, Bannerman. Most cases that you come up against, supply something, at least, in that line. This wretched case, up to the moment, reveals nothing, with the possible exception of that one word that I told you just now was intriguing me.

Over which, too, you didn't help me. Rather the reverse, in fact. Remember, Doctor?"

He drained his glass with almost as much deliberation as with which he had filled it. "I rather reproach myself for omitting to do something this morning. But I was busy and, after all, one can't do everything. I had to see Goodaker early on. He's working on the Fredericks' 'antecedents' end. I ought to have had another look at Kreutz. He's a slippery devil, that fellow, and I'm far from sure about him. I don't care about leaving him too much to other people."

"He was at his job as usual to-day, if that's any news for you. You needn't worry. He hasn't given you the slip yet."

"I know that, Bannerman," he replied good-humouredly. "At least, I think I do. Goodaker's put one of his best men on to him—at my suggestion. If he went, he wouldn't get far. He'd have a real job to hide himself. You say he was at Melsheimer's to-day? How do you know that so certainly? Did you drop in there yourself?"

I explained how I had heard.

He screwed up his face as he listened.

"And Tabernacle, you say, couldn't place him either?"

"No. No more than I."

"Pity. It was a slender chance, though, wasn't it?"

"Yes. But worth trying all the same."

He walked to the french doors and looked out into the night. It was summer at its best. Everything was tranquil, and the stark ugliness of red murder as even a possibility seemed out of place in the quiet beauty of a countryside like this.

A.L.B. jingled his loose coins. "What's this one word that intrigues you?" I asked him. "The word at which you hinted with regard to the question of motive. Tell me. I'm curious."

He turned and looked at me strangely. Several seconds elapsed before he answered.

"Vendetta," he said quietly. "*Rache! La Revanche!* Behold me polygot." He grinned that attractive grin of his.

The words had scarcely left his lips when my 'phone went, in the next room. I was afraid that it meant a confinement. There were two in the offing that I knew to be imminent. I know that I went to the noisy instrument with a certain amount of resentment. I was wrong, however. Each of my two ladies was behaving herself. The speaker was Iris Fredericks. She was agitated.

"Is that you, Doctor? I'm awfully sorry to trouble you, but it's about Donald, my brother. Is he by any chance with you?"

I told her that he wasn't. What was the trouble, then?

"He arranged to be home soon after seven, Dr. Bannerman. He's never been near. We're frightfully worried about him."

"Naturally," I responded, "but there are other places where he may be besides mine. For instance, there's Tabernacle's. Have you 'phoned him?"

She said she hadn't.

"Very well," I returned, "I'll get through to Jack for you at once. Very likely, young Donald's in there at his place having two or three drinks or something. Ring off for half a second and I'll get through to him."

I rang through and the operator gave me Jack's line pretty quickly.

"Who? Bannerman? Oh—you, Michael. I was just going to turn in. What's the game now?"

I told him. No luck. Donald wasn't there. Jack hadn't seen him since the late afternoon. Could he do anything, though?

I told him that I didn't think so, rang off and got through to Iris again. Tried to reassure her a bit and asked her to let me know at once when her brother came in. Wasn't too successful though with my spot of comfort. The little lady was refusing—very definitely.

Then I went back to A.L.B., Esq.—still standing by the two doors and looking out into the night, exactly as I had left him.

"Any trouble, Bannerman? Tell me—I'm interested!" He asked and instructed me quietly. There was a gleam in the grey eyes of him. Again, I unburdened myself. "God!" I heard him mutter, half to himself and half to me. Swinging round on to me with a suppressed excitement, he staggered me as I had never been staggered before. There was a fierceness in his voice that almost shocked me.

"Bannerman," he said, "we aren't going to see bed, you and I, for another hour yet. Get your car out, man. Don't waste a moment. I'm going to take you for a spin."

"What!" I exclaimed incredulously. "Where?"

"Taggarts Way," he replied gravely.

"Why?" I cried wildly.

The anxiety in his voice communicated itself to me. "To make sure, Bannerman."

"Of what? Of what, in God's name?"

Again he looked at me appraisingly—measuringly.

"Vendetta. Father and son."

CHAPTER IX
THROUGH THE BRAIN

I GOT the old bus going in about three and a half jiffies, and I did well over forty through Great Steeping and Chelmersley up to Taggarts Way. I can't recall that either of us spoke a word until we reached the lane itself. This is some indication of the tenseness of the situation.

As we turned into the lane itself, Bathurst leant forward silently and touched me on the arm.

"Don't run her too far up, Bannerman," he said. "Take it easy, man; keep your nerve and prepare yourself for a shock. Unless I'm very wide of the mark," he added softly, almost to himself.

It was pretty dark as I ran the car up the lane and I should have been forced to have slackened speed even if Bathurst hadn't told me. Suddenly he clutched my arm again.

"Should be somewhere about here," he said, "as far as my memory goes. Wish it weren't so damned dark. Stop here, Doctor, will you?"

I obeyed. He opened the door nearest to him and slithered out. I followed and stood at his side. He peered round for a few minutes. Eventually he found what he wanted.

I followed the line of his outstretched finger and saw what he wanted me to see. It was the path that led across the piece of waste land. The path that we had used before with Bligh and Goodaker. Few people used it now. It was a relic of the days when there had been a gun station there. Over and above that, Taggarts Way was usually given a wide berth these days; it was lonely, desolate and grim.

Bathurst took a stride away from me. Then he beckoned to me. "Not far to look, Bannerman," he said curtly. "There."

I bent forward. Screwed my eyes into the inky cloud of darkness. Very gradually they asserted themselves and I was able to pick something out that looked to me like a huddled heap of clothes on the ground. My companion caught me by the arm and pulled me towards it. A few quick steps were enough. The body in front of us was that of a young man.

He lay face downwards. His right arm was flung out despairingly, or so it seemed, in front of him. I dropped to one knee and turned him over. Only to make sure, for what I feared was only too true. It was young Donald Fredericks.

I whispered his name to Bathurst as he stood by me. He followed my example and, nodding, knelt down on the other side of the dead man.

"Of course," he muttered. "There was no doubt of that from the first. How did they get him, the devils? Throat again?"

He was wrong though, in this surmise. I told him so at once. There wasn't a scratch on the throat, as far as I could see. Like Bathurst before me, I cursed the absence of light. It made things so deuced hard for us. But I hunched young Donald, or what was left of him, on to his shoulders and propped his body up against my left knee.

As I did so, the soft hat that he was wearing tumbled off and I saw at once how he had travelled to his death. There was blood in his hair that had welled from a wound on the right-hand side of the head. From what I could see, from such a superficial examination as that which I was then able to make, Donald Fredericks had been shot through the head.

It seemed to me that the shot had been fired from behind and below. There was a hole just behind the right ear where the bullet had evidently entered. I had no doubt, when I saw this hole, that the bullet had lodged in the brain, somewhere, I thought, in the part that is known as the anterior. The skin was burnt and the hair was singed. There was little doubt that the shot had been fired at Fredericks from a distance that had been quite close.

I told Bathurst at once all that I have written down. He listened without the hint of an interruption.

"Leaden bullet, I suppose?" he asked at length.

"I think so," I said. "Pretty heavy calibre at that."

"A '45 revolver, for instance," suggested Bathurst to me.

"Very possibly," I agreed. "When I've dug for the bullet I shall be able to tell you more."

To this he made no reply. Falling to full length he crawled very carefully and slowly over the ground in the intimate neighbourhood of the body. There came neither achievement nor result. I heard sounds that were signs of annoyance. The ground was bare of clue or evidence. A little dismayed, I thought, at his lack of success, he rose to his feet, dusted his knees and swung round on to me with an order.

"Stay here, Bannerman, for a quarter of an hour or so. Look him over as thoroughly as you can. You may hit on something that has so far eluded us. I'm going to drive your car down for Goodaker, or whomever's on duty at this benighted hour. And I shan't loiter over the job, I give you my word."

Next morning we were no nearer to anything that may be termed satisfactory. All that we knew that we hadn't known before, was that A.L.B.'s surmise re the revolver was correct. I took the bullet from the young fellow's brain. It had lodged, rather unexpectedly to me, near the parieto-occipital fissure. It was leaden, of heavy calibre. Old Bligh handled it gingerly and then, without a word of comment, passed it over to Goodaker for inspection.

The latter looked it over and addressed Bathurst. "I can't get much on the dead man's movements during the whole of yesterday," he observed. "He was seen in Chelmersley during the morning and then again in the late afternoon. After that he seems to have vanished into thin air. Since his father's death, of course, he's been much more busy than he ever had been before. Naturally, there were many things that he found wanted doing. Things, too, that had to be done at once."

Bathurst nodded silently. Old Bligh, who seemed to be waiting for Bathurst to say something, and therefore a trifle disappointed, harangued Goodaker.

"That man Kreutz—the barber's-shop chap—you were shadowing him, weren't you, Inspector? What happened to your man? Had he anything to report?"

"Kreutz went on duty a few minutes before eight in the morning. He remained there all day. That's what my chap says."

Bathurst cut in here. "How can he be sure of that? Did he see Kreutz uninterruptedly for twelve hours?"

Goodaker looked a little uncomfortable. "Grainger's a fairly reliable chap, who usually knows what he's talking about. This is what he reported to me last night. Kreutz was at work in Melsheimer's shop all the morning. He saw him in there several times. About midday, Melsheimer himself went out to lunch. When that happened, Kreutz went upstairs and worked in the ladies' room, leaving a boy in the lower part of the shop. Grainger says that he must have stayed up there until closing time. At any rate, he hadn't left the premises when the place closed in the evening. The only people that came out were obviously customers who had gone in for attention."

He watched A.L.B.'s face to see how he would receive this news. A trifle apprehensively, I thought. He was justified. Bathurst became immediately critical.

"H'm! Pretty negative, all of it. Sorry to appear ungracious, Goodaker, and all that, but your man-at-arms, Monsieur Grainger, doesn't please me. He may be reliable, but he certainly doesn't coruscate. Even though (as I am perfectly willing to admit) we were trying him rather highly. We took him just a little out of his depth."

The words were uttered lightly but the look in his eyes told me a different story. I could see that Bathurst still attached a lot of importance to the movements of the elusive Kreutz.

Bligh nodded his agreement. As I have said before, the old fool nearly always annoyed me. He was never more successful, I think, than at that particular moment.

"Mr. Bathurst is undeniably right, Goodaker," he declared profoundly. "It's no good tackling a case like this with half measures. If we do, we shall be the laughing stock of the county."

"And well cast too," I thought to myself. Bathurst said no more on the subject but turned his attention to me—professionally this time.

"When was young Fredericks shot, Doctor?" he asked me quietly. "How long had he been dead, would you say, when we picked him up? Within a little, that is."

His question was by no means difficult to answer. I made a rapid calculation. "When we found him last night," I said deliberately, "he'd been dead about three hours. Certainly not more, in my opinion."

"That was what I thought," he mused. "Between eight o'clock and nine, say."

"Thinking of Kreutz again?" I asked pointedly. "After he came off duty?"

"Can't very well overlook him, can I?" he answered coolly. "Considering what we've already learned about him. The curse of the whole thing is *proving* what you conjecture. That's where my difficulty is going to lie. By the way, Sir George—"

Before he was able to complete his sentence the noise of the 'phone bell cut across the room. I noticed it so intensely that the noise seemed almost strident to my ear.

Goodaker picked up the receiver. After a moment's interrogation, he beckoned to Bligh.

"It's you that's wanted, sir. Mr. Montague Corbett. Hold on, will you, please?" he shouted into the mouthpiece. "The Chief Constable will speak to you."

Bligh, after an exchange of the usual openings, clearly frowned at the instrument. "By all means, Mr. Corbett," I heard him say. "Come round here now, if you like. Yes—whenever you please. I shall be very pleased to hear what you have to say. Oh . . . undoubtedly . . . I quite agree with you. Very terrible, indeed. What? . . . sincerely hope not . . . if so, it won't be any fault of mine, I assure you. Right you are. I'll expect you, then."

Replacing the receiver thoughtfully, he turned to me. "That was Montague Corbett, the house and estate agent. Lives in a big house up beyond Taggarts' Way. He's coming down here at once to see us. To see me really." He puffed and blew out his cheeks.

Bathurst seemed interested. "That's rather diverting. What's his particular point of view, Sir George? Does he think he's seen the murderer?"

Old Bligh was unable to satisfy him. "Don't quite know, Bathurst. Couldn't place him in that way on the 'phone. The only real impression that I formed of him was . . ."

Sir George stopped abruptly. Bathurst eyed him curiously. Bligh seemed doubtful as to choice of words.

"Go on, Sir George. You interest me immensely." The old boy chuckled. "Well, it may sound a bit idiotic on my part to suggest such a thing, but I formed the impression that Corbett's feet were most distinctly chilly." He darted quick glances at each of us who heard him. Seemingly he was delighted with the idea.

"Wind-up—eh?" queried Bathurst laconically.

Bligh nodded. "Very much so, I thought."

"H'm. Curious, don't you think?"

"I do. I haven't quite digested it yet."

"Old ass. He can take it from me that his skin's as safe as the Pope of Rome's. Unless he's a . . ." He paused for a moment. To revert to Goodaker. "What sort of a bloke is this Corbett? Details, please."

"Elderly. About the same age, I should say, as Fredericks senior. Runs a house-and-estate agent's business. A very big one, too, in Chelmersley. Highly prosperous. Lives two or three miles out. Not in Bannerman's direction, Great Steeping. In the opposite direction, towards Cressing and Saxbury. Sort of a civic big noise. Alderman, I believe, of the County Council. Has had several local honours. At least, I believe that's what they call 'em. For two or three years now has represented the Council on the London and Home Counties Joint Electricity Authority. Dark, swarthy and fattish."

"Married?"

"Widower, I believe. No family. Housekeeper."

"Big house?"

"Every time. One of the finest in the district."

"Like the elder Fredericks', something, eh?"

"Ye-es. Similar sort of man, perhaps, in more than one way. Came to the district about the same time, too."

Bathurst shrugged unsympathetic shoulders. "Well, he can read more into this murder riddle than I can, if he thinks there's a killer running wild who's out to exterminate the leading citizens of Chelmersley. There's only one chance of him being snuffed out and that, I'm afraid, is extremely remote. However, we'll wait till we see him before we say any more. There's nothing like the personal interview, you know, for giving you the true perspective."

"You won't have to wait long for it, Bathurst," I interposed. "If I mistake not, this is our man. Hark."

A car had been driven into the station yard and a shortish man in a heavy overcoat was shutting one of the doors. Although the weather had changed suddenly, and there was a nip in the air for early September, the coat was a heavier one than I should have expected to see a man wearing at that season of the year, and I wondered if Sir George Bligh's diagnosis weren't even more accurate than any of us who had heard it, had thought at the time.

It was Montague Corbett right enough. I saw his face better as he came to the door of the police station and was able to recognize it from the many photographs (authentic and libellous) that I had seen of him, fairly regularly, in the local papers. I watched him.

He came bustling through the main doorway; when he came to the door of our room, he stopped, and in a loudish voice inquired for Sir George Bligh. You could tell that he was a man accustomed to having his own way.

"Come in, Mr. Corbett." The invitation came from the Chief Constable himself, and our visitor accepted it with alacrity.

It was easy to see that he was fussy and self-important. His actions were those of a man whose platitudes must be accepted as pontifical pronouncements. At the same time, it wasn't a difficult matter to spot something else. The man was in a state of nervous agitation. You could gauge that from a full variety of signs. Outward and visible.

There was an air of excitement about him, too, and now that I have written the words, I am acutely aware that they do not convey all that his appearance conveyed to me. He laboured under something that was more than mere excitement. There was a peculiar condition of restlessness about him; hands and even fingers told the same story. Every now and then he touched the ends of his dark moustache.

He peered sharply at each of us as he stood in the doorway and faced us. little quick, sharp furtive glances that darted from his eyes in rapid succession.

I argued with myself that one of three reasons was responsible for the state that the man was in. These were they:

Firstly, that he was in a sheer blue funk of something or somebody; secondly, that he had recently undergone a terrible experience that had shaken his nerve very considerably; or thirdly, that he was in a condition that I may describe as one of nervous *anticipation*. That any minute, for example, a gun might go off close to his ear, or an enemy spring upon him suddenly from round that corner that lay just ahead of him.

He was swarthy and stocky, but his swarthiness was "sicklied o'er" with the paler cast of something I knew not of. If I call it fear, I shall get as near as I ever can to it.

"Good morning, Sir George," he said jerkily. Then, inquiringly, and a little critically, "These other gentlemen here? May I assume that—"

"All in order, Mr. Corbett," chirped old Bligh. "You can speak quite freely in front of them. I'll introduce you though, first. Mr. Anthony Bathurst, *the* Mr. Bathurst, of whom no doubt you have heard; Dr. Bannerman and—er—but I expect you know him as well as I do, Inspector Goodaker. Mr. Montague Corbett, gentle-men. Sit down, Mr. Corbett."

Corbett obeyed. He plucked the glove from his left, hand nervously; then his mind seemed to falter or wander, for the fingers that had started to remove his other glove stopped and appeared to become uncertain and lose their way. They came at last to his cheek, which he rubbed up and down two or three times before he spoke.

"Sir George," he opened at length, "I don't quite know where to begin, but I feel that the position here in Chelmersley is becoming well-nigh intolerable. . . . The news of the murder of Donald Fredericks is the last straw. That is, to me."

"Why to *you*, so much, Mr. Corbett, may I ask?"

It was Bathurst who asked the question—very softly.

Corbett seemed a little taken aback at the directness of the question. I could have sworn that the bird's feathers were ruffled and well on the flutter. I don't think he had anticipated that particular query. He went a bit blue round the gills. "Ticker not too sound," I said to myself, and amongst other things—"you'd better not run for a train too soon after 'brekker'."

He recovered a bit, however, and blinked at Bathurst as though he had asked a question that had busted the prettiest canons of etiquette, as high as Haman.

"I don't think you quite understand. I am a public man, sir—a man to whom the well-being of Chelmersley means a lot. I have always taken a prominent part in the affairs of the town. Upon the occasion of the granting of our Charter of Incorporation, when we had our historical pageant—that I may justifiably say thrilled the world—I was chosen to assume the character of His Majesty Charles the Second. I mention this merely to give some indication of my pride in the town and my own standing therein."

Bathurst bowed. "I'm sure that His late Majesty of ahem—blessed memory—would have welcomed your appointment with open arms, although he usually had them pretty full in other directions, I believe. But proceed, Mr. Corbett, if you please."

"I will, and I shall not be over-long in coming to the main point. What I am about to say, however, will not, I fear, be too palatable."

His hands worked convulsively. "There is a killer loose in Chelmersley. Two of our most respected citizens have been murdered in the most brutal fashion. Under the *noses*, almost, of the police. You'll pardon me saying that, Sir George, and you, Inspector, but that's how I feel about it, and I'm a man that says a thing to your face, rather than behind your back. I'm going to ask you this. What are you going to do about it?"

"We are doing all that we can, Mr. Corbett," replied Bligh, as stiff as the best of 'em. "And I'm sorry that I can't listen to—"

Corbett's agitation conquered his manners.

"That's all very well, Sir George, as far as it goes. But this business calls for something more than ordinary routine. Good God! Look at things for yourself. Desperate diseases need desperate remedies. For I'll tell you one thing, Sir George, if nothing else."

"Which is what?"

Corbett heaved forward in his chair and spoke words that I knew came from his heart. He was thoroughly rattled and unbalanced.

"Unless you take special steps to combat this evil, this killer will go on with his work and there will be more murders in Chelmersley. I am as certain of that as I have been of anything in my life."

"Special steps," repeated the Chief Constable with a shrug of the shoulders. "It sounds all right, I know. What would you do if you had my job, that I haven't done?"

"I'd have nightly patrols, for one thing. Instead of six police on the streets I'd have sixty. Six hundred! I'm positive that every decent-minded man in Chelmersley would come forward and offer to do his bit. The majority of them only require to be asked. I can tell you that, because I've already approached several of 'em."

Bligh nodded. "Go on. What then?"

"Places like Taggarts Way, that invite wickedness and obscenity, would have flood-lights installed, so that no murderer could hope to do his ghastly work there; it would be fatal for him to poke his nose down it. The police, too, would be armed—"

Bathurst interrupted him. "You think that there will be other murders then, Mr. Corbett? As a matter of fact, I'm inclined to agree with you. But may I ask you *why* you think so? I should like to know if your reason's the same as mine." He waited patiently for Corbett's answer. This, particularly, was when the man puzzled me. When tackled like this, he again became evasive.

"I don't know," he answered, "that I've any special reason beyond the promptings of my own common sense. My reason's what you would call a general reason—based on my experience of men, women and things. I argue it out like this: In Chelmersley, or in the district round about, there's a homicidal maniac. Living right amongst us in all probability. A man who may break out again at any time or place even, and kill somebody else. Before he has the chance of doing so, *we must lay him by the heels.*"

Corbett rose in the vehemence of his argument. "I appeal to you, Sir George, as Chief Constable of the county, to put forward every effort on the lines that I've suggested—"

Again A.L.B. interrupted him. "But, Mr. Corbett, one little minute before we leave our muttons—your muttons and mine. This homicidal maniac—to whom you referred just now—do you know, I don't think he'll hold water for a moment? Consider the facts, my dear sir."

Corbett glared and Goodaker chewed at his underlip: Bathurst proceeded unperturbed.

"You don't surely suggest, Mr. Corbett, that your homicidal maniac picked out and murdered, *by pure chance*, father and son, do you? That an *indiscriminate* killer, such as you must admit you depicted, could ever have hit on these two men of that particular relationship?"

"Hold that one, friend Corbett!" I whispered to myself as the sentence left Bathurst's lips. I waited for our visitor's reply. When it came, it was completely beside the point.

"There are more things, my dear sir, in heaven and earth . . ." He reached for his hat which he had placed on the table in front of him. "Good morning, Sir George—and gentlemen. And for God's sake, don't forget what I've said to you. If you do . . ." He waved his hand in an epitome of pessimism.

"Very interesting," murmured Bathurst a moment after his departure, "—very interesting, indeed. Now I wonder what Mr. Corbett's real reason was for coming here? If I knew that, I think it would help me a great deal."

He turned to Goodaker impulsively. "Inspector. If it's convenient to Sir George here, you and I, and Doctor Bannerman with us, will call again on Herr Melsheimer. *And* we won't waste time about it, either."

CHAPTER X
GONE AWAY

I REMEMBER that we walked down to West Street. In the circumstances, Goodaker said that he considered it to be the better policy. Cars are so easily picked out.

On the way, we ran into Jack and I could see at a glance that this second tragedy, on the very heels of the first, had hit him hard, and then harder. Goodaker and Bathurst left us alone for a moment and I asked him how Iris was that morning. Directly I mentioned the name to him, Bathurst, a few steps away, showed signs of intense interest. This was the opportunity that I had wanted. And now that it had come, I wasn't missing it.

I called him to us and made the necessary introduction. Very much as I had been, a day or two previously, Jack was immediately drawn to A.L.B. He told me afterwards that Anthony Bathurst fascinated him. I knew the truth of this as well as he did. They were soon on the best of terms and when Bathurst elicited the fact that Jack Tabernacle knew Cardinal Amadeo Vespucci, who had moved from Milan to Rome in the early part of that year, a fund of mutual reminiscence was soon established.

As we approached Melsheimer's place in West Street, Bathurst moved up to Goodaker and said something to him in an undertone. The Inspector nodded his understanding. Bathurst then came back to me.

"Goodaker and I are going right into Melsheimer's," he explained. "We've decided to leave that job to the two of us. I'm not quite sure, you see, how things are going. If we want you, Doctor, I'll send out word. I don't know how, but if it's necessary, I'll find a way."

A few paces carried Goodaker and him ahead of us and a moment later we saw them enter the shop. I will relate what took place as I had it from Bathurst himself afterwards.

When they got inside, Melsheimer himself was in the saloon. A lad was helping him. There was no sign of the man whom they knew as Otto Kreutz. Goodaker's tone on this occasion was very different from that which he had used on the previous occasion that Melsheimer had played host.

"Good morning, Mr. Melsheimer," he said. "You will remember that we called here the other day over a little matter connected with the post-office. You were good enough to supply us with certain information. This morning we want to see your assistant, Otto Kreutz. Will you tell him, please?"

The request seemed to find Melsheimer at a loss. He opened his mouth as though to answer, but no words came. Possibly unfortunately, Goodaker became impatient at the delay.

"Come on, man. We want to have a word with your man Kreutz. That's plain enough, isn't it? Where is he?"

Melsheimer's search for words was now more successful. "But that is what I myself do not know. Otto Kreutz has not been since yesterday—the lunchtime it was. He go to his lunch at the usual time but come back here, he do not. I say to myself, he ill; he sick; he have himself hurt; he will in the morning come. But no, he has not here been at all. You gentlemen can it see."

He spread out his fat hands eloquently and gestured round the shop with some degree of violence. Bathurst realized at once all that this meant. The truth of it—minus trimmings!

"What time did Kreutz go to lunch?" he asked. I think that his tone made Melsheimer answer immediately.

"At one o'clock. He always did. That was his time to go."

The Inspector looked at Bathurst, and Melsheimer attempted to interpret the glance.

"Gentlemen," he said with an ill-timed complacency, "you need not worry. Come back he will. There is no doubt. Shall I tell you why? How I know? How certain I am? Because I have not this week him paid." This last on a note of triumph.

Bathurst brushed his ridiculous avowal to one side. "Has he left anything behind here that belonged to him? Have you had a look round yet?"

"There is his jacket. His white coat that he wear while at work here. Fritz, get Otto's jacket for the gentleman. In the usual place it is hanging."

"Don't trouble," declared Bathurst before the boy could move. "Tell me where the coat is. I'll get it myself."

Melsheimer pointed to a white cabinet. Bathurst opened it and took out a white coat that was hanging there. A quick piece of handling told him that the pockets were empty.

"Take this coat, Inspector," he said. "It may pay for a little attention. Now, Mr. Melsheimer, I should be greatly obliged if you would answer me one or two questions. And as quickly as you can, please. How long have you had your assistant Kreutz?"

"About eight months. He to me came, I think, in the early part of last February."

"Where from?" He appeared bewildered. "From where did you get him?"

Melsheimer's hands again bore testimony. "In the papers, advertised. He the advertisement answered."

"From where, do you remember?"

Melsheimer shook his head. "No. I do not remember."

"Got the letter?"

"Ach—no. It is months ago, remember. The letter—I have it not."

"Did you ask for references?"

"Ja! Yes, I always do."

"Did you get 'em?"

"Yes, yes."

"Did you test them when you got them?" Melsheimer shook his head slowly. "No. I read them. That is what I did. They to me seemed good. I them accepted."

"Of course. As I imagined. You don't know who the man was from Adam." Bathurst watched him keenly to see if he would in any way betray himself. Melsheimer, however, looked transparently honest.

"All I know is that Otto Kreutz to me, he was."

"Where did he lodge, Melsheimer? Near here?"

Goodaker had intervened with the question. "I have the address, Inspector," said Bathurst. "Kreutz gave it to me when we came the time before. He lodges with a Mrs. Rhodes at Little Chelmersley. Ninety-four, Thatch Road, to be exact. How far's that from here, Goodaker?"

"A tidy step, sir. Take us too long to tramp it. We'd do better to run up in the car. We'll take the car from the station, if it's all the same to you."

Bathurst nodded and they joined Tabernacle and me on the pavement outside. We learned what had happened and their further plans.

Dropping Jack at the railway station, at his request, we were soon back at H.Q. for Goodaker to commission the larger of the police cars. Twenty minutes run brought us to Little Chelmersley and twenty-two (I timed it myself) to Thatch Road.

"Will he be in, Mr. Bathurst?" Goodaker seemed anxious.

"Lord, man, no!" replied Bathurst with swift curtness. "You're an optimist, Goodaker, if you think he'll be waiting here for us with a cup of tea in his hand. He's slipped through your fingers despite the trouble you took to hold him."

Goodaker stuck doggedly at his position. "It looks like it, sir, I admit. And it'll go against me. But I'd like to know how he did it, though, all the same."

"We've bigger problems than that in front of us, Goodaker. You'll take a chance in his rooms here, of course?" Bathurst was interrogative.

"Give it the once-over, do you mean? I shall. Most certainly. I'll chance that—don't you worry."

We slipped down Thatch Road and pulled that car up in front of number ninety-four. Goodaker rang the bell of a red-bricked villa—one of thousands of such villas that are dotted over the English countryside.

After a brief delay, the summons was answered by a thin, sharp-featured woman, with pale, watery blue eyes.

"Your pardon, Madam," said Goodaker brusquely, "I'm Inspector Goodaker from Chelmersley police station and I apologize for troubling you. But could you tell me if your lodger, Otto Kreutz, is at home?"

The woman shook her head. Habit kept her fingers round the front door, and she yielded no ground for entrance.

"No, he's not. I think that he's . . ." She came to a sudden stop.

"You think that he's what?"

Goodaker almost pounced on her in his eagerness.

"I think that he must have gone away altogether, Inspector. Left here for good, I mean. He hasn't been home here since he left to go to business yesterday morning. About a quarter past seven, it was. That was his usual time to go. Just after he'd had breakfast."

Bathurst gestured to Goodaker, and the Inspector picked up his cue absolutely on the beat.

"I'm afraid I shall have to ask you to let me have a look over his rooms. The matter I've come about is extremely important."

"You must come in, then, Inspector," returned the woman rather wearily. "But Kreutz didn't have 'rooms' here, as you said just now. He only had one room here, a bed-sitting-room."

"Please take us up there, Mrs. Rhodes," interposed Bathurst courteously. "Very likely it won't take us five minutes to look over the one room pretty thoroughly."

Mrs. Rhodes nodded her consent and we filed up the stairs behind her; Bathurst splitting Goodaker and me. I went last. On the top stair the woman stopped and turned her body towards us.

"You won't find anything up here in his room, gentlemen. I'll tell you that before you go in there, so that you won't be disappointed. I went in there this morning. When he didn't show up yesterday I was a bit worried about him. This is the room, gentlemen. This one here."

She ushered us into a conventional bed-sitting-room. Bed, table, dressing-chest and three chairs. There were no clothes, no books, no boots or shoes. Nothing personal at all.

"What he had, he's taken with him, sir." Mrs. Rhodes spoke to Goodaker as though explaining the situation.

"Had he a bag or suitcase when he went out yesterday morning?"

"He must have had, Inspector. How else could he have—"

"That's neither here nor there. Did you see him carrying a bag or suitcase? Actually see him?"

"No, I didn't see him go out, you see: I rarely did. The slam of the front door was the only intimation I had that he'd gone."

Goodaker grunted as though he were dissatisfied, but A.L.B. shoved an oar in that at once seemed to shift a considerable amount of water.

"Tell me this, please, Mrs. Rhodes," he said, "have you *ever* seen Kreutz leave here with a suitcase in his hand? Before yesterday morning, that is?"

"Oh yes, sir. Bless your heart, why yes! Many and many's the time, sir."

"Tell me more," murmured Anthony sweetly. "I'd love to hear it."

Mrs. Rhodes was sure of her ground now.

"Every time he went away for week-ends, sir, he took his suitcase with him. And at other times, too. That is to say, just occasionally. There was one day last week it happened."

"These week-end excursions you mention, Mrs. Rhodes, were they spasmodic, or fairly regular?"

Anthony was as keen as razors now. The woman's answer was rapid and emphatic.

"Regular, sir. Kreutz has been away every week-end since he came to lodge with me."

This statement caused a lot of stir. I thought that both Bathurst and the plodding Goodaker received it with some measure of surprise. The former frowned; the latter opened his eyes as though a mosquito had nestled in his knickers and put forward a business "feeler". Anthony went on again.

"*Every* week-end, Mrs. Rhodes—without exception?"

She nodded primly. "Every week-end, sir. Kreutz would go away from here about seven on the Saturday morning. He used to come straight home here from Melsheimer's shop, where I expect you know he worked, on the Friday, pack his case already for the morning and clear out to work on the following morning—that's the Saturday—carrying it. That would be the last I should see of him until late on the Sunday night. Then he'd come in usually about a quarter past eleven. That was his week-end performance as regular as clockwork, sir."

I saw Bathurst stroke his chin. "Where did he go? Any idea?"

I don't think either he or the Inspector anticipated any result from this last question. It came, however.

"Yes, sir. To a sister-in-law who lived at Friningham. He volunteered the information once, sir, when I said that I knew Friningham."

"Know the address of this sister-in-law?"

Nothing doing this time. "No, sir. I don't even know her name."

"No correspondence ever came to him from her?" This question drew the completest of blanks. "No, sir. Neither from her, nor from anybody else. As far as I know, Kreutz never had a letter or a postcard come here all the time that he lived here." Bathurst and Goodaker exchanged glances. "Rather strange that, Mrs. Rhodes, don't you think?" declared the former. "Didn't it strike you as so, yourself?"

Mrs. Rhodes attacked this last question with folded arms. "It did. Of course it did. And I mentioned it to Kreutz himself one evening, just casual like. Didn't seem to drag it in or to appear 'nosey'. But he had quite a good explanation to offer me. He said that he had all his correspondence addressed to the shop because of the time of the morning post. We get the first post here, you see, about a quarter to eight. Kreutz had left for Chelmersley long before that, so he picked his correspondence up when he arrived at the shop in case of missing anything. It's quite feasible, sir," she concluded rather defensively.

"H'm," said Bathurst non-committally. "It depends, rather, I think, on the point of view."

"Was this man, Kreutz, recommended to you by anybody? When he first came to you, I mean."

"No, Inspector. He saw my card in the window, advertising that I had a room to let, and came to the door and applied for it. He seemed a quiet and respectable sort of chap and when he offered me the first month's rent in advance, I closed with him. I would rather have let to an Englishman, of course, but in these times you can't pick and choose, and a German's money goes as far as anybody else's."

"Had you any other lodgers, Mrs. Rhodes?" The question came from Bathurst.

"No, sir. I've a little money that was left to me by my late husband, and I only need to let one room to be able to manage fairly comfortably. My daughter lives with me and she helps me too, financially. She's employed at the Beaufoy Cinema in West Street, Chelmersley."

I saw the interest light up in Bathurst's eyes. "Close to Melsheimer's saloon, isn't it?"

"Yes, sir. In the same block, as you might say."

"Tell me, Mrs. Rhodes," put in Bathurst, "was this man Kreutz on friendly terms with your daughter?"

"What exactly are you getting at, sir? Are you hinting at a romance between them or something of that kind?"

"I thought that such a thing might not be beyond the bounds of possibility."

"Well, you can dismiss that idea at once, sir. Elsie wouldn't have looked at a man like Kreutz—a foreigner. My daughter's not an ordinary girl, sir, by any means. You can take my word for that, sir. Also, I'll give him his due and be fair to him, Kreutz never so much as lifted a finger or an eyelid towards her. He knew better than to do that. He was always a quiet, well-behaved man when he was here."

"I'll take your word for all that, Mrs. Rhodes, as you ask me, but I must submit with all deference that Kreutz *might* have made advances to Miss Rhodes when they were away from here. There were plenty of other opportunities, you know. You yourself might have been kept in the dark."

"No, sir. You're wrong right through, if you think that. Elsie wouldn't have stood for it. She's not that sort of a girl. And if he'd ever given her a hint of such a thing, she'd have told me about it at once and I'd have sent the man about his business." I could see the woman implicitly believed all that she had said and she struck me, too, as a person who knew her own mind very thoroughly. She proceeded to give us a further piece of information.

"Elsie has never been a girl who could keep things to herself. Right from the time when she was a baby. She would confide in me. We have been alone together for so long, you see. Even things that happened to her at business, she would tell me about when she came home. When she had the burglary at the 'Beaufoy' she told me all about it directly afterwards."

Goodaker and Bathurst pricked up two pairs of ears.

"What was this, Mrs. Rhodes? What happened at the 'Beaufoy'?" asked the latter.

"Elsie had her desk broken open and some things stolen out of it."

"When did this happen? I can't remember having heard of it before"—Goodaker this time.

"Almost two months ago, Inspector. A little more than that, perhaps. In June some time, I think it was."

"Was the affair reported to the police?"

Mrs. Rhodes shook her head. "I can't say that. Elsie reported it to Mr. Fredericks. I do know that much, because she told me so herself. I can't say what he did—whether he took it to the police or not. But he was in a great state about it, Elsie said."

"What was stolen from your daughter, Mrs. Rhodes?" Bathurst watched her keenly as he put the question.

"Not a lot, sir—from the point of view of monetary value, that is. Elsie was more upset, I think, at the idea of the thing happening, than from any actual loss that she suffered. A wrist-watch was taken, a ring that used to belong to her father, which she only wore sometimes, and some papers."

A.L.B. was in again like a flash.

"Papers, Mrs. Rhodes? What papers?"

"That I don't really know, sir. Nothing of particular importance, I believe. I never really knew the rights of it. But Elsie herself would be able to tell you if you cared to ask her. She'll be home to-night. Late though, of course."

"Did this incident at the cinema cause your daughter any worry, Mrs. Rhodes? Unduly?"

Here I thought Mrs. Rhodes looked just a little perturbed.

"Well, sir, she certainly did seem a bit worried about it. But as I said just now, the idea that somebody was about in the cinema, who was a thief, concerned her more, I think, than the loss of anything. She said that you couldn't feel that anything was safe with people like that about."

"Forgive me if I appear to harp on the subject, Mrs. Rhodes, but did Kreutz ever accompany your daughter home here, to your knowledge? Did they ever come in together, for instance?"

Again Mrs. Rhodes denied the soft impeachment, just as emphatically as before. "No, sir. Never. Not once have I ever known it happen. Kreutz was home here much earlier than Elsie. His work finished three hours or so earlier than hers did. If he had wanted to come home here with her, look how he would have had to hang about."

The three of us looked at each other, and at a nod from Bathurst, Goodaker decided to closure the interview.

"I'll have a full description of Kreutz broadcast immediately," he said. "There's one thing," he added, "if he's anywhere near at hand, we ought to be able to pick him up pretty easily."

At that, we said good-bye to Mrs. Rhodes and climbed into the big police car.

The audience in attendance at the Beaufoy Cinema that evening was destined to enjoy a sensation that was not supplied by the screen itself.

Towards the end of the programme, at about twenty minutes past ten, to be moderately exact, the people sitting in the rear seats of the upper circle were startled by a piercing scream that was easily separable from the "talkie" to which they were listening.

In the flash of a moment, affrighted faces searched each other for explanation. Flying feet along the spaces beyond told the story that something was desperately amiss within the building. Raised and then lowered voices added to the general apprehension, and more than one woman whimpered distress. .

Two attendants barred the way through one of the exit doors, with the result that the people leaving the theatre were forced to make their way through the exit door that was placed on the farther side. But, as fire is almost always heralded by smoke, the news of what had transpired to cause the sensation, gradually found being and floated round. Whispers were weighted with fear. Shorn of the more lurid details, and reduced to the stark nudity of truth, the rumours amounted to this. The girl in charge of the confectionery counter, which lay just behind the doors of the upper circle, had been murdered. She had been stabbed, the better informed told the others, through the heart, at close quarters.

The name of this girl, it was said, was Elsie Rhodes.

CHAPTER XI
THE THIRD PROBLEM

WHEN Goodaker was sent for, through the medium of an urgent telephone call that was put through from the Beaufoy Cinema, his care-lined face reacted immediately to this third summons of tragedy. A haggard look settled on it and stayed there.

He had been hard on the Kreutz trail ever since our interview with Mrs. Rhodes and up to the moment had picked up nothing. His first step, following on this last message, was to get through to Sir George Bligh; unhappily for him, especially from the point of view of his present frame of mind and outlook, the Chief Constable wasn't at home. Lady Bligh, who answered the call herself, informed the Inspector that he had been sent for suddenly and that she wasn't able to say very accurately the time that she expected him to return home.

Goodaker thought matters over and then communicated with me. As Bathurst was again at "The Rowfants", he was in luck's way and clicked a couple of finches with one pebble. At the particular time, Bathurst was busily engaged in outlining to me a strong theory that Corbett's fears were completely unfounded because the death of the two Fredericks, father and son, pointed unmistakably to his own old and original idea of the crime being an affair of personal vendetta.

When the moment came for my 'phone to go, he was standing in the middle of my hearth-rug, picking off his various points with the stem of his pipe on the tips of his fingers.

"Jump to it, Bannerman," he said. "I don't think it will be startling news this time."

As you know by now, having read what has gone before, he was well wide of the mark. I listened to Goodaker, made one or two appropriate remarks, and then turned the message as I had it, over to Anthony Bathurst.

"I've bad news. You're wrong, old man, for once. This is murder number three. A girl employed at the Beaufoy Cinema, this time. Stabbed through the heart, so Goodaker tells me. He's going straight on there and wants us to follow. What price Corbett now, eh?"

Bathurst's face whitened as he heard what I had to say. When he spoke to me, it was with ominous quietness.

"A girl employed at the Beaufoy, did you say, Bannerman? *A* girl or *the* girl?"

I knew what he meant. "*The* girl," I replied just as quietly. "What about your vendetta theory now? This man Kreutz is a homicidal maniac and he's still loose amongst us."

For the moment he had no answer for me. At length, he made some sort of concession. "Looks as though you're right, Bannerman—you and Corbett. And, if so, I'm wrong. All the same, I'm not . . ."

He broke off precipitately. "Let's go down in the Crossley. It's faster than yours."

Goodaker was waiting for us when we arrived at the cinema and, considering the little time that he had had at his disposal, had done remarkably well.

The excessively curious had been zealously shepherded and only those remained who had something definite and tangible in the way of evidence to offer to us.

First of all, naturally, I went to the body of the poor creature whose life had been taken. She had been killed with an ordinary sort of knife; longish white handle with sharp blade, worked almost to a point. The weapon had bitten hard into the wound and had penetrated the heart. I found that there was a deep incision in the left lung and the arch of the aorta almost in a state of severance. The blow had been swift and sure and the girl's death almost instantaneous, judging, that is, from the condition of the pulmonary artery.

I do not think that she could have lived for more than a few seconds after the blow had been struck. Also, her murderer must have been very close to her when he had struck that blow. I looked up at Goodaker and asked a question.

"Was the knife in the wound when she was found?"

"No, Doctor—so I'm told, that is. It was found lying on the ground there beside her."

By the time I had been able to take better stock of the position, I saw that the girl's body was lying close to the top of a flight of stairs. Very near, indeed, to the top stair of all. To anybody coming out of the circle seats on his or her way from the theatre, this flight of stairs would be on the left-hand side.

As the knife had been driven into her left side right near to the breast-bone, I formed the opinion that she had fallen sideways on to her left side and almost on to the top step of all. There was a pool of blood under her, as she lay there, as may be well imagined.

I told them all that I thought and for a moment or two after its reception, nobody spoke.

"Who found her, Goodaker? Is the person here?" asked Bathurst.

"This boy, Mr. Bathurst."

A man, who was evidently the manager of the cinema, stepped forward rather ostentatiously. He had his arm round a small boy's shoulder. I couldn't help thinking at the time that it was rather remarkable that in the cases of the first and third murders, the first person to find the body should have been a lad. The manager was speaking to Bathurst.

"This boy found Miss Rhodes, sir. He will tell his story again."

The lad obeyed. The gist of it was this: he was a uniformed boy, whose job of work it was to sell chocolates and cigarettes to the patrons of the Beaufoy. He carried his wares in the usual manner of such mercantile princes, in front of him, on a tray suspended from his neck. It was up to him, he explained to us, to meet the incoming patrons of the circle and endeavour to do a spot of business with them. Miss Rhodes was in charge of the confectionery counter and supplied him periodically with the goods for his tray. When he wanted replenishments he went to her for them.

Her counter, let it be said, was situated in a recess almost exactly midway between the two staircases and between the two doors leading into, and out of, the circle. There were occasions, he also informed us, when he would venture into the circle itself, especially towards the completion of the programme, when incomers were beginning to be few.

This is what had happened, he proceeded to tell us, when Miss Rhodes had been murdered. He had gone into the circle by the left door as you faced it.

Just as he came out, by the same door, mark you, he had heard a scream, that seemed to him, he said, to come from the flight of stairs on his left. He had run towards it as best as he could, considering the handicap of the tray round his neck, and found the girl lying there exactly as we were looking at her now. He had gone down a little and had stood for a moment on the second step from the top.

"Did you see anybody else? Anywhere?"

"No sir." He looked at Bathurst with sturdy independence.

"Hear anything?"

"Nothing, except the scream. And then, after a little while, other people moving about."

Bathurst looked round and, with his eyes, measured the different distances. "Would any of Miss Rhodes' ordinary duties bring her on this staircase?"

The question was addressed to the manager. I found out afterwards that his name was Jenkinson.

"None. That is to say, under normal conditions. There would be no call for her to leave her counter until business was over for the evening. We always took care to see that she was well stocked with confectionery."

"What took her to this staircase, then?" interrupted Goodaker.

Jenkinson shrugged his shoulders. "I haven't the least idea. I think if we knew that, we should probably know a very great deal."

"You've detained nobody, I suppose, Goodaker?"

"No, Mr. Bathurst. How could I? It's a hundred to one that the murderer simply walked down the staircase and strolled out of the building. Easy as kiss my hand. By the time the boy had come to the body, the killer was out of the cinema and into the street."

"I think you're right, Goodaker. How was she enticed across here, though? What attracted her? That's our problem." He turned and pointed to the two doors that opened into the circle. "Notice those two doors, Goodaker?"

The inspector screwed up his face. "What exactly do you mean, sir?"

"Their position, man. Look at 'em."

"I see what you're after. You mean that they're rather nearer to each other than the two staircases are. Isn't that it?"

"It is. There is a difference in the two distances. A person leaving the cinema by the left-hand door of the circle, takes a half turn to reach the left-hand stairs or else has to cross right over to the other side. A similar half turn to the right is necessary for the people leaving on the other side."

"Well, admitting all that, sir, what are you trying to say?"

"This. If you stood on the second or third step down, say, you would be invisible to anybody coming out of the circle by the door nearer to the particular staircase on which you stood. Follow me?"

The inspector nodded his acceptance of Bathurst's point. "I agree, Mr. Bathurst."

The latter turned to the youth who sold chocolates. "What time was it that you heard the girl scream? As nearly as you can remember."

The boy thought hard. You could see the little chap straining at the leash, almost. Eventually he achieved result.

"You can put the time, sir, at about twenty-two minutes past ten, sir. That was when Miss Rhodes screamed. That would be very little out, if anything at all. The scream was—"

"Tell me this, though. How are you able to time it so accurately? I'm not doubting your word. Don't think that for a minute. But it's tremendously important that I should know *how* you arrive at your time, so that I can estimate it at its proper value. Do you understand?"

The youth brightened up considerably. "Yes, sir. I'll tell you how I worked it out. The comedy that finished up the programme comes on at ten-ten. 'Crystal Kisses' it's called. When I went into the circle, that last time, what I saw on the screen showed me that the comedy had been running for about ten minutes. You see, it's like this. When a programme has been running for two or three nights in succession, and you are in the habit of popping in and out several times during the performance, you get to know the various times, as you might say, and for how long the different films run."

He paused for a moment to take breath. To proceed again, however, even more confidently.

"You can take it from me, sir," he said, "it was about twenty-two minutes past ten when Miss Rhodes was murdered."

I cocked my eye in Bathurst's direction and was able to tell from his expression that he considered the boy's story fairly reliable. I heard him say "good" before turning to Jenkinson again.

"Tell me," he said to the manager rather sharply, "what people have crossed between that door' and this flight of stairs since the alarm was first given? Possibles, mind you, as well as actuals."

He indicated with a quick thrust of his finger the place where the girl lay and the door of the circle that served this particular staircase.

Jenkinson fluttered eyelids and showed signs of surprise. "Well, as far as I know, sir, only those of us who are here now. Young Richards did when he first ran to the body, of course. Since then, only the people who are here now. I can't think of anybody else." He looked round, rather hopelessly.

Bathurst put an immediate question to him. "This is desperately important. Listen carefully, please. What about the members of the audience when they left the cinema? Can you assure me beyond any doubt that none of them passed this way?"

"Oh, yes," returned Jenkinson. "You can make your mind absolutely easy about that. Shortly after the murder was discovered, everybody who was in the circle at the time left the house by way of the other staircase. I made immediate arrangements to that effect, and I took great care that they were rigorously adhered to. I saw that I should have to do that, if only to protect myself."

"Excellent. My congratulations on your organization, Mr. Jenkinson." I saw A.L.B. rub his hands in undisguised pleasure as he paid the man the tribute. He then went back to the boy Richards.

"You dropped your confectionery, I suppose," he said, "when you ran to Miss Rhodes' assistance? Is that right?"

"Yes, sir," replied the boy. "As I ran across, the packets went flying in all directions."

Jenkinson interposed. Evidently he regarded it as an appropriate moment. "You might pick up the stuff now, Richards. That is, of course, if Inspector Goodaker and this gentleman have no objection." Goodaker, thus appealed to, looked at Bathurst and signified assent to the course suggested. Bathurst prowled round the body again. I saw him look carefully at the soles of the girl's shoes and then heard him call out to the boy, Richards.

"Let me look at what you pick up, Richards," he ordered. "Put it all on your tray when you get it, and bring it over to me. Every tiny scrap that you can find."

The boy, on his task of salvage, scrambled up from his knees and brought the tray over for A.L.B.'s inspection.

"These what you dropped?" he asked him.

"Yes, sir."

Bathurst made audible inventory of the tray's contents. "Five packets of milk chocolate, three bars of ordinary chocolate, and one carton (damaged) of mixed or assorted chocolates. Missing contents of this last item, recovered, in detail, and placed on tray. Nine clean and intact, and one—a pink soft centre—squashed on carpet. Thank you very much, Richards. There is an eloquence about your tray that I find most fascinating."

For a moment, he stood on the top step, thinking hard. Then I saw his eyes look down to the strip of carpet that ran across the floor where we were standing.

"This—er—carpet," he said to the manager, "seems to me to have been pulled in some way from its true alignment. Look here, at this, if you don't believe me. All of you."

He knelt on the carpet in demonstration and ran a critical eye along its two edges. Jenkinson, the inspector, and I, followed his example. It certainly was a little way away from the straight. I said so directly I spotted it, and both Goodaker and Jenkinson agreed with me. Not much—but just a little.

For the life of me, however, I couldn't see what the hell Bathurst was driving at. Also, having already established a common basis of agreement with regard to the carpet amongst us four men, I was more amazed than ever when he thought fit to demand young Richards' opinion on the matter.

"Come down here, Richards," he called. "Kneel down there in front of me. Just there, where I'm pointing. Look carefully at that carpet edge. See where I mean? Would you be prepared to swear that this particular strip of carpet is in its usual position?"

The boy, however, was a pretty cool hand and took bags of time before he answered. He screwed one eye up, and then the other, perpetrated a complete dynasty of perfectly appalling grimaces, and then announced that in his opinion the strip of carpet upon which the inquest was being held was very much as usual.

Bathurst nodded, thanked him and dismissed him. Then, rising to his feet again, he approached Jenkinson.

"I am rather interested," he said, "in your two staircases. We will descend this one and see what we find. All of you come along, please."

By this time, we were all thoroughly under the influence of the blighter's personality, so we prepared to follow him without the slightest demur. But he waited, linked his arm in mine, and instead, we twain, Bathurst and Bannerman, actually followed Jenkinson and Inspector Goodaker down the flight of steps.

A dozen or so of these steps brought us to a spacious vestibule. Wicker lounge-chairs and a divan stood within it. To my utter astonishment, Bathurst gazed across the space thus reached, nodded approvingly, but said nothing at all. This silence he maintained for an appreciable period.

Emerging from it, he beckoned to Jenkinson to come across to him. "There's just a chance that the suggestion I'm about to make may bring us to something tangible. Let me tell you that I'm moderately certain that the man who murdered Elsie Rhodes got up from his seat and left the circle at a time approximating twenty-one minutes past ten. Now my idea, amplified, is this. The dying girl's scream came very shortly after that and must have been heard by hundreds, in whose memories it will live for a long time to come. *What if one of those hundreds remembers somebody who rose from the next seat and made a way out a few seconds before that scream was heard?* We have a definite indication of *time* you know! Do you follow me?"

His eyes burned with the fire of eagerness. Jenkinson signified his understanding and I formed the opinion that he was considerably impressed by the possibilities that Bathurst's suggestion had opened up.

"I take it that you will have 'feelers' put out then, for something of this sort, eh?" he queried. "How do you propose to—"

"Inspector Goodaker will see to that part of the business for us. I have strong hopes that it will yield good results. All clear, Goodaker?"

"I get the idea, Mr. Bathurst, and I'll have what you want done, directly we get back. As a matter of fact, I had thought of the possibility myself." A.L.B., waving us into a half circle, favoured the group with a demonstration. "Just give me two minutes, gentlemen. I will reconstruct the crime for you. The murderer, who had probably made an appointment with Miss Rhodes for somewhere about ten-twenty, left the circle in the manner I have already indicated, lured her to the flight of steps, where he stabbed her. He then descended the staircase, crossed this vestibule where we now stand, ascended the other staircase and entered the theatre again. I should say, if I were asked, that he entered the circle at almost the same moment that young Richards came to the body of Elsie Rhodes. Richards, of course, had his back towards him, and before re-entering the circle he took two steps towards the staircase where the girl lay, and listened."

Just as he finished speaking, in bustled old Bligh. Late as usual!

CHAPTER XII
DEMONSTRATION BY BATHURST

GOODAKER went to the old man's side and lost no time in putting him wise as to all that had occurred. Bligh punctuated the inspector's recital with nods of the head that I think he intended should be taken to indicate the profundity of his own wisdom.

"Mr. Bathurst has already formed certain theories, Sir George," the inspector concluded. "No doubt he will tell you of them."

A.L.B. smiled. "I'm not going to allow that. Hardly theories, Goodaker," he rejoined. "Much more than that, you know. Certain data, shall we say, with which I have been furnished most fortunately, have disposed me to accept certain conclusions. When there are only two possibilities, and one of them is probed and shown to be an impossibility, only one remains, because the other has been subjected to elimination. That is the principle which I applied and which led me to the announcement that I made to you."

He paused, seemingly inviting old Bligh's inevitable question. It came right enough. A real stone-ginger.

"What is this theory of yours, then, Bathurst? I confess that I shall be interested to hear it."

"Accepting the word 'theory' under protest, Sir George, I shall be delighted to pass my conclusions on to you. They are as follows."

Bathurst repeated to Bligh the account of the murderer's movements with which he had just favoured us. The old boy listened keenly.

"You are confident of the soundness of your position, Bathurst?" he asked.

"Absolutely, sir. If you will allow me, I'll more or less prove it to you. Will you come upstairs, please?"

Old Bligh gestured his willingness and we trooped up the staircase again, one behind the other. As we came to the body of Elsie Rhodes, Bligh paled a bit under his tan. I remembered, in his justification, that he was getting on in years, and say what you like, it was by no means an agreeable sight when you first came on it. Jenkinson had placed a towel over the girl's face, but, despite this, the Chief Constable, after the first glance, averted his gaze resolutely. Bathurst halted us when we reached the circle landing and turned to the manager.

"Let me have a word with that boy, Richards, again. Send for him, will you?"

Richards was requisitioned and was with us in a brace of shakes. Bathurst beckoned to him.

"Bring me everything that you dropped from your tray when you heard the scream and ran over to Miss Rhodes."

The boy seemed overcome by doubt. "Everything, sir? Do you mean—"

"I mean exactly what I said, Richards. Everything! All that went overboard. Damaged goods as well."

The boy turned and went to the ledge of the confectionery counter that I have described previously. I watched him—every movement. I was rather keen to see what he was about to do. I hadn't the least idea, you see, at this juncture, what the surprise was that Bathurst was staging. The youngster messed about for a moment or so with packets of sweets, replaced others on the counter, placed a number on his tray again, and then sauntered over to Bathurst.

"Here you are, sir," he volunteered, "everything is here just as it was all picked up."

Bathurst bent forwards towards the tray. He smiled. Then he signalled to us to gather round him. We did so, old Bligh pushing well to the front. He wasn't the man to miss a bus, let me tell you, if shoving other people out of the way counted.

"When Miss Rhodes screamed, gentlemen, this boy Richards ran to her help. A very natural thing for him to do. He was the nearest to her and, other things being equal, would be the first to reach her as she lay at the head of this flight of steps. As he ran to her, he dropped several of his packets of chocolate and chocolates. They fell from his tray. Just as you would expect to happen. If you don't believe me, try running with that tray suspended from your neck. One of the cartons containing chocolates fell, and its weight caused it to break open. Several of these chocolates were thus scattered over the carpet. Very soon afterwards, one was trodden on just there. You can see the flattened smudge quite distinctly if you look. Squashed chocolates—pink at that—are messy affairs."

He pointed down at a spot on the carpet. The mark was there right enough—plain for all of us to see. Bathurst waited for our recognition of it, before proceeding.

"If any gentlemen here harbour any doubt as to whether that is the actual spot where the chocolate was trodden on, I can dispel it immediately, because I saw Richards pick up part of the cream from there. Where are we, then? Well, I think that we are enabled to establish the following facts: Inasmuch as the sweet was trodden on *after* the murder of Elsie Rhodes, it must have been trodden on by one of the following. Listen carefully to the goodly fellowship. Richards, Mr. Jenkinson, Doctor Bannerman, Inspector Goodaker, myself, any stray member of the audience, *or* one other. Now, note the location of the smudge on the carpet, that little blurred blot of pink cream. Approximately, it is four inches the staircase side of that door. Which fact eliminates any and every member of the audience, because Mr. Jenkinson will tell you, as he told me, that the whole of the audience was very carefully shepherded through that farther door and down the staircase on the other side. In other words, none of them was near enough to that spot of carpet to have trodden on that chocolate. In addition, we are able to eliminate Richards, Jenkinson, the doctor here, the inspector, and, finally, myself."

He looked at us almost mischievously. Old Bligh fell for it with commendable fortitude and made the purchase.

"Why? How?"

"Because I have looked at the soles of all the boots and shoes concerned," replied Bathurst sweetly. "Each is clean."

I remembered then how we had knelt down in front of him. Bathurst continued:

"There remains, therefore, that 'one other'. The only possible . . . that '*one* other'. The murderer himself, gentlemen, trod on that chocolate. Just there—on the spot at which you are looking. Which enables me to assert with the confidence, parented by certainty, that having stabbed Miss Rhodes on the one flight of steps, he sped down them to the common landing that we have just left, crossed it as rapidly as he knew how, ascended by the other staircase, reached the top just as Richards had got to the body, took perhaps three of four steps to the right, listened for a second or so, and then passed into the circle again. At the psychological moment, too, for unnoticed entrance. *When everybody was looking at everybody else and seeking for an explanation of the scream that they had heard.* In fact, nobody but the murderer *could* have trodden on the chocolate, as I see the chain of events."

He was right, I thought—undeniably right. He had flushed a little under the stress of the explanation, but he saw my look, that I had followed him, with appreciation, and he flashed me a quick glance of gratitude. Bligh nodded pompously—true to type. Goodaker frowned; the manager, Jenkinson, fingered nervously the ends of his "toothbrush" moustache. Bathurst, however, went on again, to tell Sir George of his idea of getting into touch with anybody who had been in the theatre and could remember a neighbour rising from a seat just before the scream was heard.

Bligh lifted his hands and gave his blessing to the suggestion at once—without discussion or criticism of any kind. Goodaker also received appropriate instructions, and I told him, besides, to make the usual arrangements for the removal of the girl's body.

Bathurst turned to me when I went back and rejoined them. "I'm coming along with you, Bannerman. I don't think that we can reasonably do any more now."

"Righto," I retaliated. "That suits me."

"Sir George," he proceeded. "There's a very remarkable feature of this third murder. I must inform you of it. It sticks out most aggressively."

Sir George stared owlishly. "What's that, may I ask?"

"Simply this. My investigations into the two previous cases led me to no less a place *than the house of this dead girl*. I had already interviewed her mother. Most extraordinary, don't you think?"

Bligh's stare became a gape. "I do. I do, most decidedly. You had, and you have, a definite theory, then?"

It seemed to me that for once Bathurst finessed. "It's like this. In a way, you see, I'm already in the dead girl's circle, which gives me an undoubted initial advantage. I shan't be forced, or will the inspector, to inquire for the usual preliminary associations. Which, if nothing else, must mean a saving of time. Valuable time. As to your question concerning my possession of a theory re murders one and two—I can only say this: this murder of Miss Rhodes becomes definitely disturbing. I may, or may not, be forced to shift my position. What have you to say about that, Bannerman?"

His eyes held mine, almost hungrily.

"I know what you mean, Bathurst," I said stoutly. "It's difficult to read 'vendetta' into this third murder. That's what you mean, isn't it?"

"As you say, Doctor. Just so. I am inclined to admit that it's brought me up with a jerk."

His face held a far-away look as he held out his hand to say "good night" to Sir George Bligh. Seemingly, absent-mindedness was the cause of his holding the old boy's hand for a longer period than was usual.

"I wonder," I heard him whisper to himself; and then, in the moment of recovery, "Good night, Sir George."

Chapter XIII
CORBETT BRINGS EVIDENCE

LITTLE sleep came to me that night. Nerves don't trouble me much in the ordinary way, but this string of murders, so close at hand, was approaching the limit of ordinary human endurance. I was less easy in my mind if only for the fact that I knew beyond question that Anthony Bathurst, too, was troubled. As the affair sorted itself out to me, since the stabbing of Elsie Rhodes, it seemed that on the main issue, Montague Corbett had been right and Bathurst wrong.

The idea that the latter had held, that this danger threatened the Fredericks family only, had by now been definitely dispelled, and Corbett's contention, that the entire population of Chelmersley and district was in danger, and needed extra protection, had received rather gruesome confirmation.

I was by no means too fresh, therefore, when I threw the bedclothes back on the following morning and followed A.L.B. into the bathroom. To my surprise, however, he seemed to have exchanged his doubting for a mood of moderate optimism.

"Morning, Bannerman," he chirped cheerily, and the salutation was succeeded by a confident expression of opinion. "Do you know," he continued, "I've been doing a hell of a lot of thinking in my waking hours. I don't consider that we are any the worse off. Cast your mind back, Doctor, to that little conversation we had at Ninety-four Thatch Road. With Mrs. Rhodes. Arrived?"

He had travelled a wee bit too rapidly for me. I tried to recall the various points of what the woman had told us, but failed, from the point of view of my own satisfaction, to pick on anything that seemed more important than the rest. I shook my head non-committally and put my inability into words.

"I'll whisper to you, then, while you do your morning stropping act. In the first place, concentrate on that interesting little burglary that we were told took place at the Beaufoy Cinema—the burglary which caused Elsie Rhodes so much concern. Concern, too, which her mother was at a loss to explain. Note also, in connection therewith, that this dutiful daughter, who was always making her mother her confidante, did not do so on this occasion. Add to those contents the illuminating fact that Master Otto Kreutz deliberately chose the Rhodes' establishment for his apartments. Allow mixture to simmer gently for two hours, and add flavouring to taste."

He rubbed his hands, semi-challengingly.

"You think that your theory still holds, then," I declared rather lamely.

"I wouldn't altogether say that. It may do. It may not. We shall have to wait for further data. At the same time, I see no valid reason why I should discard it until I have something better to put in its place. But I won't talk to you any more now, Bannerman. You may cut yourself, and your personal beauty trembles on too slender a thread to risk antagonisms of that kind. Let me unto the door and I'll get out."

We had breakfast and I was just inspecting my professional diary to see how I could best and most conveniently arrange my consultation programme for the day, when that infernal telephone-bell rang again.

It was Inspector Goodaker at the other end, as I had half expected when I went to answer it. I listened, told him that it would be all right, and replaced the receiver.

"News," I informed my companion. "Your suggestion has already borne fruit, Bathurst."

He was all interest at once. "Full details, Doctor, please."

"I'm sorry. Can't give you them yet awhile. But there's something being spilt at the station now. Goodaker wants us both to go down. I'd very much like to, but I don't know that I can. There are one or two patients on my list whom I simply must see some time this morning. There's no reason, though, why you shouldn't get down there yourself at once. You can take the Crossley."

"I'm in agreement with you, Doctor. You mustn't neglect your patients any more. All the same, I could bear to hear everything that Goodaker is hearing. If I'm not very much mistaken, it will turn out to be as eloquent as anything we have yet heard. See you later, then."

Bathurst told me, when I saw him again at dinner that evening, that his first feeling upon arrival at the police station was one of surprise. Fate, however, is always staging little dramas of coincidence, and Goodaker's attempt to get into touch with members of the "Beaufoy" audience had been rewarded in an extraordinary manner. For, lo and behold, it had beckoned Montague Corbett from the wings and installed him centre stage. Not that the invitation had appealed to eyes that were myopic.

Directly he had become aware that the authorities desired evidence of the particular kind that had been indicated he had come down to the station without a moment's delay.

Bathurst found him with Goodaker and Bligh when he arrived. The following is what he had to contribute to the book of words.

He had attended the "Beaufoy" on the evening previous. It was his habit to go there at least once a week, he said. Very often twice. Liked pictures better than he liked the theatre, and as he grew older was getting to like them more and more. Far greater scope there than on the boards, you know. Bathurst, here, had intimated that he did. Corbett, a wee bit abashed at the corroborative remark, proceeded.

According to Bathurst, the little interruption that I've just mentioned served to put Corbett temporarily out of his stride. The semi-cultured accent that he habitually affected incontinently escaped, and it soon became very apparent to the listeners that Corbett had less of polish and more of veneer. "A thousand aitches in his sight," observed Bathurst dryly as he picked up a stick of asparagus, "were in a morning gone."

Boiled down to the bones of facts, Corbett's further contribution amounted to this: He had arrived at the "Beaufoy" on the evening before, at about half past seven, and had paid for a seat in his usual place—the circle. When he had reached his seat, in the wake of the guiding attendant, the circle, at a rough computation, was half full. His seat was on the right-hand side of the circle as you faced the screen and in the very back row.

"Near a gangway?" asked Bathurst.

"Yes. One from the end of the row."

When he had first seated himself, this end seat next to his had been occupied by a young lady who had, however, vacated it somewhere about nine o'clock, he thought, when the big picture had finished. An exceedingly well-dressed young lady.

A little while after this young lady had gone out, the seat had been taken by a man. Corbett had noticed this person particularly—seated next to him, he had had ample opportunity. At Bathurst's request he described him. These were the more important points of description. I will dissect them as Bathurst did for me.

The man was dark, of average height, fairly stout, and wore spectacles. His clothes, Corbett said, were ordinary—similar clothes to those worn every day by hundreds. Dark suit—blue serge, he fancied—linen collar, hard hat, and roughish black shoes. And gloves, he added, light-coloured wash-leather.

He had been in a position to notice the man's shoes particularly, because of the manner in which the man had sat with his legs crossed during the interval, when the theatre had been lighted for the programme to start again.

He called the shoes "roughish" because they looked coarser and heavier than most of the shoes that the young men wore nowadays. Here Corbett added a farther hint.

"In my opinion, that pair of shoes was never made in this country." This man, Corbett went on, although not coming in until very late in the evening—five minutes past nine, say—had risen and left his seat only "a moment or so" before the murdered girl had screamed.

Hereabouts, so he told me, Bathurst had probed him pretty severely. Corbett's story was so important that of very necessity it had to be tested rigorously and stringently. Bathurst was unsuccessful, however, in shaking him with regard to any material point. Corbett had stood the fire of Bathurst's questions admirably and had yielded no real ground. Like many others of the audience who had heard the scream and been alarmed, he had attempted to seek its origin, with the natural idea, he explained, of rendering help should it be required. But when he had reached the exit door nearer to his seat in the circle he had found it barred on the inside by attendants and had eventually been escorted across the circle, out of the farther door, and down the farther staircase.

This, as Bathurst already knew, from the statement made by Jenkinson, the manager, was what had actually happened. There was no reason, as far as he could see, why Montague Corbett should have been afforded different treatment from the rest. At the finish of the interview Corbett had departed, declaring, with dominating vehemence, that what he had taken the trouble to warn the police against had taken place. In time, he affirmed, the whole population of Chelmersley would be murdered, one by one. Then the police would wake up.

Goodaker had naturally taken a detailed account of Corbett's statement, as he had also done from two other people who had presented themselves at the police station later on in the day and volunteered statements of a somewhat similar nature.

In each of these instances Bathurst had thoroughly examined the information that had been preferred. One emanated from a motherly old soul, rejoicing in the somewhat plebeian patronymic of Muggeridge. The story that she had to tell (labouring under great excitement) was this.

"A few minutes"—mark the words that Mrs. Muggeridge used—before she heard that dreadful scream, a very beautiful and charmingly dressed young lady, seated two or three places from her, had made her way rather hastily along the row, and gone out. Mrs. M. was able to furnish only a vague and quite indefinite description of this person, but concluded on a hopeful note with the assertion that the young lady had used "lovely scent". Different from the cheap muck that so many of the hussies use nowadays, to hide other and worse odours.

Statement number two came to Goodaker via a middle-aged man named Lewis. This man said that he was a clerk, engaged at the goods depot of Chelmersley railway station. Here again, Bathurst asked me to notice carefully the details of what was said.

"About five minutes" before the general consternation caused by the scream, Lewis had noticed a big, fair man ascend the carpeted steps of the circle, obviously on his way out. He had come, he thought, from somewhere near the front row. Lewis had noticed him, he said, because he himself had been seated at the very end of a row, and the fair man had brushed Lewis's shoulders with his sleeve on. the point of passing.

"These three informations," said A.L.B. to me over a glass of Clicquot, "make up the sum total that has rewarded Goodaker's toil. Up to the moment, that is."

"And what do you make of them?" I asked, as I drained my bubbly, and fingered the delicate stem of the glass that had held it.

"I expected you to ask me that, Doctor. As a matter of fact, only one of the three interests me. But that particular one intrigues me beyond the wildest dreams of Gaboriau. Lecoq would have loved it." He rubbed his hands enthusiastically. "Gaboriau, that apostle of secret scandal and family intrigue. Where would Monsieur Lecoq have ever been without the sins of the fathers?"

"Which interests you? Corbett's?"

He nodded. "Corbett's. For if I mistake not, my dear Bannerman, once again, if Corbett be speaking the truth, we cross the trail of Otto Kreutz. And for the third time, mind you. Consider, if you please, the description given by Montague Corbett of the man who left the circle *only a moment or so* before Elsie Rhodes was murdered. In every detail, as I see it, it speaks of Otto Kreutz, the man whom you and I met in the hairdresser's in West Street, the man who lodged at ninety-four Thatch Road."

At that moment I decided to let him have my bombshell.

"Something I want to tell you, Bathurst," I said nonchalantly—"something I discovered to-day. The murdered girl was within a couple of months of maternity."

He turned and regarded me intently. There was a light in his eyes. It seemed to me, as I looked at him, that it was a light of satisfaction.

Chapter XIV
CONSTERNATION

After these happenings, Bathurst hitched his waggon to my star for good. What traps he had brought with him to Bligh's in the first place he lugged round to my show and generally made a stay of it. The arrangement certainly suited us both. He was free to come and go when he liked, and I could mingle ordinary work with "sleuthing" to my heart's content.

There was one great barrier, however, to progress. Kreutz, whom fingers itched to hold, had, to all intents and purposes disappeared from the face of the earth. The statement may sound incredible, but it is true all the same. Goodaker enlisted all the services and resources that the police authorities had at their disposal. But all to no purpose. This man, of unusual appearance, to say the least, who, we had every reason to believe, had been in the heart of Chelmersley on the previous evening and had murdered Elsie Rhodes in such a place as the "Beaufoy" Cinema, vanished as effectively and as completely as though he had never known existence. Neither Melsheimer's nor Mrs. Rhodes' establishment heard a whisper of him.

Bathurst was in touch with Goodaker almost hourly and the 'phone, which, come to think of it, had been in it since the jump-off, was going incessantly. But it brought us nothing. I was disappointed, but Bathurst imperturbable. One might almost have imagined, from his outward manner, that he was pleased with the way that things were going.

On the second morning after the third murder, I had left Bathurst alone at "The Rowfants", barring the Ramage, of course. A woman over at Little Steeping had sent for me urgently to look at one of her youngsters, and I had discovered, when I arrived there, that what she had been afraid was erysipelas was nothing more than an alveolar abscess.

The kid's face was considerably swollen, but it was a case for a dentist in the very near future, and I was able to allay maternal fears and forebodings and breeze back to "The Rowfants" by lunch-time.

Upon arrival, I saw that there was something doing; there was an air of excitement amongst the people that I found in my little dining-room that spoke eloquently of activity on all fronts. Bathurst and Goodaker were there, with Jack Tabernacle and a man of Chelmersley whom I knew as Torrelli.

His full name was Pietro Torrelli and he kept what was usually known as the "posh" restaurant in West Street. This restaurant was the very next building to the "Beaufoy". I knew him fairly well, if only for the reason that I had sometimes dined there, and had also bought my last bus off him six months or so previously.

I quickly gathered from the conversation that our three guests had not arrived in one party. Jack had drifted in to see me on his own, and Bathurst had explained the position to him. He had elected to wait for my return, and the inspector and Torrelli had come in upon them later.

Here I will digress for just a moment. I said just now that Torrelli's restaurant was a "posh" one. What I really mean is this.. It wasn't a palace of pleasure, but you could get a bottle of really good wine there, if you wanted it; a very decent grill; anything you chose to ask for as an entree; absolutely topping hors d'oeuvres . . . and the cooking was par excellence.

He was an able man, Torrelli, who had worked hard to establish his connection, and by now, it had become the common thing for parties from Chelmersley and district to wind up their "dos" and have little dinners at "Torrelli's".

All this will, I hope, help you to understand the particular kind of man that Pietro Torrelli was. A foreigner, who looked the part all over. He was short, plump, and altogether comfortable-looking. It was he, it transpired, who was the primary cause of this morning conclave at "The Rowfants".

I toddled on to the stage at what the novelists call the psychological moment. Also, I shall never, if I live to the age of Methuselah himself, forget the look of anxiety that I saw on Jack's face as he, with Bathurst at his side, listened to Pietro Torrelli's story. I don't blame him either; when I heard it and realized, right at the conclusion of it, the exact direction in which Torrelli was heading, I shared his anxiety. Anxiety—that's a moderate word to use. Consternation would express my condition very much better.

"You're in the nick, Doctor." That was Bathurst's greeting to me as I strode in. "Go back a little way, Mr. Torrelli, please. I'm sure you won't mind repeating your most interesting story for Doctor Bannerman's benefit. After all, we owe him something, you know. It would be ungracious on our part to forget that. We're occupying a moderately substantial portion of his ancestral hearthrug."

Torrelli flashed a half-smile in my direction. The humour wasn't of his kind. I'm not sure either that he was too bucked at Bathurst's suggestion.

"I will, sir." His English was good, excellent, almost always. "I will start again at the beginning that the doctor may hear all that there is to hear. Doctor Bannerman and I are friends, as he will tell you, if you care to ask him. When I—"

Jack cut in here. Impatience seemed to have rubbed him somewhere into rawness. "Get on, Torrelli, for God's sake!" he interjected. "You've told us something already, and I, for one, must know more. It means a lot to me. Don't waste any more time."

I thought this was decently cool on the part of Master Jack, seeing that I had heard nothing and was in complete ignorance of what was doing. But I knew for a certainty, from my first glance at him, that he was on edge and made allowances accordingly.

I said nothing, therefore, and waited for Torrelli to get the move on that Tabernacle had requested. He took Jack's heat very well for one of his race, I must say, and was smiling when he started to speak again.

"It's like this, Doctor. You remember a few days ago when Mr. Fredericks was murdered? Mr. Walter Fredericks? Well, a little thing came to me this morning, about something that happened in my place on the evening previous to that murder. My head's busy with so many things, that, for the time being, I had forgotten it, and if I had not told a friend of mine about it on the night when it happened and he had not told me something that I did not know before, I do not think it would ever have come back to me. Perhaps. Perhaps not. Who can say of these things? But listen. Because we cannot be sure of a thing like that, I am going to tell you now. You must know that in my restaurant, I have a large room below and a number of smaller rooms above. There are three floors altogether. A big staircase leads from the main room downstairs, up to the other floors. It is on the right as you enter, about two-thirds of the distance down the room.

"On the first floor, as you turn the corner, there are, on one side, lavatories for gentlemen, and on the other, tucked right away in the far corner, a telephone cabinet. Now I will tell you the important thing. The evening before this murder of poor Mr. Fredericks, a lady engaged a table for two, in one of the small rooms upstairs, in the name of Mrs. Cotterill. She ordered one of my very best dinners; everything just as it should be; she has what you call irreproachable taste; five courses, and every one of them just right."

"August thirty, Bannerman," interpolated Bathurst, "the lady's birthday. A little celebration. Don't worry. It helps to prove Mr. Torrelli's point. Go on, Mr. Torrelli."

"When she came, she came with another young lady. Very pretty and very attractive. Quite charming. But not like the lady calling herself Mrs. Cotterill. Oh—no. She—Mrs. Cotterill—has such glorious eyes, such long lashes with them. Altogether, an air. You call it . . . you know . . . like a queen . . . regent . . . no, no—regal. I was surprised that the other young lady should come with her."

Torrelli shrugged his shoulders and went on to explain. "I should have expected a gentleman like one of you to have been with her . . . your pardon, you know what I mean. The lady was so beautiful that she must have many admirers. It is only right."

Nobody made response; so, disappointed somewhat, Torrelli glanced round and then proceeded a little more slowly. I don't think he quite understood us.

"Just as the two ladies were finishing dinner, the beautiful one, Mrs. Cotterill, made a request to the waiter who was attending to her. Would he please delay the coffee for a few minutes? She desired, so she said, to make use of the telephone. So she made her way out of the room to my telephone. I have explained to you where it is. Now listen, gentlemen, please, because this is where the important part comes in. The very important part. As I came down from the top floor of all, where I had been to speak to a gentleman concerning how his wine was to be cooled, I passed the telephone just as Mrs. Cotterill must have been finishing her conversation. She was speaking very audibly. Her voice is very clear and it—what is it that you English say?—it carries well. I could not help but hear what the words were that she was using. In a way, I wish I hadn't. Knowledge, very often, is double-edged—dangerous."

Torrelli shook his head meaningly and approximated reminiscence, I thought. "She said this: 'Once and for all . . . please understand. This is final. I'll see you to-morrow night as you wish . . . for the very last time. I've told your daughter all about it this evening.' As I started to descend the last flight of stairs, I heard her say something else. 'I'll see you dead first. Dead at my feet'. Then she laughed. It was a low, cruel sort of laugh, as though she were anticipating almost what she had just hinted at."

He turned in his chair and spread hairy hands over big knee-caps. I could have welted the blighter a fourpenny-one in the mouth as he spoke his last sentence. Confounded insolence! The idea of it indeed! What was the fool driving at in the name of goodness? How could he know for certain to whom Rosemary had been speaking, unless he had since put police inquiry on to the point and they had found out something.

At this juncture, uneasiness seized me and I indulged in a "spot" of thinking. This conference must mean something, I argued. I hadn't heard it all yet, either. Besides there was Jack ... the look on his face. I switched from him to Goodaker and from the inspector to A.L.B. He, however, was waiting again for another contribution from Torrelli. It came.

"Well, gentlemen?" The man leant forward, fussily important. I loathed him more than ever now. "For some while, I thought no more about that little telephone talk. As I told you just now, I'm a busy man and, in these hard times, business must come first, second and third. Even Mr. Fredericks' murder didn't revive the thing in my mind. I never connected the incident with that for a moment. To-day, however, my brain woke up. I tapped myself on the head and said, 'Pietro Torrelli, you damn-blast fool.'" He looked round and dropped his voice a little. "I'll tell you why. Listen. In Chelmersley to-day—this morning early—I saw a young lady in a motor-car. She was dressed all in black. I recognized her as the young lady who had dined with Mrs. Cotterill. And then a friend of mine who was with me said something that almost made me jump from my skin."

Torrelli, with all the native drama of his race, raised expressive hands. "The young lady that I tell you about was Miss Fredericks. Miss Iris Fredericks, my friend told me. There, gentlemen, what do you make of that? You see all that it means, don't you?"

I hated the man with a seething hate as he put the question to us. It was framed in a leer of consummate craft. Goodaker, however, was quick to answer him.

"You mean that if Mrs. Cotterill—"

Torrelli's eagerness, however, was in spate. It brooked no denial. "If Mrs. Cotterill said on the 'phone, 'I've told your daughter all about it this evening', words which I heard her say—I'll swear it on this—then she must have been talking to Mr. Fredericks and it must have been Mr. Fredericks whom she threatened."

As he spoke, Torrelli held up a medal of the Immaculate Conception that swayed gently on a faded blue ribbon. He made the sign of the Cross. The gesture completed, he glanced round at us, one by one. They were quick, darting glances. Almost furtive. It seemed that he was striving to discover the various impressions that he had made upon each one of us.

Goodaker showed no hesitation. He accepted Torrelli's point with avidity. "We can check up on all that, Torrelli. There won't be any difficulty there. Also, I'm not surprised. I thought there was a woman in it all the time."

"There is, Inspector, undoubtedly." The intervention came from Bathurst. We all waited for him to continue. Somehow, I think, he made us do that. Personality again. "But she's the *right* one. We don't want any superfluous women knocking about. They'd merely get in the way."

Goodaker and Torrelli stared at him. He met the stares with a disarming smile. "Well, gentlemen, why the thunderous applause?"

Jack pressed him. "How d'you mean—superfluous women?"

"Isn't my meaning crystal clear, then? Where's the snag that protrudes so offensively?"

"What do you mean—the 'right woman'?"

"Elsie Rhodes, of course. Who else, among women, could it be? At this stage of the case, the murder of Fredericks tells us a great deal. The death of his only son—only remaining son, mark you, tells us very much more. They are as one card built delicately upon another. 'Built,' I said. 'Making something.' If you like it better, 'Hinting at a definite pattern in the carpet that is being trailed in front of us.' There is just a faint tracery beginning to shape."

He paused. The grey eyes appeared to be looking at something which only they saw. We others, who listened to him, were miles away. He continued: "But, just as this tracery begins to appear, Elsie Rhodes is murdered. Cleverly, too, by a criminal who is as ruthless as he is cunning. Who strikes hard and who strikes home. Which incident blurs my pattern. But does it, after all? Let us make sure. Short of considerations of vital data, we may come to that opinion and yet be wrong. Given the data of the right kind, and fortified by the unerring factor of the science of deduction, the pattern we seek may be there all the time if we can only find it. Clearer, more defined, and its visibility . . ."

He stopped with an abruptness that was almost shattering and turned to me with a smile. "The winds have blown them all away, Doctor. Where are the girls of yesterday?"

We who had been following him so keenly and so closely, seemed like struggling men who had been given a lift halfway up a hill, like Sunrising Hill, for example, and then been left quite suddenly to fend for ourselves over the distance that remained.

Jack was a little impatient at Bathurst's deviation. "Yet all the women may not be so superfluous as you imagine, surely?"

The grey eyes of Anthony Bathurst regarded him almost lazily. "No! Let me see if I agree with you. Do you allude to Miss Fredericks, by any chance?"

This time, Jack's impatience manifested itself more clearly. "Of course I don't. I was speaking entirely generally. I had no one in mind. Her, last of all. I am engaged to Iris, as you probably know by this time. If you knew her as I know her, you'd know at the same time that she is incapable of injuring a fly."

Bathurst nodded. "I expected you to say that, Mr. Tabernacle. And, of course, all honour to you for the expression of loyalty."

Jack blushed a bit at the compliment. Like most of us, when a bouquet comes our embarrassed way, I suppose.

"This is all very well," exclaimed Goodaker. "Why drag Miss Fredericks across the trail? It seems to me a sheer waste of time.

Torrelli's statement never indicated that in any way. Surely he turns the searchlight of inquiry on to Mrs. Cotterill. I don't follow Mr. Bathurst when he darts away from the truth, like he did just now. Mr. Tabernacle, I think, was perfectly justified in what he said."

I was astounded at the look that I saw on A.L.B.'s face. No words of mine are adequate to describe it. It was as though he had separated his soul from his body by some wonderful occult process, and launched it into space, to watch it again, wonderingly, on its amazing way. Then, as I watched, I saw his jaws stiffen and he came back to normality again, with a light in his eyes that had never been there before—at least, during the time that I had known him.

"Thank you, Inspector," he remarked quietly. "You have brought me to book and I deserve all your censures and all your criticism. As you say, why drag Miss Fredericks across the trail? 'Twould be the epitome of foolishness. Doctor, concentrate, please, on the evidence that came to us in the Beaufoy Picture-house. It speaks for itself. And I've been as blind as a battalion of bats. Torrelli!"

He swung round on to the restaurant proprietor with dramatic vehemence. The fool blinked at the sudden change.

"Yes, sir. What is it?"

Although I was more or less bewildered at the turn things had taken, my dislike of Torrelli had, if anything, increased in force. His deliberate accusation that Rosemary was in some way involved in the wretched affair and had threatened Walter Fredericks had absolutely incensed me. I could have pushed my fist into his fat face with a positively unholy joy and made mince-meat of it.

Bathurst swooped on him and pinned him down. "Tell me the name of this friend of yours to whom you repeated Mrs. Cotterill's telephone conversation and who pointed Miss Fredericks out to you in Chelmersley this morning. His name—quick."

Torrelli was stung into alert reply. "Melsheimer—my neighbour in West Street. Why?"

Bathurst looked at the inspector and motioned to Jack and me. "Very natural, I suppose, too—in the circumstances."

Walking to the window, he stood there, looking out into the garden. There was a quietude about him that tended to puzzle me. Suddenly he turned. "Inspector," he said, "I'll tell you something that may interest you. Above Melsheimer's saloon there is an empty, unfurnished room with a door that communicates with the restaurant adjoining. I wonder to what purpose it has been put."

CHAPTER XV
MISS FREDERICKS AT HOME

SHORTLY afterwards, Torrelli and the inspector cleared out. Jack and Bathurst stopped with me. We had lunch and, by arrangement, not another word was said relative to our problem. On the other hand, Bathurst descanted at some length upon the excellence of the Ramage salad-dressing.

"Congratulations, Bannerman," he said, "upon your possession of a very valuable retainer. The longer I stay with you, the more I realize what a lucky man you are. One very seldom finds, for instance, the right proportion of mushroom ketchup in a dressing of this kind."

Jack chimed in an agreement and then, somewhat to my amusement, the pair of them waxed eloquent upon the three varieties of roux—white, blond and brown.

"The last simply must have that rich nut-brown tint," declared Bathurst, "which only comes from prolonging the frying process." He embarked upon explanation in support. . . .

When we'd finished lunch, it occurred to me that he'd grown despondent. I rallied him. "It's this fellow Kreutz that worries me," he explained to us. "You've a clever devil against you there, Bannerman. I'm afraid he'll get clean away this time. There's no doubt that he has a ready-made hiding-place somewhere. Both convenient and handy. He'll run to earth there and stay hidden in all probability while the hue and cry are red hot. Otherwise, why wasn't he found before? He should be so easily recognizable, surely? I don't like it, Bannerman. Not a little bit. How's that for a double negative, eh?"

His despondency cleared a bit at that and he grinned at us in the old way again. Jack did something then for which I was unprepared and which I thought was very decent on his part.

"I owe you half an apology, Bathurst. Although, to be fair to myself, I've a certain amount of excuse. But I misunderstood you just now. And I'm only just beginning to understand now. I think that I was all kinds of a silly ass and that I jumped to an entirely wrong conclusion. You meant to tell me, I think, *that Miss Fredericks was in danger*. I'm right there, am I not?"

Bathurst nodded. "I'm very much afraid so, Tabernacle. That's how I read the problem and that's what I tried to tell you."

"What can we do?"

"Wait and watch. This time we are, to some extent, forearmed, where we weren't before."

"That's all very well; but whom do we watch? If we knew that—"

"We can watch *her*, man, can't we? The tiger-hunter, you know, builds his *machan* in the tree nearest to where the great lord of the jungle has left his kill. Then, rifle in hand, the hunter ascends to his little platform and waits for the brute to come back—on the night of the morrow, as a rule. He always does come back. He's swift and he's silent and he's strong and he belongs to the shadows. He is part of them and they are part of him. But he comes into the open at last. The meat of his kill draws him there. So will our murderer. When that happens, we shall do our job of hunting."

Jack was clearly disappointed. His face and manner united to show it. "And all the time Iris is in danger, while I've got to—"

Bathurst clapped him on the shoulder. "That's hard, I know, old man. Nobody knows it better than I. Waiting is always the harder part, especially when the pads are on for a long time. But I promise you, Tabernacle, that if Miss Fredericks can be saved

I'll do my very best on her behalf. I can't say more than that at the moment."

Here, I took a hand in the conversation—to help Jack out, I think, more than anything else. I could see that the news .that Bathurst had given to him had affected him considerably. After all, it's a bit of a kick up the pants to hear that the lady of your choice stands a distinctly healthy chance of having her throat cut. I essayed a quick review of the situation. If Torrelli's story had anything in it, and if Corbett's yarn of Kreutz being in the "Beaufoy"—which Bathurst seemed to regard as extraordinarily important—were also authoritative, how did it affect such a person as Iris Fredericks? I strove for a reasonable interpretation of Torrelli's prolixity.

"Bathurst," I cried. "What did you make of *Melsheimer* in Torrelli's story? I can't forget, you see, that Kreutz was with him, working in his shop, under his orders. Here he is, cropping up again after Kreutz has left him and disappeared. Don't you think it very significant?"

His reply was a counter question. "In what particular way, Bannerman?"

"Mayn't he have something to do with the murders—know something, perhaps?"

"In one way, he had a lot to do with the *first* murder. But only the first one, I fancy."

Jack and I stared at him incredulously. Jack's incredulity translated itself into words and dashed itself against Bathurst's imperturbable personality.

"You speak as though you have found the murderer," he cried. "How can you say what you did, when you don't know—"

"So much?" Anthony smiled at his eagerness and completed the sentence for him. "Perhaps I did sound dogmatic, Tabernacle. Forgive me. Now for something much more tangible. Can you help me, you fellows, this afternoon and evening?"

The change of subject was precipitate. I knew the reason of it. Bathurst had a sudden visualization of activity and, as was his invariable custom, he was shedding the mantle of meditation for the cloak of clash.

"What do you want of us?" I inquired. Jack followed suit, as ready and willing as I. "Say the word, Bathurst—and I'm your man."

"Very many thanks, you fellows. I knew that I could rely on you. You've a car, Tabernacle, haven't you?"

Jack nodded affirmatively.

"I thought you had. I wonder if you would mind running up to town for me? To New Scotland Yard. I 'phoned Sir Austin Kemble this morning and he's expecting an emissary of some kind from me. I must have someone whom I can implicitly trust. Give him this, will you?"

He handed Jack a letter.

"I'm sending him a full description of both Otto Kreutz and Melsheimer. It's just possible, I think, that Berlin may be in a position to help us. Von Eisenhofer is in my debt on one or two accounts. The Commissioner may ask you to wait. If he do, you can bet your bottom dollar that things have started moving. Fit?"

"O.K., Chief," replied Jack satirically.

"Thank you. Now you, Doctor. How long ago was the Chelmersley pageant? Can you give me any idea?"

I stared at him, I confess, with sheer amazement in my eyes. What hare was he coursing now? I pulled myself together. "Seven months ago, about. In February. Why?"

He grinned. "Don't quite know yet. Not sure. But just a glimmer. Clutching therefore, at straws. Would it be possible for you, do you think, to get me a full list of performers and their costumes? I suppose there's a record of the show kept somewhere?"

"Oh yes, I should think so. It was semi-official. For instance, the people at the Town Hall might be able to help. The Town Clerk was the big noise."

"And all the Municipal jackals, eh? Did you take part, Bannerman?"

I flushed. It was by way of being a sore point with me. "Yes. I was Guy Fawkes, if you must know. He had Chelmersley associations, you know. At Eastbury Grange—that's the name of the actual place. The plot itself was hatched between Chelmersley and Cressing. Nobody seemed keen on the part, though, and I was badgered to take it. There's a mug born every minute."

He grinned. "So you think poorly of friend Guido, do you? I'm not sure that he hadn't his finger on the pulse of a great truth. Who knows? Now tell me. Were the Fredericks in the pageant? Either of them?"

I shook my head. "Neither of them, as it happens. Neither Walter nor Donald. Iris was and so was Duncan, the elder brother. Jack here, would be able to tell you exactly what they were. Something with a healthy touch of importance, you bet. Sorry, Jack, and all that, but you know what I mean."

"You know what these country places are, Mike. Why worry?"

"Never mind the details. Can you answer me this, either of you?" Bathurst was in again. "Were any of the pageant scenes enacted in modern costume?"

"Yes," returned Jack. "I can answer that. There were two scenes that were laid in the market place at Chelmersley. August fourth, nineteen hundred and fourteen, was the time of the first. War declared—a recruiting stunt. You know the idea. 'Chelmersley's Manhood Answers the Country's Call.' The second one was a huge success. One of the most loudly-acclaimed of the whole show, I should say. A batch of Hun prisoners being marched through the town on the way to a prison camp over at Cressing."

Bathurst rubbed his hands. "Ah! Now that's most interesting. Well, Doctor, do your best to get me a full list of performers from somewhere, will you? Then we can go into it thoroughly."

He turned away deliberately and Jack and I took this as our cue for dismissal. I rolled off to the old public offices, now raised to the questionable dignity of Town Hall, by the mere change of the name and description over the doorway, and interviewed Mittick the Town Clerk.

Jack turned his car towards the office of Sir Austin Kemble. The time then, would be about half past two in the afternoon.

At a few minutes to five Bathurst rang the bell of the Fredericks' household just off the Great Steeping road. It may be remarked that he did not approach the front of the house in the ordinary way—from the road. He came to it, on the other hand, from the back of the house itself. Iris was in. Rosemary Cotterill was with her. Fate stages such strange scenes sometimes, doesn't it? A.L.B., however, was unperturbed at the conditions. This proves what an extraordinary man he was. Few men are at their best in the presence of the girl who has turned them down years before and whom they meet again suddenly and unexpectedly.

Bathurst told me afterwards that, taking everything into consideration, the proximity of Rosemary pleased him immensely. I can understand that part of it as well as any man. It always did me. She was beautiful—as a summer morning is beautiful in its "immaculate hours". Serenely cool, with the lazy promise of the glory to come. She was tall and she was slender. She was magnificently vivid. Creamy skin, red lips, and white even teeth. Her hair in shadow was brown, but when the light caught it and played on it, it gave it threads of sparkle. She had a habit of raising her eyebrows that gave her a suggestion of whimsical solicitude. Her voice was perfect—musical but crisp. Once you had heard it, it sounded perpetually in your ears.

She gave Bathurst the tips of her fingers after Iris had given him her hand. "This is an unexpected pleasure, Mrs. Cotterill," he said. "I had no idea that I should find you here. I anticipated finding Miss Fredericks alone."

"I'm staying here," she replied quietly. "You shouldn't be surprised," she added; "Iris has need of me."

Bathurst bowed. "I can well believe that."

She smiled a little at this. "You are not entirely changed, then?"

He adroitly disregarded the overture and addressed her companion. "You will have heard of the murder of Miss Rhodes, of course. Because of that—mainly—I have come to you for help, Miss Fredericks. Will you give it to me? Only you, I think, are in a position to give me what I want."

Iris raised her eyebrows. "I don't know what you mean. But what I am able to tell you, you know you have only to ask me." With a strange calmness the girl folded her hands on her lap; she waited for Bathurst to continue.

"How long have you lived here, Miss Fredericks?"

"Nearly nine years. I was a little girl of fourteen when we came here."

Rosemary's face was in serene repose as Iris talked. Even her eyebrows were passive, which fact, I assure you, was most unusual.

"Before that, Miss Fredericks? Where did you live before you came here?"

"Abroad. At a place called Jacintos, near Antofagasta, South America."

"How long were you there?"

Iris frowned over a spot of thinking. Bathurst has told me since that he positively loathed having to tell her what he had come to say.

"Nearly fourteen years. I was a baby in arms when we went there first of all."

"Did your people go to South America from this country, do you know, Miss Fredericks?"

She nodded. "Yes. I have heard my mother say so. She died when I was nine."

Bathurst came to the point. "Your people went abroad then between twenty-two and twenty-three years ago?"

"Yes."

He rose and went to a photograph. He had mentioned it to me before.

"Yes," affirmed Iris. "That was taken when we were out there."

"Yes. I understand, Miss Fredericks."

Rosemary became critical-eyed. If she were trying, however, to deprive Bathurst of his ordinary ease and composure, the endeavour was utterly unsuccessful. Realizing this, she threw back her head and there flickered in her eyes for a second, perhaps, the faintest possible light of a comprehending and resentful smile. Anthony caught it but decided to ignore it. This was no time for finesse; there was urgent need of actualities. Although he was on his guard, his grey eyes showed no sign of emotion. He seated himself on the arm of the leather chair next to Iris Fredericks and with calculated deliberation took a cigarette from his case.

"Have I your permission?" he asked.

"Of course."

With the same studied care, he spoke to her. "Miss Fredericks, I want you to listen to me very attentively for a moment."

She looked up at him, as though measuring the situation, and nodded. "I understand. I will try to do as you desire me."

"I could sympathize with you if I so chose. That is to say, being interpreted, I could waste a certain amount of time on the expression of mere words of sympathy. You have lost your father and you have lost your brother. Both your brothers now."

It seemed that he was purposely hard upon her; attempting to lash her from acquiescent subjection into defiant activity. That cruelty, however, was to parent kindness. She nodded again and looked at him mutely and cloudy-eyed. Bathurst continued as he lit a match and held it to his cigarette.

"I want you to realize, with the full instinct of every sense that you possess, that you yourself are in grave danger. Very grave danger indeed."

"I think I know it," she whispered. "That's one reason why Rosemary's here with me now. She knew that I needed her, so she came."

"With all due respect, Miss Fredericks, that is not enough."

The eyebrows of Rosemary Cotterill asked a question and a shadow took possession of the eyes beneath. She was unable to resist the temptation of comment. "Really? Now, isn't that too bad?"

Bathurst accorded her the semblance of a bow. "Consider the forces that are arraigned against you." His voice grew stern and unassailable. "If you would question the quality or accuracy of my judgment, consider the murder of Elsie Rhodes. And then search your hearts and ask yourselves if I am not right."

He clasped his hands, and his eyes met those of Rosemary. She bit her lip. There was a touch of severity in this new Bathurst that was unknown to her. I think that she understood, at that moment, that she had over-assessed her self-control, and her natural aptitude—talent, rather—for dissembling.

"Do you really think all that?" She spoke lightly. Her tone was doubtless intended to convey the politeness of convention. As she spoke the words her eyes flickered towards his again and the teeth went to her lips with annoyance. She had trusted too much, she realized at that moment, to her adroitness of parry and her deftness of thrust, and because of that she had allowed this man, who had once loved her, kissed her, used to her the words and ways that lovers use, to make her betray herself into a petulant resentment.

"I do," he rejoined. "And, because I do, we must take immediate steps to deliver Miss Fredericks from the power of the dog."

She tried to become amiable, unembarrassed. But her pretence at amiability merely developed into feigned severity.

"Well, then, my dear Anthony, accepting your suggestions at their face value, what do you propose? Have you anything like a definite plan in your mind or are you just throwing out a general ..." She paused.

"My plan is excessively simple. That, I hope, will be one of its greatest strengths. Miss Fredericks must leave Chelmersley. At once. That is all I desire. And secretly. Her destination must be kept from everybody. The only people that may know it are those of your most intimate circle—Doctor Bannerman and I myself."

"Am I included?" Here was sovereignty.

Anthony considered and marvelled at the old imperiousness. He gestured rather gallantly. "You, Mrs. Cotterill, I include in Miss Fredericks' most intimate circle."

"That is charming of you. I wondered. That was all." She gave a light little laugh and with that there came a brightening of the eyes and an inclination of the head.

Bathurst approached actualities. "Have you anywhere that you can conveniently go, Miss Fredericks?"

Iris began to shake her head.

"Have you no relations in this country?"

She began to explain. "I have heard my father speak of a brother that he had—he would be my Uncle Marcus and a little younger than my father. But I believe they lost touch with each other when we went abroad, so it's no use thinking of him. I haven't the least idea where he is to be found now."

Bathurst tried again. "Friends, then? People with whom you would be happy and safe? Surely you can conjure up somebody, somewhere?"

No response came to this. Rosemary watched her and after a period of waiting, entered the breach.

"Couldn't Iris come with me? Would that suit your Highness?"

Anthony shrugged his shoulders—almost imperceptibly. Otherwise he ignored the taunt. "With you? You are vague. It depends very much upon the locality. It's not the slightest use taking Miss Fredericks to your place here, for instance. She might just as well remain where she is. But if your suggestion could be—"

She intervened with some eagerness. Her tone was less frigid. "I didn't dream of staying in this district. That wasn't my idea at all. Supposing I took her to town?"

"Where?"

"To an hotel."

"Depends again—on the hotel. Locality—other considerations."

"Which would you prefer?"

"I haven't any particular bias—only this. The bigger the better, and the nearer the heart of things the better, too. I wouldn't countenance anything that wasn't—"

"Let me make a definite suggestion, then. How would the 'Florizel' suit? Supposing I take Iris there—I can, quite easily. There's nothing on at the moment to keep me down here. We'll keep it dark. I'll look after her—you needn't worry about that part of the business."

With a swift grace, she turned to the girl.

"Are you agreeable, Iris? Will you trust yourself with me?"

Iris Fredericks had pluck in plenty. "Suits me, Rosemary. I should welcome any chance to get away from here and from all that's been going on. But will you sanction it, Mr. Bathurst?"

He pulled at his lip. "Yes—under the conditions that I specified a little while ago. The address to which you go must be known to those only whom I mentioned. When can you go? At once?"

"At once?" Rosemary echoed his words questioningly. She continued, "That's giving us rather short notice, isn't it? Make it to-morrow."

"Let it be to-morrow then. But not later," returned Bathurst.

Rosemary rose to her full height. It annoyed her to be reminded that, even then, Bathurst—seventy-four inches of him—towered over her. To her surprise Anthony had other words for her. Words, too, that were the reverse of comfortable. When the full understanding of them reached her brain, her feeling of indignation struggled for mastery with her feeling of amazement.

"Mrs. Cotterill," he said to her quietly, "there's another most important matter about which I feel that I must speak to you. Believe me, it is in your own interest. Otherwise I wouldn't bother you with it."

Although the cool pluck of her showed in the lines of her lips, she wilted a bit under his steadfast scrutiny. For a moment or two after he spoke there was silence. Iris, watching the scene that they were playing, felt an almost over-powering desire to scream. Then Rosemary attempted recovery and pulled herself together a little. She was white and she was worn, but she faced the music and the man who had just addressed her.

"Well," she said, "what is it?"

"I feel that you ought to know, Mrs. Cotterill, that the police at Chelmersley have a piece of information in their possession that intimately concerns you."

"Concerns me," she gasped. "What on earth are you talking about now?"

Bathurst amplified his statement. "And by the police, I mean those of them who are working on the three murders. Particularly Inspector Goodaker."

Her teeth bit into her lips as she realized the full significance of his words. When she spoke again, there came, too, a flash of anger. Her eyes glistened and met his fearlessly.

"Are you seeking to frighten me? Is that your plan? To make me say something or do something to incriminate myself?"

Bathurst's tone grew sterner. "Please don't behave absurdly. I am not setting traps for you, if that is what you mean. I am not a dealer in subterfuge. I would never stoop to tricks to use against you. You—least of all people in the world."

She did not answer him. One could think that she was suddenly extending a hand to steady herself against a wall that was almost invisible to her, but which she knew very well was there, and which she could find if she persisted.

"Well?" he questioned.

"What did you mean—me—least of all people?"

Bathurst shrugged shoulders at the interrogation. "Surely the meaning is there—plain to see? If not for the world in general—for you and me. Am I likely to relinquish the eminence upon which I stand and from which I look down upon you? Am I likely to forgo the advantage that I have over you? An advantage which you presented to me some years ago? The word I used was 'tricks'. I chose it with deliberation."

Her hand went to her throat and she laughed. A hard, mordant, ironical laugh. "Have it your way, Anthony. I think I catch your meaning. We will not enter into details, please. After all, we aren't alone and Iris might fail to appreciate the delicacy of the situation and feel most appallingly *de trop*."

"I entirely agree. We will return to that statement of mine that you found a little, shall we say, disconcerting. Shall I repeat myself? It concerned certain information that the police hold."

"I care not," she interrupted proudly, "for anything the police know. For the best reason in the world. They can know nothing to my discredit."

"That is a relief," returned Bathurst quietly.

"For you?" she flashed.

"On the contrary—for you."

She was taken aback at the rejoinder. But her discomfiture was no more than momentary. She fixed her eyes unwaveringly upon him and betrayed no resentment in either looks or feeling.

"I will explain the position fully now that you have given me that assurance. I am sure that Miss Fredericks will see that I have no option and will, therefore, understand. The police are aware, Mrs. Cotterill, of your 'phone message to Walter Fredericks on the evening of the day before he was murdered. The message that you sent from Torrelli's restaurant. That is what I felt that I must tell you."

Under fire, she was magnificent. "I am sorry, Iris," she said, "that I provoked Mr. Bathurst to say that in front of you. Forgive me, dear, please. Tell me that you do."

She went to her impulsively and Iris caught her hand. "Thank you, Iris."

Rosemary Cotterill then turned again to Anthony Bathurst. She remained magnificent. "Thank you too, Anthony," she said. "Thank you for telling me what you have done and forgive me for having been so ungracious. You've been *warning* me, I suppose I ought to say. Rest assured that although there have been many things in my life which have caused me to reproach myself most bitterly, my association with Mr. Fredericks was not one of these. His attentions were unwelcome to me, that is all. Just before he died, I was forced to tell him so. I have nothing further to say."

She walked to the door where she halted for a second. "The Florizel Hotel, then, Anthony—from this time to-morrow afternoon. If we can't manage to book up there, I'll let you know."

When he got home to my place, I pressed him for further details of the lurid past. All he did was to grin and shake his head.

"It's no good, Elizabeth," he returned banteringly. *"Infandum, regina, jubes renovare dolorem."*

CHAPTER XVI

PAGEANT FRAGMENTS—AND OTHERS

THE allusion to Gloriana tickled me tremendously.

"Sorry, old man," I apologized. "Put it down to my insatiable thirst for knowledge. Don't condemn me as curious." I emerged from the past and entered the present. "Which shall it be first? My story of this afternoon or the remainder of yours?"

It was a totally different Bathurst who answered this last question of mine. He pulled at his lip consideringly and then cocked his head to one side.

"Yours, I think, Bannerman. I have told you of what I did up at the house of Miss Fredericks. The rest can wait for a time. You shall have the honour."

I patted my pocket for the list that I knew was in there. Before I could retrieve it, however, there was a ring and a second or so afterwards the Ramage ushered in Jack to us. He grinned cheerfully and plainly looked at A.B.L. for further instructions. At least, that was my interpretation of matters. Bathurst gestured him to a seat.

"Sit down, Tabernacle, if you don't mind. The Doctor is the first turn on the bill this evening, then—you."

"Before Michael starts, Bathurst," cut in Jack, "I must ask you one thing. What about Iris?"

Anthony held up his hand. "Don't worry about Miss Fredericks. I've given her certain specific instructions from which she has promised me faithfully not to depart one iota. From the moment I go out to-night, she will be under my personal care. Until—"

"Until when?" I asked.

He chose carefully the words of his reply. "Until she is safe for always. There, Tabernacle, I can't promise you anything further than that, can I?"

Jack nodded gratefully. The relief on his face was apparent. "Thanks, old man. It cheers me up no end to hear all that."

"Now, Doctor," chimed Bathurst, turning to me again. "Have another shot."

I captured my elusive paper. "I saw Mittick," I explained. "Not a bad sort of chap for a local official. Doesn't indicate the parish pump quite so vividly as the majority of them do. He listened to my bleating accents very patiently and then came to heel quite amicably. Eventually, a dewy-eyed typist laboured and brought forth this."

I tapped document No. 2. "Here we have a complete list of Chelmersley Pageant performers with full particulars of costumes worn, scenes, etc., attached."

I held it out to Bathurst for him to take. "Have a look at it yourself. It's well arranged and well indexed."

Bathurst spread it out on the table and we other two gathered round him. He ran a patient finger down the fist of names. There were, of course, several people included there who were familiar to me and several whom Jack knew. Every now and then, Bathurst would pause significantly, and his finger come to a dead stop.

His first pause of this nature came at the name of Sir George Bligh. The second and third were at Iris Fredericks and Rosemary Cotterill respectively. Then we had Duncan Fredericks, Goodaker, Elsie Rhodes and me. The last two finger stoppages were at Melsheimer and Montague Corbett.

"Gentlemen," said Bathurst meaningly. "Melsheimer! Melsheimer again, of all people. Highly interesting, don't you think."

"What did he wear?" asked Jack.

"I can't remember," I answered thoughtfully. "Can't place the blighter for the moment."

"Soon find out," said A.L.B., running his finger across the typed page. "Here we are. 'German Soldier (private). Infantryman. Episode II.'"

"That was the scene I was telling you about," put in Tabernacle. "Melsheimer must have been in that without us knowing. One of the crowd—no doubt. There were several crowd scenes in the pageant. It was impossible to memorize all the performers in them.”

I shook my head with a healthy quantity, I’m afraid, of despondency. “Jack’s quite right. But where the merry hell we’re getting to I don’t know. Supposing Melsheimer *were* in the show, and supposing, also, that he were a German infantryman, how does either of these facts affect the question of who—”

“I’m testing a little theory, Bannerman. It may or may not lead me anywhere. That’s the substance of the whole thing. Don’t be hard on me. What I’ve learned so far out of the brew of the Pageant cauldron is moderately informative. For the moment, we’ll leave it at that, and take item number two on the programme. Tell us how you got on, Tabernacle.”

Jack slipped into his story with immediate ease. That’s one thing for which I’d always give him credit. He was invariably the coolest of cucumbers.

“Well, I ran up there and after interviewing a hefty sort of bloke named MacMorran, I think it was, I was shown into the august presence of Sir Austin Kemble himself. I explained who I was and handed him the letter you had given me. He read it, asked me a question or so about you and Sir George Bligh— what you were doing and so on—and then asked me to wait for a little while in another apartment. When he came back, after about half an hour, I suppose, he told me that ‘chits’ were being prepared to be submitted to Berlin, Vienna, Prague and Budapest. There’s an idea, I think, up at Victoria 7000, that Kreutz may be an Austrian. Directly the Commissioner receives anything about either Kreutz or Melsheimer, he will immediately communicate with you. If he gets nothing much, he’ll let you know that he’s trying his luck elsewhere. He insisted on me telling you that. Everything O.K.?”

Bathurst added his thanks. “I’m eternally indebted to you, Tabernacle. Let’s hope your visit will bear fruit—and quickly at that. I told the Doctor here, before you came in, how I had fared at the house of Miss Fredericks. I’ll just recapitulate the anthem for your personal benefit. Apart from your own natural desire to hear of our doings, it’s no use letting a man in on half a story.”

He told Tabernacle of his interview with Rosemary and Iris as he had told me a few moments previously. Although I had heard it before, I listened attentively. Jack, even more so. Which was natural—he was hungry for news. Iris was deeply implicated here, don't forget.

"They're going away together, then," he said, when Bathurst's recital came to a conclusion.

"Yes. It's best, don't you think?"

He shook Bathurst's hand. "Absolutely. Darned good idea! If you hadn't suggested it, I can assure you that I should have done. I had it in my mind when I came in."

"To which hotel are they going?" I asked.

"The 'Florizel', in all probability, Doctor. That's the idea as I left it with them. If they can't fix up there comfortably, and are forced to go elsewhere, I shall be informed."

Jack and I nodded in unison. "What else did you do," I asked, "besides your visit to the ladies? You were going to tell me the rest of your programme after I had switched on to mine."

He eyed me queerly, I thought, for a moment or so, saying nothing. Then he commenced to pace the room, hands thrust deeply into pockets.

"I revisited the 'Beaufoy' cinema this afternoon for a definite reason." He paused—to proceed almost at once. "On one occasion, my dear Bannerman, the immortal Holmes threatened to tell the world the story of the politician, the lighthouse-keeper and the trained cormorant. An intriguing triangle, don't you think? Much more so than the comparative prosaic triangle that consists of the cinema attendant, the German hairdresser and the pink chocolate cream. My luck, you see, compared with the master's. One day, perhaps, I shall have the glittering good fortune to—"

He broke off as suddenly as he turned to us. Jack looked amazed. I thought I had better explain matters to him. Anthony Bathurst, however, held up his hand to check me.

"Look here, Tabernacle," he said. From his breast pocket he produced an envelope from which he shook a tiny something into the palm of his left hand. When I saw what it was I knew that I had seen it before. It was a flattened fragment of pink cream. "The murderer of Elsie Rhodes, Tabernacle, trod on that chocolate. I am as certain of that fact as I am that night follows day. He may *know* that he did so. On the other hand, *he may not*. Whether he does or not isn't tremendously important at the moment. For several reasons."

"Where did that come from?" asked Jack with eager interest.

"From the 'Beaufoy'," I answered on Bathurst's behalf. "Bathurst was able to prove what he has just told you when he was called there on the night of the murder."

"How?" asked Jack.

"By the science of deduction," grinned A.L.B. "You can't beat it, you know."

"I suppose it's a big thing in this sort of job," conceded Jack; "but all the same, I don't see how it's going to help you over much. The boot that trod on that chocolate would surely satisfy you more than the chocolate on which the boot trod. If you could put your hand on that, now . . ."

Bathurst grinned at him again. "It's tongue would talk, eh? Don't make me lick my lips, Tabernacle. The fruit rarely falls from the tree into the mouth, you know. Life isn't as Utopian as that."

He balanced the flattened fragment on the palm of his hand. "Nevertheless, gentlemen," he said quietly, "that little piece of confectionery that you see here in my hand is going to bring a man to the gallows, and somehow I don't think he knows how or when he trod on it. I have strong hopes that that's the position."

I looked at him, and as I did so I knew that he meant every word of what he said. Jack seemed unconvinced.

"Do you really think that?"

The grey eyes of Bathurst grew thoughtful. "Yes, I do. At any rate, I am becoming very confident of a successful termination to our case."

My 'phone went as he spoke. I walked to it to answer it. "Bathurst," I called to him. "You're wanted."

"Who is it, Doctor?"

"I don't know. I didn't recognize the voice." He picked up the receiver and listened. "Miss Fredericks' maid," he whispered, his hand over the mouthpiece. "Either Miss Fredericks wants me, or . . . yes, yes. Anthony Bathurst this end."

We watched him as he listened. "Right," he replied. "That's understood, then, Miss Fredericks. Mind now, remember what I said, and above all, obey me implicitly. I'll write you in the morning. Good-bye. What? Oh, I'm sorry, *au 'voir*, then."

He replaced the receiver and stood there thinking. "Gentlemen," he said quietly as he turned to us, "Miss Fredericks and Mrs. Cotterill have been able to fix up at the Florizel Hotel. Be discreet to the *n*th degree. Take care that no action or careless word of yours leads the enemy to them."

Jack nodded acquiescence and quoted softly, "A man's enemies are the men of his own house—sometimes."

Bathurst's eyes gleamed. "Do you know, Tabernacle," he said, "you've helped me more than you know. Of his own house—eh?"

CHAPTER XVII
THE THIRD WARNING

I HAVE rarely known Bathurst as silent as he was at breakfast next morning. I gave him a glance or two, and reflecting, decided not to disturb him by attempting to force matters. This policy eventually bore fruit. Suddenly he turned to me, egg-spoon poised and almost admonitory.

"Much on to-day, Bannerman?"

"Not a great deal. There are five patients whom I should visit, but none of 'em's on the danger list."

"Nor likely to arrive there?"

"With ordinary progress, there shouldn't be an earthly. One of 'em—a labourer in Little Steeping, needn't be seen at all. Lives in one of those tumble-down cottages on the right-hand side of the marketplace. I can always get to him without any trouble."

"What's the matter with him that you needn't see him?"

"According to his own version, it should be sub-acute rheumatism. But my diagnosis is 'pendulum plumbi'," I returned. "He has it every September and every March. Telegraphic address—regularity." A.L.B. grinned at me. "Go on. What's the idea? The rise and fall of the year?"

"On the Contrary," I replied, "the falling due of certain liabilities. Rates, insurance premiums—"

His grin broadened. "Clubs? Sickness benefit?"

"You've hit it. He's in five to my knowledge, and draws his full whack from all of 'em."

"Interesting bloke. I'd like to meet the joker." His words set me thinking. "There's one thing," I said, "that's moderately obvious to me. The murderer we're after must be a homicidal lunatic. I don't think that there's the slightest doubt on that point."

He cracked the shell of his third egg.

"Don't you agree?" I pressed him.

"Not altogether." His words came slowly as he continued. "Of unbalanced mind—yes. But if you mean that any doctor would regard the murderer as certifiable—well then, no."

I joined issue. "But your own phrase, 'of unbalanced mind', clearly indicates that the man is abnormal—or even sub-normal. Therefore, I'm perfectly justified in saying that if—"

"I don't think you would be. I know what you were going to say. In my opinion the mind of our murderer is unbalanced in one direction only. In all other respects, I would venture to predict, he or she is as sane as you or I. Pardon my egotistical—"

I began to shake my head. "A healthy body," I commenced, "must perforce be—"

He smiled. "Oh—no, Doctor, please! Would you assert that good health is an absolute necessity to a brilliant mentality? Man—you can't. How does it apply to genius, for example?"

"How do you mean?" I asked.

He smiled again. "I was afraid that you would quote friend Schopenhauer when he talks of the broad shoulders that characterize the men of genius. On the other hand, it would be easy to mention literary celebrities who were but meanly endowed with physical strength. If you had quoted Schopenhauer that is how I should have countered you."

"Consider that I did, for the sake of argument. Tell me of your instances. It is not naturally in order. I'm the firmest of believers in the old Latin tag, *Mens sana . . .*"

Bathurst took me at my word. "Will you believe me, Bannerman, if I tell you that the modern fashion is to connect genius with epilepsy?"

"Why? What's behind it? There must be something definite and—er—concrete, for such an idea to be ventilated."

"There is. Don't you worry about that part of it. If I were to supply a reason for it, it would be this: Putting on one side the historic example of the great Julius, 'who bled for Justice' sake' on a certain March Ides, we have had the comparative modern instances of Gustave Flaubert, the brothers Goncourt, add the incomparable Dostoievsky. These are all reputed to have been epileptics. Victims of the falling sickness. You probably knew this?"

He waited for my answer. "I have heard it rumoured—hinted at, if you like."

He eyed me shrewdly. "You can see, of course, what has fortified the idea, can't you. Evidence that has gained strength out of sheer accumulation. They were contemporaries. A coincidence— nothing more. But it is not wonderful that the coincidence has given rise to a certain amount of controversy, is it? It would have been surprising, I think, had it not?"

I nodded. "I agree. I won't quarrel with you there."

His eyes twinkled. "I will make a concession, however. It would be but fair. In the case of Dostoievsky, the connection of epilepsy with genius seems to have been fairly well established. His criminology was doubtless derived from his involuntary associations with the Siberian prisoners. His vivid descriptions of epileptics, however, that occur in his books, are doubtless due to his own personal experience. It is highly probable, I think, that he drew from his malady a most remarkable sense of insight and an extraordinary sense of power. Consider his epileptic in *The Idiot*. In one of his fits he finds that the sensation of life and of conscious existence is multiplied something like tenfold. Think of that, dwell on it, and marvel at the ways of the Almighty! Have you had much practical experience of epilepsy in your time, Doctor?”

“Not a lot. Two or three cases have come under my notice—not more.”

“Well, there’s little doubt, I should say, that in Dostoievsky’s case those extraordinary seizures from which he suffered increased his psychological power to such an extent that ultimately, in what we will describe as the ‘tracking of motives’, he was more or less clairvoyant. He suffered from a sort of *frayeur mystique*’. Lombroso himself, I believe, has something very pertinent to say on the subject. I’ll look it up one of these days and read it to you. That will satisfy us both.”

As he finished, the homely Ramage entered, fair, fat and flushed. “A young lad at the door, sir.” She addressed her words to me.

“What’s he want, Mrs. Ramage? Did he say?”

“He wouldn’t say, Doctor. All he says is that he wants to speak to the gentleman who’s staying with Doctor Bannerman. Said he wasn’t sure of the name.”

“What’s that?” Bathurst was in on us like a flash. “Somebody wants me?”

The Ramage, after the manner of women, transferred her attention to him at once. “Yes, sir. A young lad, sir. Shall I ask him in here, sir? Or will you come out and speak to him?”

A.L.B. threw a quick glance at me as though assessing the situation from more than one point of view. “I think I’ll go out and speak to him, Doctor, if it’s all the same to you. After all, we don’t know him and we don’t know what he wants—yet.”

I concurred with the suggestion and, simultaneously, Bathurst slipped from the room. For five minutes, I should think, I kicked my heels on my own carpet. I was surprised at the impatience which came over me. A week ago I should have been quite different. The Ramage, naturally, had gone back to her own regions and left me alone.

When Bathurst returned, I saw at once that something important was afoot. "Here's an offer to you! A sporting one. A dozen guesses as to who that was, Bannerman?"

He eyed me with sharp interrogation. I wasn't having any. "I'm a non-runner. Open the can."

"A boy. Surname, Pope. Christian name, William. Porter of lacteal fluid from moo-cows. Bustles round in the early hours, he tells me, with bottles of it. Cans are prehistoric."

I stared. I was surprised. Not at the boy coming to my place, but at his particular identity.

"That's the very boy—"

"That found Fredericks senior in Taggarts Way. Exactly, my dear Watson. It struck me, too, as a curious coincidence."

"What did he want, Bathurst?"

He fished in his pocket and threw an envelope across to me. "Brought that. Call it an S.O.S. and you won't be far out, Bannerman."

The tone of his voice stirred me. If it were humanly possible for Bathurst to be rattled he approximated that condition now. "Know what it means, Bannerman? I'll tell you. The rag's going up for the first scene of the last act."

"The *last* act?" I repeated after him wonderingly. "Yes. It's on us, Doctor, and we must prepare for it. Read what's enclosed, and then give me all the best of your brains. For I'm dead certain that I'll need 'em, as much as I've ever needed anything in my life. It's all wrong, Bannerman . . . wrong to blazes. That's the curse of the whole business."

He watched me keenly as I read what the boy Pope had brought to him. The first thing I pulled out of the envelope was a piece of notepaper with a few lines of writing scrawled on it. I recognized the fist at once. It was Rosemary Cotterill's. I saw too, directly I looked at it, that she had written in a very great haste and under conditions of acute disturbance. The message ran as follows:

My dear Anthony,

I am sorry to trouble you so soon after our interview of yesterday, and having regard to the arrangements to which we came. But something has happened since then and I am desperately afraid. That must be my excuse for worrying you. Forgive me, please. I received this by this mornings post and I am frightened. Will you please tell me what I am to do? Do the arrangements that we made together still stand or are they to be cancelled and others substituted because of this happening? Please let me know what I am to do as early as you possibly can, as I am very nearly at my wit's end. I have not told Iris anything of this last business. I dare not. The poor kid has enough to worry her without me adding to her burden. I shall remain here until I hear from you.

Yours sincerely,

Rosemary Cotterill.

The words "as early as you possibly can" were heavily under-lined. I next turned my attention to "this". It was in another envelope addressed to Mrs. R. Cotterill. The postmark was London. Immediately I clapped eyes on it, its setting and atmos-phere—if I may use the words in this connection—were familiar to me. I had gazed on its fellow before, when Goodaker had held it in his hand and showed it to me. It was a typewritten message and, as in the previous instance, the machine that had been used was a fairly old one. Several of the letters had been struck more than once so that they should be properly legible.

I read it. No wonder the girl to whom it was addressed was afraid. I'm dead sure that I should have been scared stiff had I been in her place and it had come popping through my letter-box.

Dear Madam (it ran),

There have been ladies in my life whose eyes would be over-joyed to read my signature or my name at the foot of a letter to them. There was Elsa of the Königstrasse, Rosa of old Heidel-berg and Gretchen of the beer-garden at Wintenberg. And others too numerous to mention. I am far from sure, however, whether this pleasure will be yours. I write to inform you that I am leaving Chelmersley within a day or so, my mission more or less accomplished. I have but two more calls to make. Upon a certain gentleman and then, in sweet finality, upon yourself. After these calls, both you and he will be famous, or shall I say, notorious? Like M. Hanaud, you will have headlines. For when the admirable Press of this accursed country refer to you in relation to the case, you will in turn be described as "the victim" . . . he—that other—very certainly will be the fourth victim . . . you most assuredly will be the fifth victim. Also, you will have no warning as to when and how the blow will fall. Aren't you lucky?

Faithfully yours, neither "The Eagle" nor "Aquila" now, but this time plain "Otto Kreutz'. ~~Murderer, Lunatic,~~ Avenger.

The words "murderer" and "lunatic" had been typed and then crossed through exactly as I have shown them here. The whole thing struck a chill at my heart. Before I could make comment, Bathurst began to speak—rapidly and anxiously:

"You heard what I said just now, Bannerman, didn't you? The damned thing's all wrong. Utterly and completely wrong."

He paused, his lips tightly pressed. Then I heard him almost whisper to himself, "Or else damned clever. The question is which? And Elsie Rhodes may have—"

I intervened. "What are we going to do, man? We can't stand here and dither. If we wait and do nothing, we may be too late."

"Yes. You're right. You must be right. If I could only give him some of his own devilish medicine. But no English jury would look at the facts as I am able to."

He swung round to me. "I'm going to Mrs. Cotterill at once, Doctor. I'll go in the Crossley."

My blazing curiosity overcame my tendency towards discretion. "Why do you say it's all wrong? I don't quite get you there. Say what you like, Bathurst, there's a consistency about the actions of this man Kreutz if there's nothing else. Here's the warning again. Judging by antecedents—to my mind, just what we might have expected."

He shook his head decisively. "Oh, think, Bannerman, think! Why the inclusion of Mrs. Cotterill? Where does she enter his particular gallery? Fredericks, yes! Young Donald Fredericks, yes! Every time! Even Elsie Rhodes. . . . But then after that, Iris Fredericks surely! Certainly not Mrs. Cotterill. His cleverness is inhuman, Bannerman, or else my psychology's all wrong." He whispered again "Iris Fredericks".

"You forget," I warned him in attempted extenuation of my own point of view, "it's not merely Rosemary who's receiving the warning. There's somebody before her in this heritage of death, remember. A man. A 'certain gentleman'. Is that utterly wrong too? You've got to decide, Bathurst!" There was no doubt whatever that I had scored this time. I saw his face twitch with anxiety. "I know all about that, Bannerman. And all about Mrs. Cotterill. My knowledge may tell me that she and this unknown 'he' are in deadly peril, but my *reason* tells me that Iris Fredericks is most surely in a like condition."

I sensed the purpose in his tone and accepted the position. "All right, Bathurst. I won't keep you yapping here if things are as you say they are. You'll go to Mrs. Cotterill's now, I suppose?"

He nodded. "It's imperative. I must get there as soon as I possibly can. Damn it all, man, I can't let an appeal of this kind fall on deaf ears, can I?"

He tapped the letter that young Pope had brought and turned on his heel.

"Of course not. I understand perfectly."

"Thank you, Doctor."

At the door, on his way out, he turned again to speak to me. "It's possible, I think, Doctor, that there may be developments while I'm away. I can't indicate their particular nature, but test everything that comes along pretty thoroughly. You know what I mean. It's so uncertain how the next move will come. But don't get drawn into anything like a trap."

I demurred. "What's the idea? Why should anybody attack me?"

"The person we're after may attempt to divide our forces, Bannerman. An old dodge, I know, but still effective for all that. At any rate you're wise to it now and won't be off your guard. Cheero!"

He waved his hand to me and after a few minutes I heard the Crossley on its way to Rosemary Cotterill's. From the speed at which Anthony Bathurst was driving I knew that as far as he himself was concerned he had spoken no idle words. Things were getting desperate.

Chapter XVIII
CHELMERSLEY IS RATTLED

FOLLOWING upon his departure, I hung about for an hour or so; after this I began to chafe at the inaction and decided to see two of the five patients whom I had mentioned to Bathurst. The nearer case was a run of a couple of miles or more. As I walked towards the garage to dig the car out I was overjoyed to see Jack coming through the front gate. I'm moderately gregarious, I suppose, but I can't remember a time in my life when I felt the jolly old urge for companionship more than I did on that particular morning.

"What's doing?" I called to him. I would have bet the Koh-i-noor to a crumpet that he had heard something in the way of news that was more or less fresh. His face was both expressive and eloquent. As it happened, I should have been right.

"Come inside, Michael," he said. "Something doing."

I followed him indoors. "Well," I repeated when we heaved-to inside, "what's this last word in bad news?"

He regarded me curiously. "Why, Michael? What makes you so confident that I am the bearer of sticky news?"

"Your mug, my dear chap. It's as eloquent as a hen bazaar-committee. I'm doing no Sherlock stuff, I assure you."

He grinned as he flopped into the most comfortable of my chairs. "Well, it's like this, my dear chap. You can call it bad news if you like. I don't know that I do, when all's said and done.

But Chelmersley's pretty badly rattled. That's the gist of what I've come to tell you. Where's Bathurst?"

"Gone to Mrs. Cotterill's. But what's your real point in regard to Chelmersley? Had I been asked, I should have said it had been rattled for some little time."

"Very likely. I'm not denying it, Michael. It has been rattled! Now it's *badly* rattled. There's a difference, young feller-me-lad."

"Out with it. What do you know?" I could see that there was more in his statement than met the eye. He took his cigarette-case from his pocket and with irritating deliberation selected a cigarette. I puffed at my old briar, waiting for him.

"Chelmersley is more excited than at any previous time in its history. With the possible exception, perhaps, of the hectic period of the pageant. It has decided to form a 'Protection and Vigilance Committee'."

"What's the idea? Patrols?"

"You've hit it. Every street and turning in the town is to be patrolled after sundown. At least that's the suggestion. The patrols are to work in pairs. They won't knock off till dawn. Also, my lad, they will be armed. And when they shoot, they'll shoot to kill. Over a thousand men have volunteered for the job already. The patrol starts to-night. A second idea is the installation of flood-lights in certain of the more remote places, but no definite decision as to that has been reached yet."

"What about the outskirts? The places and houses just outside Chelmersley?"

"If they get sufficient numbers of dutiful citizens the present intention, I believe, is to patrol as far as Little Steeping on the one side and Cressing on the other."

"They'll work in shifts, of course?"

"That's the idea, Michael. Shifts of two hours each."

"Have you signed on, Jack?"

"Not yet. I gave old Corbett a sort of half-promise when he tackled me, though. He was devilishly insistent."

"Corbett? Montague Corbett, do you mean?"

"No other. He's the power behind the throne, let me tell you. Or, in other more pertinent words, he's the moving spirit of the whole business. Keen as mustard to get the thing in proper working order."

I nodded. I remembered the earlier occasion when Corbett had come to us in the police station and had asked for similar action to be taken. There was something in the man after all. A quality of determination, resolution—call it what you like, I don't mind—to fight this murderer in our midst and stay his bloody hand, if at all possible. I remembered too, what old Bligh had said at the time and how Anthony Bathurst had received the original idea.

"I'm glad," I said to Jack, "that the patrol operations are not to be confined to Chelmersley absolutely."

"Why? Why particularly?"

"For a thundering good reason. As you'll agree—when you hear what it is."

He looked dead scared, and I knew why. He was remembering what Bathurst had prognosticated after Elsie Rhodes had been murdered. I hastened to put him right.

"Not what you're thinking," I explained, "so set your mind at rest on that point. It's Mrs. Cotterill. At least, that's my opinion."

"What the hell are you talking about now?" he snapped at me. "How in the name of goodness does Rosemary Cotterill come into it?"

"I'll tell you 'how', although I can't tell you 'why'. Otto Kreutz has included her in his list of correspondents. She sent the news up to us here this morning, *via* the milk-boy. Young Pope. She's afraid, Jack. Dead scared! Candidly, I don't wonder at it." I supplied him with the story.

"Neither do I," he returned gloomily. "I should think it damned funny if she weren't."

"That's why Bathurst has gone up to her place now."

"He thinks it's genuine, then?"

"Without a doubt. Friend Otto has been far too successful in the past for his epistles of warning to be treated lightly or disregarded. Otto's got a way with him that's effective."

"It's a good job they're getting out of it, Michael. That little excursion to town wasn't arranged a day too soon. Thank God for Anthony Bathurst."

"Amen to that," I rejoined, "and I don't suppose we're the first people to think it, or say it either."

I fell to pondering on men, women and things. On the definite search for the physical seat of what is called the soul—the inmost essence of a man. It lies not in his hands or in his features. A man of mental nobility may be turned into a creature of obscene bestiality from a mere gross physical cause, such as the fall of a tiny spicule of bone from the inner table of his skull on to the surface of the membrane by which his brain is covered.

And yet, when all is said and done, the picture has a reverse side. When I was at Charing Cross, I had an interesting would-be suicide, who shot away the front lobe of his brain and lived to repent bitterly the inaccuracy of his aim. Fate had been kinder had his aim been true. I contrasted the murderer whom we were hunting here in Chelmersley with Anthony Bathurst, the man who directed and headed the hunt. After all, I argued to myself as I advanced down the avenue of introspection, the old school of philosophy that located the soul in the pineal gland may have been much nearer the mark than has been imagined. No chance observer can put a finger on the chink of weakness in a piece of human armour. It may be in the body; it is equally as likely to be present in the mind. A grand strapping fellow one day and then a little vascular change may charge him with every degenerate and debasing tendency.

Another man, splendid in rough rude health to all appearances, may be visited with G.P. or mistake the lightning pains of *locomotor ataxia* for intercostal neuralgia. A beautiful woman, dazzling and glorious to look on, may be utterly and absolutely rotten with struma or eaten with serpiginous ulcers. All part of the Designer's secret scheme and plan, in which we groping and stuttering mortals can have no potent hand.

I wondered then, as man has wondered ever since he scribbled upon papyrus with sepia. As he will continue to wonder until the end of time. Until he has real saints to draw from and "splashes at a ten-leagued canvas with brushes of Comet's hair".

Jack, standing at the window and looking out, jerked me back from my thought adventure to a contemplation of the normal. "Here's Bathurst," he said quietly, "on his way back, I presume."

He pointed a distance down the road. The Crossley was flying along, at times swaying like a cardboard box almost in the deeply-rutted country road that stretched past "The Rowfants". He drew up outside my place and sprang from the car. I caught Jack by the arm before Bathurst could reach the door. "Tell him the news of Chelmersley at once. Don't forget. It may make a difference to his plans."

Jack nodded. "You're right, Michael. If he knows that we are on a watching stunt down here it may release him more to guard Iris where she is."

A.L.B. was no sooner in than I gave Jack the tip to unpack the parcel. Bathurst listened attentively. Once or twice he punctuated Jack's story with a sharp, decisive nod.

"Tell me, Tabernacle," he said at length, "when does this suggested patrol system start?"

"To-night. At least, it's hoped so. Moreover, Corbett's taking his share of the work with all the others. He was actually engaged in drawing up the rota when I left him."

Bathurst rubbed his cheek. "I wonder," he said thoughtfully, "if that bruise has gone yet from the thumb of Otto Kreutz." Jack and I looked at each other blankly.

CHAPTER XIX
MRS. RHODES AGAIN

CORBETT, dominant and masterful, had his way. His organization was effected so speedily, and volunteers responded so splendidly, that the patrols started their work in Chelmersley and its environs that same night. In addition, there was a partial beginning of his second plan. Two huge flood-lights were installed under the authority of the Electrical Engineer of Chelmersley and worked from sundown. One was placed at the eastern end of the borough, in Chelmersley Great Park, and the other had its position in the old Abbey meadow, just behind Wedlock's flour-mill.

I remember that I was alone that night. Bathurst had departed on some mysterious errand. I say "mysterious" if only for the fact that, for once, he had not taken me into his confidence. I can remember, also, that I walked to the french doors of my dining-room and looked out into the night as Bathurst had done on the evening that Donald Fredericks had been lured to Taggarts Way and there murdered.

There was a difference, however, in the outlook to-night. A sensible difference. Now, from my place, I was able to see with little difficulty across the country the flood-light that was operating in the meadow hard by the bridge and the old flour-mill. I mused to myself, as I gazed at its cold bath of light that whitened and wintered all that was close to it and turned the green grass into a sickly imitation, that the murderer was probably watching it from somewhere, even as I watched it. It was a sign to him. A sign that had a double meaning. It was both a message and a warning. It told him unmistakably that the men and women of the world that he had outraged were in arms against him with hands linked against his evil. It told him that civilization and the forces which it could command were at war with him and that before long he would find that the dice were loaded against him.

As I meditated, I half thrilled too at the sight of that great white light. Bathurst told me the next day at breakfast that it had affected him somewhat similarly. I will try to put down what he told me, then, in his own words as far as I am able to remember them.

His destination, when he had left me, had been 94, Thatch Road, Little Chelmersley, the house of Mrs. Rhodes. The house that we had visited, in strength, before. Ever since Elsie Rhodes had been murdered he had meant to give the house a second visit, and he chose this evening to put his desire into effect. He intended, as far as he found possible, to test a theory with which he had been coquetting for some little time. "Never discard the eminently reasonable," he said, "because certain evidence that you hold may seem to discount it or disagree with it. Those contradictory pieces are much more likely, in the end, to be false themselves. Logic must invariably triumph. Its value is there for all to see, and through its use ignorant minds are taught to consider *all* the facts and not only those which are convenient for them to consider. Treat logic as a science, impeccable and infallible, and you'll gain in power all the time."

This, then, was the line of his argument, as he put it to me over the grape-fruit. I will try to reproduce it *in toto.*

So far, three people had fallen victims to this murderer whom we hunted. A father, a son, and a girl attendant employed at an ordinary picture-palace in the town that had harboured the two murdered men. Father and son moved, it may be presumed, in more or less the same circle. They lived in the same house, and no doubt had many acquaintances and friends of each sex who were common to each of them. What was the connection, however, that Elsie Rhodes carried with *(a)* Fredericks senior, *(b)* Fredericks junior, or, as a remoter possibility *(c)* the two men *together*? It seemed to Anthony Bathurst, at this stage of the case, that Elsie Rhodes presented the line of least resistance, and because of that he made up his mind to attack in that direction, as always.

Mrs. Rhodes' face registered something akin to surprise as she answered the door to his summons. "Well, now, sir," she said, "come in, please. And if this isn't the strangest of things. Come into this room here, sir, and sit yourself down."

Anthony smiled at the cordiality of the invitation. At any rate that's what he tells me he did. If it were the same sort of smile that I so often see light up his old dial when I'm jawing to him, I can well understand the heart of Mrs. Rhodes warming to him, in spite of the terrible blow which it had recently suffered.

"What's this thing that's so strange, Mrs. Rhodes?" he asked her, as he lined up east of the Joanna and north of the aspidistra.

"Why—you're coming here again, sir. To-day, I mean. It's strange in this way: If you hadn't come to see me, I should have tried to have come to see you."

Instantly, he appreciated the inner meaning of what she had said to him. "What for, Mrs. Rhodes?"

A peculiar look took possession of the woman's eyes. There was, however, a definite interval before she answered his question. "For help, sir, and also to bring to you certain information." The words of her reply were chosen with care. "Concerning Elsie, sir—my poor girl."

Bathurst waited for her to add to her statement. Mrs. Rhodes, though, seemed at a momentary loss. She hesitated again, as though uncertain as to where Jo start.

"You have found something here?" His tone was eager. She was startled out of her indecision.

Her eyes betrayed the sureness of his touch. She wondered, as she looked at him, whether in any way she had, as it were, invoked his question.

"How did you know?" she whispered.

He responded as far as he was able to the present mood of the woman. "I hardly *knew*. It would be wrong of me to claim knowledge. Let me say, rather, that I anticipated something of the kind had happened. Quite frankly, Mrs. Rhodes, that is why I came here to see you. I was going to ask your permission to look for something that I thought *might* be in the house. You, evidently, have found it already. Before me." He smiled again.

She shook her head, unable to understand him properly. "That seems very difficult for me to believe. What were you going to look for, then?"

"Similarly, that is more difficult for me to answer. Anything— that I might have been able to find in Miss Rhodes' room . . . or in the room of Otto Kreutz . . . anything that might have helped me to link her up with . . . all that has gone on."

She understood now. "If you know all that, tell me what you think I have found."

Anthony finessed. "Possibly that which was stolen from her out of her drawer at the Beaufoy cinema. The thief may now have replaced it. It may by now—you see—have served its purpose."

He made a movement of the shoulders. Mrs. Rhodes shook her head. "No. Not that. I think you are wrong there. As far as I know, Elsie never recovered what was stolen from her at the cinema. Something else."

"Tell me, then, Mrs. Rhodes. I'll throw myself on your mercy. When I know all I shall be the better able to judge of its importance."

A spot of defiance flaunted itself in each of her cheeks. The woman achieved dignity. "No doubt you know that Elsie, had she lived a little longer, would have been a mother. Doctor Bannerman is sure to have told you."

Bathurst gave her a nod of silent acquiescence.

"In that case, sir, please look at this. It will explain a lot." She took a small box from the mantelpiece and opened it in front of him. As she removed the lid he saw at once what the box contained. It held a plain gold ring, attached to a loop of white silk ribbon. A wedding-ring, undoubtedly.

"Look inside, sir," she said. "Inside the ring itself. There's an inscription that you may read." Bathurst held the ring so that he could read what Mrs. Rhodes had indicated. Inside the ring had been cut the words, "To my darling wife, Elsie, with eternal love."

"My daughter was married, sir, you see. She had married secretly. I was wrong when I told you that she had no secrets from me. I beg your pardon."

Anthony waved a sympathetic hand. "To whom, Mrs. Rhodes?" he asked. "Who was this man she married?"

"I am as completely in the dark as you, sir. That's what hurts me a little. Especially when I think how Elsie died. Why hasn't his grief at her loss made him come forward?" Her voice broke for the first time since Anthony had come to her.

"And you suspect nobody? There is nobody that you can remember . . . that you can associate with her in the days that have gone? Seen her with? Seen talking to her? During last year, for example?"

Mrs. Rhodes shook her head. "Nobody, sir. I haven't the slightest suspicion of the kind that you mention. I couldn't put a name to anybody. If I could, I would."

Bathurst probed hard. "Not to your lodger of a week back . . . Otto Kreutz."

"No," she cried with vehemence and some of her old spirit, "never! Otto Kreutz, least of all. Certainly not Otto Kreutz, if he were the only man in the whole world."

"But why, Mrs. Rhodes," he insisted almost despairingly, "why are you so certain about this man? Why are you so *obstinately* certain that she could have had nothing to do with him? Surely, in the further light of what we know now, you cannot be quite so certain—"

"I cannot prove it," she interrupted him stubbornly. "I know that. But I shall be able to later, I know. Just as surely. Kreutz was not the kind of man to hold any attraction for Elsie. I speak as her mother."

Anthony shrugged his shoulders hopelessly. "I *think* you're right. I want to, because I *know* you're right, if I can trust my reason. But, you see, I can't *build* on conjectures and prejudices, can I? I must have stronger foundations."

"I am sorry." She stood before him, dry-eyed and white-lipped.

He rose and faced her. "Perhaps you would allow me to see your daughter's room. I can't tell beforehand, but I may be able to help."

She nodded silently and beckoned to him to follow her. Outside the girl's room he stopped and spoke softly to the mother.

"Tell me, Mrs. Rhodes," he urged her, "why do you think Elsie was killed? For what reason? Try to be clear-headed . . . forget the irreparable wrong that has been done you . . . and think. *Why* was she removed . . . after those two others? What can have been the motive?"

The woman looked out into space, right over Anthony Bathurst's head. Her eyes, wide open, seemed unseeing. "I think," she said, after a pause, "that she was murdered by the man that she had married. That he wanted her out of the way. Like that horrible 'Brides in the Bath' man. They married in haste, and he repented at leisure. And, besides losing his affection for her, perhaps she knew something about him that he didn't want made generally known. He was frightened of what he had told her about himself. Frightened that she might expose him. That's all I can think," she added softly.

"Is that why Walter Fredericks and Donald Fredericks were killed as well, then? Did they know this same secret?"

She was in no way deterred by the question. "Perhaps. Very likely. In some way that you and I are unable to see now, but which might be very clear to us if we knew just a little more."

He motioned to her to lead him into the room.

"I've been through all the things," she said. "I went through them when Inspector Goodaker came the day after Elsie was . . ."

He nodded. "This isn't where you found the wedding-ring, I presume?"

"Oh no. That was on the top shelf of the cupboard. In an old bag. Neither the inspector nor I found it the first time we looked. You can look again yourself. In the drawers or in any of the boxes. If you wish to, of course."

He walked round the apartment, his eyes searching every-where. "No letters, Mrs. Rhodes? Papers? Correspondence of any kind?"

"No, sir."

"Photographs? Picture-postcards?"

"No. Nothing."

"That's the reason, no doubt, why the thief, wanting what I want now, turned his attention to burglary at the Beaufoy cinema. He'd toiled here and caught nothing. Which tells us pretty conclusively who the thief was, doesn't it?"

He regarded her quizzically, head to one side, assessing the reception of his question. He soon saw that he had startled her from what he termed her "Kreutz" complacency.

"Who? I don't understand?"

"Why—it's as clear as daylight. Kreutz, of course. Otto Kreutz. Who else could it be?"

"How do you know that, sir?"

"Consider the circumstances. Anybody desirous of stealing from Elsie would naturally first turn his attention to her own room in her home. The place where she would normally have kept her valued possessions. The odds on that happening are a good ten to one. Now who but Kreutz had such a golden opportunity to do this? Nobody has broken in here from outside; therefore, the search was carried out, without your knowledge. By your lodger, Otto Kreutz."

"Yes . . . yes . . . that would be so. I see that now."

Bathurst went on. "Having failed here in his first essay, he then tried a second line of country—your daughter's place of business. Shall we call it the second most likely place of conceal-ment? There, as you know, he was more successful. He got what he wanted so badly."

She stared at him, this time open-mouthed. Anthony hast-ened to press home his advantage. "Believe me, Mrs. Rhodes, there isn't a vestige of a doubt about it."

"You'll find her husband for me, then, Mr. Bathurst? Who was he? And if he murdered her—"

Anthony Bathurst patted her lightly on the shoulder. "I'll find out all you want to know, Mrs. Rhodes. You can rest assured of that. I've another job to do also." His face grew hard and grave. "That is to save another young lady's life."

She looked at him fearfully. "Another?" she asked in a whis-per.

"Yes, Mrs. Rhodes. Another. And, unless I'm very much mistaken, the attempt to murder her will be made within the next three or four days."

She shook her head as he left her—she was bewildered.

Which of the three men, he asked himself? For there were, he argued, as he swung the Crossley round a corner, three distinct possibilities. There were an old man, a young man, and a third man who might be fairly described as coming some-where between the other two.

It was at this point of the case that Anthony Bathurst considers that he made his greatest mistake. But once again—to mention it in justifiable defence of him—there was a factor operating which he could not possibly have foreseen; he was forced to protect those whom he knew of a certainty to be in danger. Others, that might wander into the criminal's vicious circle, could not be considered. For one thing, there was little time for finesse, and, for another, he had pledged himself to the safety of Iris Fredericks. The peril that overhung Rosemary, you will observe, seemed to him of a lesser menace. Note that particularly at this stage of the affair.

It was late that evening when he got back to "The Rowfants". He went straight to bed.

After brekker, Jack turned up again. We had a spot or so and our companionship seemed to afford A.L.B. a glow of pleasure. "Stout fellows," he said, as we sat there. "It warms the cockles of my heart to be with you again. The Chelmersley countryside is scarcely the most charming of places these days. Especially when a bloke's motoring, as I was last night, alone. Even these searchlights, friendly auxiliaries as we know them to be, gave the whole show an eeriness that made you dither right down from the nape to the coccyx. I tell you chaps that I was damned glad to get back home again."

He helped himself to a Scotch, found his favourite chair and deposited his lithe length in it.

"Listen, you fellows. This is monstrously important, as old Dogberry might have said." He leant forward to us and we pricked up our ears and listened. "First of all, I want your co-operation. Help. Bags of it. Three of 'em, full! I want you to place your two selves in my hands unreservedly. It's a big order, I know, to ask that—but there it is. I'm asking for it because I want it so badly. You're on, of course."

His grey eyes searched our faces anxiously. Jack, impetuous as always, exclaimed at once: "Of course—every time. Anything you want. I'm in your hands. Command me."

I contented myself with merely nodding. Bathurst saw the nod and accepted it.

"Good. As we three know, Mrs. Cotterill and Iris are a good few miles away from here. They are in town, at the Florizel Hotel. We three, too, are alone in possessing that knowledge. Mark that. I have taken the most careful precautions to ensure that condition. Mrs. Cotterill, also, had specific instructions from me on the matter, so, you see, we've a thundering good card up our sleeve. I fail to see how the man whom we are after could have possibly traced the two ladies to the place where they have gone. But—in spite of all that I've done—well, I won't say that I'm excessively worried, but—I'm not satisfied."

He rose from the armchair and began to pace backwards and forwards in front of us, hands thrust deeply into pockets.

Jack looked up at him. "Why? Why should you be dissatisfied? If you've taken all the precautions that you say you have—"

Bathurst shook his head. "It's not that. Don't misunderstand me. I'm not apprehensive with regard to the possible miscarriage of my plans. But last night taught me a lot. I'm doubtful of what goes on in that saloon of Melsheimer's, for one thing. So close to Torrelli's restaurant. Communication, the easiest thing in the world."

"What do you mean?" I asked him.

"My dear Doctor, consider the situation. A hair-dresser's saloon, of all places in this transitory world! An exchange and mart of all the news and gossip that the town knows, wants to know, or will ever know. Can you think of a likelier place on the face of the earth for taletellers to congregate?"

"I agree with all that you've said—but I don't see how you can circumvent it. You can't very well close the man's premises. If he's as dangerous as you seem to imagine he is—why not have him arrested?"

"On what charge?" He eyed me queerly.

"Don't ask me," I returned. "I always thought that trifling charges could usually be found and referred against a man when the police wanted him or something really big."

"Found—yes! Not manufactured! When there are grounds, Bannerman, definite grounds, for making them. Lord, man, what have we actually got against Melsheimer? That he employed Kreutz?"

"I'll give way to you," I conceded, a little sulkily I'm afraid. "You've had more experience of these things than I have."

"Shut up, Michael," intervened Jack; "don't get stuffy. What Bathurst said is perfectly true. Let's come to the point and hear what he wants us to do."

"Thank you, Tabernacle. I'm going to ask you something pretty big. I want one of you to join the two ladies at the 'Florizel'. I leave it to you which one it is."

I looked at Jack and Jack returned the compliment. We stared at one another.

"If it's all the same to you," I said after a short interval of studied staring, "I'd rather you took on that job. There are one or two people on my list down here whom I simply must drop in and see before they—"

"I understand, Michael," he said promptly. "Send me to the 'Florizel', then. I'm your man. It's immaterial to me either way."

"That settles it then," declared Bathurst. "I'd like you to report yourself up there first thing in the afternoon. Keep the two ladies under your unremitting care and supervision. As far as is humanly possible, don't let either of them out of your sight. If anything go wrong, the slightest thing, mind you, 'phone through to me here immediately you become aware of it. Don't take the slightest scintilla of a risk. If Bannerman or I don't happen to be here, leave the message with Mrs. Ramage, but be sure to see that she gets it correctly. As regards general instructions—you don't require much help from me in that direction. Keep your eyes skinned, your ears receptive, and use the brains you have, in every way, all the time. That's about all, I think. Sufficiently comprehensive?"

He grinned cheerfully as Jack rose and faced him. "What about Michael?"

"I'm going to put Michael on to the 'general precautions' fatigue. His special job of work will be to identify himself as closely as he can with Corbett's 'Citizen Protection Committee'.

In that way, I fancy that he may rub shoulders with one or two people who count. Certainly—one."

"Including the murderer himself?" I queried.

"That contingency, my dear Doctor, I regard as extremely likely. It's one of my reasons, you see, for asking you to attach yourself."

He turned to Jack. "Cheero, then, Tabernacle, and the very best of hunting."

Chapter XX
WHERE IS IRIS?

THAT same afternoon I reported to Montague Corbett's "vigilance committee" or whatever the affair called itself. I had hoped to see the man himself, as I was inclined, from what I had seen and heard of him previously, to value the strength of his personality and the quality of his initiative somewhat highly. I happened, however, to be unlucky; I was forced to be content with an interview with a comparative underling. I followed Bathurst's instructions completely and implicitly. The man whom I interviewed, after I had presented myself, informed me that Mr. Corbett wasn't able to attend the Town Hall every morning and afternoon, but had never missed an evening's enrolment since he had first projected successfully the patrol and searchlight idea. Mr. Corbett would certainly be there that evening for an appreciable period, he said, and would also, equally certainly, go out on patrol himself for a stretch of at least a couple of hours.

The bloke at the desk—conspicuous for an apparently chronic dysphagia—took my name and address with great solemnity and then addressed me rather familiarly.

"Nothing doing last night, Doc. No more murders. I fancy that we've put the fear of the Almighty into the blighter at last. He'll think twice, I reckon, before he tries his tricks again. I'll let you know your place and time on the rota in due course. These little things take time to be arranged, you know. You must have organization on a job like this if you want it to be successful. Can't move an inch without it. If you try to—absolute chaos."

He wagged his head and I nodded. The man was a crass cocksure fool, I thought. I don't suffer his tribe gladly. Never have done. Probably never shall. He annoyed me. They always do. I think I nodded twice before I became articulate. When this condition eventually materialized, I think that I intimated that I would do my best to be efficient when the time came for me to commence my self-imposed duties.

He assented genially and then made a supremely fatuous remark to the effect that I had been guilty of the expression of an extreme and catholic platitude. I left him with the feeling that his head was fat and juicy and my knuckles hard and vindictive. He was still swallowing when I turned and gave him a last lingering look.

Before I returned to "The Rowfants" I paid three duty calls, and as I passed Rosemary's, and then Jack's place on my way up, I realized that each was empty, by reason of the threat of the killer. Rosemary, protecting Iris, had been threatened herself, and Jack had been sent by the master hand directing our forces to protect them both.

A.L.B. was in when I arrived. I expected him to be there when I entered because the Crossley was stationed outside my place. It looked to me, as I glanced at it, that it had done good service during the last few hours.

"Hullo, Bannerman," was his greeting as I barged into the dining-room. "How did you get on?"

"Oh—fixed myself up as you told me to. Nothing definite yet as to when I'm actually going on. That part's due to arrive later."

"Good!" he exclaimed. "Eminently satisfactory."

"Saw your car," I said. "Been far?"

"So, so. There's one advantage, Bannerman, from conducting an investigation in the country that you don't get in the town."

"What's that?" I chipped in.

"There may be more gossiping tongues abroad, but there are certainly fewer prying eyes. In this instance, I find that latter feature on the distinctly comforting side. It's cheered me no end."

I wondered what the hell he was driving at, but knew better than to apply for greater detail. He went through some papers in front of me without saying another word. The appearance of Mrs. Ramage, however, with a tray of tea and muffins seemed to remind him of something. He waited for her to close the door behind her and then addressed me.

"No message has come through, I suppose?"

I was surprised. "Wouldn't you have—"

"I know what you're going to say. But you're off the map. As a matter of fact, I had been in the house exactly a minute and a half when you arrived." He smiled.

"I didn't see you in front of me."

"I've been out twice. On the second occasion—without the bus."

"I see. All the same, you can rest easy. If the Ramage had had a 'phone call she would have told me so directly she saw me. She's well trained, laddie."

"Righto. If you're satisfied, Doctor, I am."

After a cup of tea and a muffin, he selected a cigarette and lit it. "Who was the chappie you saw performing at the Town Hall? Any idea?"

"No. Don't remember ever having seen him before. Why?"

He ignored the question. "Tell me what he told you. Exact words if you can remember them, please."

I obeyed. He listened with the utmost attention, and several of my statements were punctuated for me by him with a nod of approval. I had barely finished when the telephone rang. I caught the gleam in his eyes as I moved across to answer it.

The first three words that I heard were enough for me to make a decision. "Come here, Bathurst," I said to him quietly, "it's Jack speaking from the 'Florizel'. He's ran into several spots of bother."

He was at the 'phone in a flash. He remained there in conversation for at least three minutes. Listening for most of the time, but occasionally interjecting a quick exclamation or a sharp command. Eventually I heard him come to his final injunction.

"Oh—good man. And bags of thanks for what you're doing. Now, listen! Don't worry about either of the apparently big things that you've just told me. Hang on tight where you are till you hear from me again. Keep on exactly as you've been doing. Don't vary your method one iota. That's your job, Tabernacle. Not very exciting, but damned useful. If you hear any more of the gentleman you mentioned don't be kidded away from where you are on any account. Stick to your post. Those last four words heavily underlined. Want to speak to the doctor again? He's busy with a mouthful of buttered muffin. No? Cheero, then."

He replaced the receiver and came over to me. I scanned his features inquiringly. "You seem pleased," I said. "What's doing?"

It was a minute or so before he replied to the question. "In a way, perhaps, I am pleased. Satisfied, though, would be the better word. Satisfied—because things are going very much as I expected they would."

"Tell me."

"I'm going to. Tabernacle, as you intimated, has run into deep waters. Two important things, so he reports, have happened up at the 'Florizel'." He paused and watched me. I rose to the bait.

"Namely?"

"Kreutz has been seen prowling about there and Iris Fredericks has disappeared."

I nearly leapt from my chair. The coolness with which he made the announcement amazed me. "What?" I yelled. "No wonder Jack's gibbering. I thought he sounded pretty well all in when he spoke to me. What are we doing about it?"

He flicked the ash from the end of a cigarette. "At the moment, not a very great deal."

I stared in astonishment. "Why not?"

"Which am I to answer? Concerning which particular trouble? In re Kreutz or in re Miss Fredericks?"

"Either. Both. Iris, then."

"There is a complication in regard to Miss Fredericks that I haven't yet told you. It is, perhaps, just a little reassuring. It depends, I suppose, how you look at it. Mrs. Cotterill has received a message from her, since she disappeared, to the effect that she is safe and well. Mrs. Cotterill is begged to make no further inquiries, as any activity may endanger Miss Fredericks' safety. In this communication, I may say, Miss Fredericks gives no address."

"And you believe this message?" I cried rather wildly. "Surely it may be false? A trick to keep you from the scent; coming, not from Iris, but from the murderer himself?"

His nonchalance astounded me. "Perhaps. But on the whole, Doctor, I think not. I'm inclined to bank on its veracity. After all, one has to take one's risks, you know. I've had to do that many times in the past and I must be prepared to do so again."

He regarded me gravely. "I realize the truth of all that," I said eventually, my heat subsiding a little, "but, all the same, I'm frightened. This man has already killed three people, and—"

"And what?"

"He has since threatened Rosemary Cotterill. He—er—has a knack of carrying out his threats."

"I can't lay him by the heels, Bannerman, until I've absolutely *got* him, *in flagrante delicto*. I know what you mean—none better. But, you see, I realize that while he's at large one person is in very great danger. Perhaps even two people. Of that second possibility, I'm not quite sure. I harbour certain suspicions—that's all. But, to save the life of the one person whom I am determined to save, I am forced to take definite risks. There may be another life lost . . . but that will be the last . . . and my protégée will be safe—which is my main objective. I have a choice of evils, you will observe, in front of me. By no means a pleasant position."

"Who saw Kreutz at the Florizel Hotel?" I asked him.

"Two of them have seen him. Mrs. Cotterill first, and then Jack himself."

I thought a moment. "Does she know him to recognize him?"

"Possibly not. But she has my description of him. I took extreme care that she should have it and gave it to her before she left Chelmersley. Besides, Tabernacle has seen him up there too, as I told you, so there's no doubt about the authenticity of it."

"Where was he seen? In the hotel itself?"

"No. On neither occasion does he seem to have been actually inside the 'Florizel'. Mrs. Cotterill saw him watching the hotel from the opposite side of the street. Jack says he saw him loitering behind a pillar-box with his eye on one of the hotel windows."

"What did he do?"

"Stopped at his post." Bathurst chuckled. "Like the good lad he is. He has his orders from me and Otto Kreutz won't get him away by showing himself hiding behind a pillar-box."

"Just fancy," I grumbled, "Kreutz is a wanted man. His description posted up outside every police station. Goodaker's hot after him, and yet he can walk about a London street as large as life and utterly unperturbed. What a ridiculous position," I concluded bitterly.

"My dear Bannerman," returned Bathurst, "the police are not infallible. Don't be unjust or unfair to them. Think of the population of London alone. One man, amongst all those millions. Like many another wanted criminal, Kreutz has managed to elude temporarily the net that was spread for him. That's all it amounts to. I don't consider it a surprising fact."

"Perhaps not," I admitted still bitterly; "all the same, it doesn't make you feel any too comfortable when you know things like that are going on."

He patted me on the shoulder. "Don't worry too much, Bannerman," he said to me. "From one point of view, perhaps, we're better off than we were. We know where he is ... which we didn't know before."

He lit another cigarette, and as the flame of the match flickered in front of him turned his head in my direction somewhat carelessly. "I went to see Bligh this afternoon, amongst one or two other things. Went over to his place."

"How is he?" I inquired listlessly.

"Like Chelmersley itself. Rattled, Bannerman. At least, that's how he appears to be to me. Most distinctly rattled. In touch with the Commissioner, he tells me, almost daily. I'd like to hear Sir Austin's comments. They'd be worth filing and bequeathing as a rich legacy to one's heirs. I'm dining with Bligh to-night, by the way. So don't expect me home here until fairly late."

"At his private house?" I inquired.

"Lord—no. At Torrelli's."

I stared. "Your suggestion?"

"Which? The invitation or the venue?"

"Both."

"Well, I told him that there were several aspects of the case that I desired to discuss with him. He suggested a 'pow-wow' over a bird and a bottle. I agreed and nominated Torrelli's. Put it down that I had a special fancy in that direction. Its convenience appeals to me."

I glanced at him sharply, but he gave me no indication that he desired to pursue the subject. "I'm going out for half an hour," I said. "There's an old lady over at Cressing whom I want to see very particularly. To all intents and purposes, if a diagnosis go for anything, she should be dead by now. But she refuses to die and I want to find out why. When I tell you that she's eighty-eight next birthday—"

"Feminine cussedness, Bannerman. They all have it. I found that out years ago—only some more than others."

Bathurst shook hands with Sir George Bligh, outside Torrelli's, at approximately 10.45 that night.

"A very nice dinner, Sir George," he said. "I hope that you enjoyed it as much as I did. Torrelli was most attentive to us. Did you notice how he hovered over us between the courses?"

"Most solicitous," grunted Bligh. "I believe that I caught him listening to us more than once. That sort of beggar is invariably confoundedly curious. Still—one can't have everything. Here's my car and there's yours. I'll see Goodaker about that other matter in the morning. Good night, Bathurst. Thank you for taking me into your confidence as you have done this evening. I'll pop in there on my way home as you have suggested."

He stepped from the kerb into his limousine and his chauffeur shut the door behind him. As Anthony Bathurst swung into his own car the ghost of a smile flitted across his face. To disappear almost as quickly as it had been born.

He turned the car in the direction of the villages of Cressing and Saxbury. A mile or two the Chelmersley side of Cressing he turned down a lane and brought the Crossley to a standstill a short distance from a large, old-fashioned house. A drive led to the front door and the light of a lamp illumined the porch.

Anthony Bathurst squared his shoulders and rang the bell. After a few moments delay, a maid answered the summons. She listened to him with intelligent quietness. About to reply, she was interrupted. A man's voice sounded in the hall behind her.

"Who is it, Kitty? I've told you to be careful. Don't listen to anybody who—"

Bathurst stepped forward from the circle of light. "You know me, I think, Mr. Corbett. We met, first of all, at Chelmersley police station. I was with Sir George Bligh, the Chief Constable. My name is Anthony Bathurst."

"Come in, sir," said Corbett. "I didn't recognize you as you stood there. Come into the library. It's all right, Kitty, you can go. You can leave this gentleman with me."

Bathurst followed Corbett into the room indicated. "Take a seat, Mr. Bathurst. What do you want of me?"

Bathurst leant over towards him. Corbett thrust his hands into his pockets.

"What time do you intend to patrol this evening, Mr. Corbett, or to-morrow morning?"

"From twelve to two, Mr. Bathurst."

"With whom? It's customary for you to work in pairs, I understand."

Corbett referred to a typed list that he took from his pocket with his left hand. "My companion to-night is Melsheimer, the barber in West Street."

Bathurst rose from the chair into which Corbett had waved him. "Mr. Corbett," he said, "if you take my advice, you will not patrol this evening, or on any evening afterwards."

Corbett sprang to his feet. His face was white with strain. "What do you mean, sir? Why do you say such a thing? If I wish to—"

Bathurst yielded not an inch of ground. He bent down and spoke in the man's ear. Few words, but ominous, and heavy with threat. "An excellent reason don't you think?" whispered Mr. Bathurst. "Personally, I can't think of a better."

The pallor of Corbett's face testified to the soundness of the opinion. He faced his visitor, but could find no words with which to answer him. "Sit down, Mr. Corbett. I want to talk to you. Then, I hope, you will talk for a little while to me."

CHAPTER XXI
MEN ON PATROL

AT ELEVEN o'clock that same evening I was seated in my cosiest room, in my own particular armchair. Looking backward now, I presume that I expected Bathurst to come in at some time between eleven-thirty and midnight. The words that he had used to me had been "don't expect me until fairly late". I had interpreted them as I have just indicated.

Drawing a roughish bow at a roughish venture, I suppose that I went to bed at about twenty minutes past twelve, taking a generous helping of Scotch up stairs with me. Rosemary Cotterill, on the same evening, had gone to bed shortly after ten o'clock. We learnt that later, when the last tragedy came to be investigated.

She was able to substantiate this time by the fact that she had said good night to Jack in the lounge of the Florizel Hotel, a few minutes after the clock on the mantelpiece had chimed ten. Iris—well, not knowing then where Iris was in hiding, we'll omit the particulars that apply to her until the arrival of a more favourable moment for their recital.

Sir George Bligh, as he had promised Bathurst, when he had left him earlier that evening, called, on his way home, at the offices of the Vigilance and Protection Committee. Upon being informed that Corbett himself had not yet put in an appearance, he announced his intention of staying there and waiting for him.

Montague Corbett, the man for whom Sir George Bligh waited, took some time, however, to recover from the effects of Mr. Bathurst's visit. The extent of Anthony's knowledge had not only been a great shock to him, it had amazed him. More than once, he had nervously fingered a revolver that he had taken from a drawer of the big roll-top desk in the room that he regarded as entirely his own.

"He may know all that," he half muttered to himself, "but he can't know all. Or have anything like definite proof. It is impossible for anybody—in so short a time. I can't stay at home in the house. I'm going through with it—I shall be safer that way."

The result was that Sir George Bligh was eventually informed that it would be useless for him to wait any longer that night for Mr. Montague Corbett. The last-named gentleman had 'phoned through to the offices of the Vigilance Committee from his own house, to the effect that he would go straight on to his patrol at the appointed time and place without first calling in at headquarters as was his usual custom. That message was conveyed by the diligent citizen on duty to Sir George Bligh, who, having thanked his informant, re-entered his car and gave orders to be driven straight home.

Corbett left his house at a quarter to twelve. It is significant, in this relation, that he travelled on foot. It is more significant that he made his exit from his house from the back thereof and not, as ordinarily, from the front door. Careful and furtive though, as his every movement showed, he was, nevertheless, not alone as he made his way down the road. For the reason that a man followed him. Followed him for a little distance, before turning and then running in the opposite direction.

Corbett's patrol that evening consisted of a stretch of main road between Chelmersley High Cross, on the outskirts of the town, and the beginning of the Cressing Road. In length, not more than half a mile at the outside. It was at least ten minutes past twelve when he picked up his companion patrol, waiting patiently at the rendezvous.

As he looked at the time, and realized that he was late on duty, he anathematized a certain Anthony Bathurst. In those ten minutes, he argued to himself aggressively, anything might have happened and perhaps even . . . At that minute, when Melsheimer stepped from the shadows and accosted him, his good spirits partly returned.

"Mr. Corbett? So! We're working together, I think."

"Yes," he returned jerkily, "that's so, Melsheimer. Pleased to see you. Sorry I'm a little late. I was—er—detained. Hope I haven't kept you waiting very long."

"A little, Mr. Corbett. That is all. It is a dark night. A likely one for the killer, I think."

Melsheimer's face gleamed in the darkness and his teeth showed prominently. Corbett saw the man's features and shivered. Well he might, for at that very moment the killer was very near to one of them. I will outline the position.

They had begun to walk in the direction of Chelmersley High Cross, intending to turn again upon reaching the limit of their territory. The car that ran by them down the road seemed to be part of another existence. A hundred yards or so down the road there is a piece of wooded country—thickly wooded at that. The hedge that separates it from the road would be, I should say, at a rough estimate, somewhere about seven feet high. There had been two bad car smashes hereabouts due to drivers having been unsighted.

Suddenly Melsheimer stopped, stood quite still, and caught his companion's arm. "Hark! Did you hear?"

"What?" whispered Corbett. "I heard nothing. Come on. We don't want to hang about. It's asking for—" He moved forward a few steps.

"*Nein,*" whispered the German in his excitement, "something I hear. Certain I am. Over there." He nodded and waved a vague hand upwards in the direction of the height of the hedge. "A cry, I hear. Faint. Like what you call a whimper. But over there, certainly."

This time Corbett pulled up short in his tracks. "Are you sure, Melsheimer?"

Again Melsheimer nodded. The two men listened, but all was silent. "It may be nothing, Melsheimer. Nothing to do with us, I mean."

Melsheimer took a step or two away from his companion. "What are you going to do?" Corbett seemed anxious.

"Over that hedge to go—and find out. So!" The German turned to the hedge and caught hold of the thick twigs at the top of it. Corbett, staring and apprehensive, watched his movements fascinatedly.

"You'll never get over that, Melsheimer," he cried. "It's too high by far. If you're going, you'll have to go round by the road. Look. Round that way. It will be quicker too."

Corbett pointed down the road that led towards Chelmersley, and Melsheimer saw that, a little distance farther along, a rough path deviated from the road that they were treading, and broke away into the wood. Another quick glance at the height of the hedge convinced him that Corbett was right and that the way that he had suggested would turn out to be the quicker.

As his eyes came away, both he and Corbett heard a low moan that sounded on the other side of them and the blood seemed to thin in both as they looked at each other. Melsheimer, the more courageous, broke away from his companion and ran with all his might towards the path that Corbett had indicated to him. It left the main road not more than thirty yards away. Corbett made no attempt to restrain or to follow him. He watched him running and then saw him turn away down the rough path. It was at that precise moment that Corbett seemed to brace himself . . . to become a different man. Bathurst's words of a short time ago came home to him and, as far as he was able, he reacted to them. He moved towards the secret darkness of the hedge . . . the hedge that, for all he knew, held horror . . . or was about to hold horror. Another moan reached his ears. This time it seemed to be very close at hand.

Melsheimer, by this time, well in the clinging bushes of the little thicket, pushed forward vigorously and fearlessly towards the spot from where he thought the moaning sounds had come. He failed to see a dark form wriggle along and slink stealthily from a bush behind him. There was a raised arm and Melsheimer, struck down all unawares, staggered under the blow and fell heavily to the ground. His assailant gave him one quick, sharp glance and, turning like lightning, ran swiftly back in the direction of the Chelmersley highway.

A second pair of altruistic citizens reached Chelmersley High Cross at approximately three minutes to two. After waiting there a quarter of an hour for the appearance of the two men whom they had hoped to relieve, they decided to put in an effort of investigation.

When they had covered the whole stretch of highway as far as the Cressing road their moderate perturbation changed to a condition of undoubted alarm. At the start of the Cressing road, where their patrolling activities were presumed to finish, they turned to make their way back. More steadily and more carefully this time, scrutinizing, as far as was humanly possible, every step of the way.

When they reached the wooded tract of country where Corbett and Melsheimer had come to a halt about two hours before, the man who was leading and using an electric torch for examination of the ground, gave a sudden sharp exclamation.

"Here, Morgan. Come here. Come and look." As he spoke, he trained the light of his torch on a definite patch of ground hard by the hedgerow. "What's that?"

The man who was called Morgan was quick to see and quicker to understand. "It's blood, Lucas. A pool of blood. There's been trouble here, man. We must get busy—there isn't a moment to lose."

Lucas shook his head. "Sounds all right, but that's always easier said than done. This business may have happened an hour ago. Or even longer than that. The man that did the job may be miles away by this time. Probably is. Still, we must do our best, I suppose. I'll keep the torch on this side of the road. You work the other in the same way."

Thus they proceeded, until they came to the path down which Melsheimer had turned after he had broken away from Corbett.

Lucas halted and called across to his companion. "Morgan! Do you think it would be worth while having a look round here? We didn't see much as we came down the road in the first place, remember, and that pool of blood is quite close to the hedge. What do you say?"

Morgan crossed over to him and mentally surveyed the various possibilities. "Perhaps you're right," he eventually conceded. "If there were any dirty work to be done I should think that this would be a very likely place. The searchlight isn't over effective just here, for one thing, and it's as quiet as hell for another. You could be here an hour and not meet a soul. Hark."

He held up his hand in silent emphasis of his statement. The two men stood and listened. It was as Morgan had said. Scarcely a sound disturbed the eerie quietude of the night. Lucas looked to where the many dark masses of bush and bramble swayed backwards and forwards in the breeze. "I'm going to have a look round that plantation, Morgan," he said. "That pool of blood may mean a body hidden somewhere in there. Come with me and keep your eyes skinned."

They crept forward slowly. Searching every inch of the ground at their feet, as they were bound to do, their rate of progress seemed to get slower and slower. Suddenly, Lucas felt his arm jerked. "What's that just ahead, Lucas?" whispered his companion.

Lucas looked as he had been bidden and the two men could see the dark form of Melsheimer prone in their path. They ran towards it. Lucas dropped on one knee and raised the man's head.

"He's dead!" exclaimed Morgan. "Look here at his head. At the blood." Melsheimer's head showed an ugly gaping wound. As Lucas moved him, however, he uttered a low moan. The man was still breathing.

"He's alive," muttered Morgan in agitation. "Pray God, we've come in time." He turned to see Lucas regarding him queerly.

"I say, Morgan," Lucas whispered, "I've just thought of something—where's Mr. Corbett? He was with Melsheimer to-night, wasn't he?"

The two men looked round, scared and wondering. But there was no sign of Montague Corbett. Search of the wood and of the road beyond revealed nothing. Corbett had disappeared from that half-mile stretch of highway between Cressing and Chelmersley High Cross.

Chapter XXII
BLIGH ARRIVES EARLY

BEFORE I rolled down to breakfast on the following morning, I discovered that Bathurst had not yet returned to "The Rowfants". His bed had not been slept in and there was no other sign whatever, in any part of the house, of his proximity.

By the time the Ramage had prepared her creatures of bread and flesh and I sat down to the bacon and kidneys, I had worked myself up into a state of mild wonderment. This condition, however, was but ephemeral, was destined to be appeased very quickly and subsequently dispelled. The hands of my little carriage-clock that I had removed from its case and stuck on my dining-room mantelpiece (mainly for lack of any reliable other) showed twenty minutes past nine when I heard the Crossley's wheels come to a standstill outside.

I went to the window and waved to the old devil getting out, for, not to put too fine a point on it, I was no end bucked to see him. You got like that with A.L.B. when you had worked in double harness with him for a time, as it were. You felt like a fish out of water when you had to carry on alone. I'm perfectly aware that I'm guilty of a metaphorical cocktail, but what I've said indicates how I felt, so I'm going to let it stand and damn the consequences.

He came in with a grin on his face that put heart into me. "Dirtiest of stop-outs. Been up all night?" I queried.

"More or less, Bannerman. Chiefly more. Mustn't mind though. Got through several spots of most useful work."

"Have some brekker," I returned. "Grapefruit on the sideboard and I'll ask Mother Ramage to bring in another consignment of mixed grill."

"Hear what comfortable words St. Michael saith." He collared a grapefruit and came to the table. "Consciousness, my dear Bannerman," he said with a soupçon of whimsicality, "can only crawl forward on the legs of the past. It has been demonstrated to us that mind and matter may be split apart. By that, I mean that they may be separated from each other entirely. Let me put it like this. Pure mathematics, for example, is surely governed by a law of predestination, whereas you and I have been blessed with that possibly doubtful gift, free will. If I thought that I had been doomed since the beginning of time to demolish this most excellent grapefruit . . ."

"The grapefruit—like most good fruit that comes your way— is the doomed part of the combination," I interrupted, "if my opinion's worth a couple of hoots. Hallo! Who's that?"

The sound of a step on the gravel outside had caught my ear. Suddenly the door behind me opened violently to admit Sir George Bligh. I was favoured simultaneously with half a glimpse of an aggrieved Ramage bringing up a stalwart and protesting rear, but catching her eye, I motioned her to clear out. Happily for the peace of mind of all concerned, she melted away like a bank balance at the beginning of the flat-racing season. I was soon, however, to sit up and take notice.

"Bathurst," exclaimed Sir George, "you will pardon my butting in on you like this, and you too, Dr. Bannerman, but I presume from your general attitude that you have not yet heard the news?"

He paused, like a child will, when he thinks he has said something bright and brainy, to watch the effect that his statement would produce on us. I cocked a look at Bathurst out of the corner of my eyes. For a second—not more—he whitened a trifle, but then seemed to give himself a kind of mental shake and discard something that had troubled him for perhaps just a fraction of time. It seemed to be a shake that threw away a husk of doubt and betokened self reassurance. He answered Bligh with a quiet composure.

"What is it that you have come to tell us, Sir George? Doctor Bannerman and I have heard nothing."

Bligh sank into the seat that I had just occupied. "You know Corbett's patrol idea?"

I nodded. Bless my soul too, if old Bathurst didn't sort of wince again and lose part of the composure that he had just regained. "Yes, Sir George," he almost rapped. "What about it?"

"Corbett himself, with Melsheimer, the hairdresser of West Street, was due to patrol this morning, or last night, whichever you prefer, between Chelmersley High Cross and the Cressing road. Time—from midnight to two o'clock. At two o'clock, they were to be met at the Cross by the relief pair. Two fellows who live in Chelmersley—don't know anything about either of 'em—by name Lucas and Morgan. Well—when these two chaps reached the rendezvous point at the High Cross—there was no sign of Corbett and Melsheimer. No sign of either of 'em. They waited for a little while and then naturally they decided to have a look round. Well, there's no earthly use in my spinning the whole yarn, so I'll cut it short and tell you the part that matters most. Towards Cressing, on the way to Corbett's house, mind you, there's a piece of wooded land—clumps of trees and bushes and so on. Goodaker tells me it's known in the locality as Castor's Corner. Attracted by a pool of blood at the hedge-side, Morgan and Lucas found Melsheimer there—he'd been bashed on the head."

Bligh licked his lips, as though the taste of the telling tickled him. "Of Corbett, there was no sign at all." He repeated himself. "And of Corbett—so far eight hours since the happening of which I've told you—there has still been no sign. He hasn't returned to his own home. We've established that fact. Nor can we find his body anywhere. We are still searching—the whole stretch of road between Cressing and the High Cross. I've had everyone on who could be spared. The killer's score is now four, Bathurst." His tone held reproach. His lips were pursed.

The remark roused Anthony Bathurst from his ordinary imperturbability. "Sir George," he said doggedly, "I can't protect the whole of the population of Chelmersley, if that's what you're trying to say. They must help me by protecting themselves. Neither can I arrest, or advise the arrest, of a man simply on the strength of suspicion. But the web that I shall spin round this spinner of webs will in the end lure him and hold him and finish him."

He wheeled round and a strange glint showed for a moment in his grey eyes. "I could bear to hear more of this, Sir George. This affair of Castor's Corner. Tell me of Herr Melsheimer. Is he dead? I am interested to know that, particularly."

"Mercifully, no, Bathurst. Doctor Honeywell, that's the doctor whose place is on the Cressing road, if you remember, thinks that he has a splendid chance of recovery. Morgan and Lucas carried Melsheimer to Honeywell's surgery and fortunately found the doctor at home. Melsheimer's a strong, robust fellow, with a cast-iron constitution."

Bathurst rubbed his hands. "So Melsheimer's not likely to die, you say? Has he been able to make any statement yet? How he was attacked? Who attacked him? And why?"

Sir George waved a deprecating hand, as though making a futile attempt to stave off this fusillade of questions. "My dear Bathurst. One at a time, if you please. My brain is moderately alert, I think, but really! . . . I will endeavour to satisfy your torrential curiosity, question by question. You will find, I am of the opinion, that a general statement will probably cover all the points that you have raised. Melsheimer regained consciousness at about a quarter to five this morning. The doctor in whose surgery he lay, communicated at once with Inspector Goodaker, who had, of course, been sent for soon after the man had been conveyed there. Honeywell satisfied himself, I suppose, that Melsheimer was well enough to stand being questioned. Goodaker went up post-haste for the second time and took a statement.

"According to Melsheimer, he and Corbett were passing Castor's Corner at about twelve-fifteen. When they reached the part where the hedge is at its highest, Melsheimer says that they heard a weirdish sort of noise. Moaning or groaning, he says, would be the most fitting description of it. Quite frankly, he told Goodaker that his own opinion, when he heard these sounds, was that the murderer had walked abroad again and that, behind the hedge, lay his last victim, not dead but dying. At any rate, he dashed round to give a hand, if he should have found it necessary. He left Corbett standing on the road side of the hedge. As he was making his way across the wooded space, towards the spot from which he fancied the noise was coming, somebody came behind him and cracked him on the head. That's about the sum total of what he knows. He lay there unconscious with his head hard against the hedge-roots for two and a half hours or so. Until Morgan and Lucas came along, picked him up and carried him to Doctor Honeywell's surgery. That's the story, Bathurst, as Melsheimer gave it to Goodaker and as Goodaker passed it on to me."

Sir George stopped in his narrative. It was obvious that some of his usual pomposity had deserted him. He seemed to be inviting Bathurst's comments on the information that he had just supplied. As I expected, A.L.B.'s first comment was a definite question.

"What weapon does Doctor Honeywell think was used to put Melsheimer out of mess? Can he suggest anything?"

Old Bligh fidgetted forward. "Oh—that's my fault. I forgot to tell you. We've found something over at Castor's Corner. One of my chaps picked it up. A length of lead piping. There's blood on it, so there's little doubt that it was used on Melsheimer."

Bathurst began to whistle softly. Under his breath almost. "D'ye know, Sir George," he ventured at length, "I find a lot here that attracts me. But before I go into that, I could endure hearing something more from you. There seems to be a part missing that is very relevant. Whilst they were introducing the lead piping to Melsheimer, what of his companion of the patrol, Montague Corbett?" His eyes searched Bligh's face.

"We don't know a great deal about Corbett. Only what Melsheimer is in a position to tell us. In his opinion, Corbett was dead scared, even before they first heard the noise and especially when he parted company from Melsheimer at Castor's Corner. That's something we'd like to find out—what has become of Corbett."

"H'm. All of it vaguely presented and vaguely disconcerting. Does anything significant occur to you, Sir George, from this welter of information?"

Sir George denied the suggestion. Bathurst wheeled round to me for my opinion. "What about you, Bannerman?"

I faced him. He proceeded: "Is there anything that strikes you?"

"What are you getting at?" I came to grips with him. I always found it the best course to pursue.

He smiled a little at my open methods. "Well . . . this is how it appears to me. Listen for a while. Let's be psychologists. What sort of a fellow would you take our mass murderer to be? In disposition?" He glanced quizzically at our faces as he used the last word. "No. I'm not rotting. Far from it. I'm dead serious. See my finger wet? For instance, being more precise, what adjective would you apply to him if you were asked. One only, mind you. Assume that you were absolutely nailed down to one."

"Bloody-minded," cried Bligh, punching a hand with a fist.

I thought for a moment. "Ruthless," I declared with as much conviction but less vehemence.

Bathurst beamed. "Exactly," he almost whispered. "Just my point. Yet Melsheimer—at the man's mercy almost—lives to tell the story of how he was attacked. Our killer has never been so merciful before, has he? Get that fact well into your bonnet. Only one more blow needed, you know, to finish the prostrate Melsheimer! Weapon in the murderer's hand! Ideal place for killing! A murderer distinguished for his savagery. That's a fair statement, I think, taking all the known facts into consideration. Yet Melsheimer's alive to-day."

Bligh shrugged his shoulders and essayed explanation. "He may have thought that Melsheimer was dead. That the first blow with the lead piping had finished him off."

Bathurst's eyes never left Bligh's face. "Besides," I exclaimed, as the point flashed into my intelligence, "he had Corbett to consider."

Bligh agreed. "And also, there was the other—"

"The other what?" Bathurst almost hurled the question at him.

"The other body. The person whose cries or moans were heard by Melsheimer. There's no trace of anybody else there. Or even traces of anybody having been there."

Bathurst held up his hand. "Stay a minute, Sir George, please. Let me listen to Doctor Michael for a moment. The point that you were about to make in respect of Corbett, Bannerman? Amplify it, do you mind? I want to hear it fully."

I obeyed the instructions. "The man who hit Melsheimer didn't know how far Corbett was away, did he? He couldn't waste too much time over Melsheimer in case he found Corbett on top of him, could he? How did he know, for example, that Corbett hadn't followed Melsheimer round Castor's Corner. If he had, and it's a perfectly reasonable proposition, Corbett was in a damned good position to lay the bloke a stymie. That seems to me to be the very thing that he would have expected. Put yourself in the man's position."

I saw old Bligh staring at me as though I were the tender spot on the fat lady at the fair, but I didn't care two hoots for him or his looks. Anthony Bathurst caressed his chin.

"I see your point, Doctor. But unfortunately it blows itself up—spontaneous combustion. It founders on the reef of reason."

"Why?" I queried bluntly.

"You know your book, Doctor, and you may know your Hoyle, but you don't know your Corbett. I can't blame you." He walked to the window and looked out. "We've another visitor," he said quietly. "Here's the indefatigable Goodaker outside and, judging by appearances, there's something lurking in his bosom that he'd very much like to be shut of."

MRS. Ramage performed again and Goodaker entered. He touched his cap in a salute to the Chief Constable. To Bathurst and me he accorded a half bow. The man was excited and inclined to be uncontrolled.

"Good morning, sir. Good morning, gentlemen." He favoured me with a sentence all my own. "Your housekeeper's getting to know me, Doctor. There was a time—not so long ago either—when she used to follow me right into your room. Now she gives way when I'm clear of the front door."

I nodded. Bathurst gave a glance at old Bligh and the latter replied to it with a quick movement of the head. "Well, Inspector," said Anthony, "you haven't come to 'The Rowfants' to tell us about your Ramage *status quo ante*. I'm confident of that. What is it that's haunting your tortured soul? Open the can."

Goodaker blew out his cheeks and did so with a vengeance. "The body of Otto Kreutz was taken from the Chelm this morning. Just below Wedlock's mill. Where the river's at its deepest. He's in the mortuary now, waiting for Doctor Bannerman. No wonder we couldn't lay hands on him."

"What?" blazed Bathurst. "Do you mean to tell me that . . ." He stopped precipitately and waved to the inspector with a gesture of apology. "I'm tremendously sorry, Goodaker. I interrupted you. I beg your pardon. It was wrong of me. Please go on with your story."

"The body has been lashed round the ankles and also round the wrists. What I mean, gentlemen, by that statement, is that the ankles and wrists have, in each case, been tied together. He had no chance whatever in the water tied as he was." Goodaker looked at us carefully. I could have sworn that he was holding something back from us.

"It's murder again," declared old Bligh aggressively. "Not a doubt about it."

Goodaker accepted the statement of his superior without comment, but his eyes sought Bathurst's for some expression of opinion from him. A.L.B. understood his look. He shook his head, however, and, for the time being, Goodaker was sent empty away.

The inspector hesitated briefly and then went ahead again. "There is also a tight cord round the top of the head and the point of the jaw. After the manner of the old-fashioned night-cap."

I stared wonderingly. "Not your kind, Bannerman," said Sir George. "He means the night-cap sartorial."

Before I could reply, Bathurst had sprung to his feet in an excess of excitement. "What did you say Goodaker? Say it all again, man, slowly!"

Goodaker, flattered, I think, at the sensation he was causing, repeated his statement with studied deliberation. When he had finished Bathurst paced the room, vivid words tumbling from his lips.

"Of course, Inspector. Of course. The rope would have to be round the skull and jaw. That was essential. Otherwise—the water would have . . ." He turned and stared at Goodaker. "Have you seen this body, Inspector?"

"I have, Mr. Bathurst. It was taken to the mortuary on my instructions."

"Have you done anything to it? Touched it in any way, for instance?"

"No. I want the Doctor here to have a look at it before I do anything of that kind."

Bathurst rubbed his hands. I recognized the symptom and drew comfort therefrom. Things were moving at last.

"Tell me, Goodaker," proceeded the now irrepressible Anthony, "by what intricate process of imagination did you identify this body as that of Otto Kreutz? Did it have a notice to that effect pinned to the jacket? Printed in block capitals?"

Goodaker flushed at the thrust, but the smile in Anthony's eyes tempered its sharpness and I think the inspector saw it and understood. And *tout comprendre, c'est tout pardonner*.

Bligh emitted a curious exclamation, the reason for which I failed to fathom. Goodaker commenced to answer Bathurst's question.

"I admit that a drowned man looks funny, Mr. Bathurst. I've seen too many in my time not to know that. Features swollen and all that, and I admit too, that I've only once before had a good look at Kreutz. Anyhow, listen to the evidence that I've collected and you'll see. The body is dressed in the white linen jacket we saw Kreutz in before; there is a pair of spectacles in the pocket; it has Kreutz's thick, black hair, black moustache and . . ." Goodaker paused. It was a subtle pause, intended for effect.

"Yes?" Bathurst's question was short and sharp.

"The remains of a bruise on the nail of the thumb of the right hand. The blueness of the nail is plainly to be seen." Goodaker shot him a shrewd glance from the corner of his eye. "Satisfied, Mr. Bathurst? Good enough, eh?"

"Oh, that touch of the vanishing bruise and that body of Kreutz that is still! Delightful—unquestionably—but a trifle outré, don't you think? No, Goodaker, answering you quite bluntly, I'm not satisfied. Far from it. Who would remove friend Otto in this fashion? And Melsheimer in dock nursing an injured head." He turned to the rest of us and the raillery left his voice immediately. "Put your hats on, gentlemen, please. We've an appointment at the mortuary. A rendezvous with Death. There's something vitally wrong in this latest development and I think I know what it is. But, until I've seen the body that has come from the waters of the Chelm, I can't be absolutely certain. Your car, Bannerman, and mine too. We'll go not singly, but in battalions."

We followed him in a body, nobody questioning the wisdom or otherwise of the policy. As I've told you, you were like that with Anthony Bathurst. You took what he said for granted.

A quarter of an hour later saw us in the mortuary. Goodaker led the way, and as we passed through the door of the building he motioned to me to come forward to do my stuff. Bathurst and Bligh ranged themselves at my side as I advanced to the slab upon which lay the soddened body of Otto Kreutz, wrists tied, ankles tied and a cord round jaw and head. Exactly as the inspector had described to us. He had been taken from the water to be given back to the earth.

CHAPTER XXIV
REVELATION

"MAY I, Sir George?" queried Bathurst, with a lift of the eyebrows and a nod towards the dead man.

"Certainly," acquiesced Bligh. "Go ahead. It is permitted. I'm quite content to place myself in your hands. What are you going to do?"

"Untie the cord that's tied round the point of the jaw. Goodaker, will you please? Carefully, man. Then I'll show you something. You don't mind, Doctor, do you?"

I shook my head and the inspector bent himself to the gruesome task. The cord was wet and slimy and his fingers picked uncertainly at the knot under the dead man's chin. Eventually he straightened it out and was able to remove the cord from the man's face.

"Here you are, sir. Do you want it?" He held it towards Bathurst. The latter shook his head.

"Put it on the slab, Inspector. At the side there. Let me have a good look at this man here."

He bent over the body and I saw that light begin to dance again in his grey eyes. Then he straightened himself and rubbed his hands—surest sign of all of satisfaction within. He beckoned to me. "You can delay your particular job of work for a little while, can't you, Doctor? Watch me."

We all stared—fascinated. He bent again over the dead man and we saw him slightly raise the head. The fingers of his right hand worked quickly somewhere at the base of the skull, whilst those of his left hand seemed to push at the dead man's forehead. Suddenly the dark hair shot upwards, and there in Anthony Bathurst's right hand, was a wig of bluish-black hair— the wig that had belonged to Otto Kreutz.

At the same time, denuded as it was, the face of the man on the slab seemed completely changed and the shock of true identification came to me immediately. For there in front of us lay the man whom we had known as Montague Corbett. There was something unusual about his appearance which I couldn't place, but you could tell that it was he. Goodaker uttered a stifled exclamation and Bligh looked as though ghosts had called upon him for immediate interview.

"There you are, Inspector," cried Bathurst, "there's your Otto Kreutz! Also, you needn't worry your head about finding Corbett. I can see that you've recognized your man."

I detected something in his tone that made me watch him intently. I was certain that he had seen more than any one of us others had. What was it? That was the question I asked myself.

"I can't believe it," moaned Bligh. "Corbett masquerading as Kreutz? How is it possible? Is Corbett then the murderer of the other people? If so . . . who has killed him? Is Kreutz dead? And Corbett dead, too?" He passed a hand across his brow wearily. "I can't piece it together. It's beyond me. Can you, Bathurst?"

With a curious sort of movement, Anthony shrugged his shoulders, and before he could answer the Chief Constable cut into the conversation.

"What's different about him?" I indicated the corpse on the slab. "There's something, but I'm hanged if I can say what it is."

Bathurst looked inquiringly from one to the other. "Well, what is it?"

As he spoke the truth came home to me in a flash. "I know," I exclaimed, "Corbett's moustache has been cut and trimmed; it's much smaller than it was when he was alive. Don't you see? Of course."

"Congratulations, Bannerman, on the accuracy of your observation. It had to be so. It was a vital necessity. Just as was the cord round the point of the jaw, to prevent the Chelm waters from washing the wig off." He swung round to Sir George Bligh with a fierce eagerness. "I will endeavour now to answer some of your recent questions, sir. Corbett is *not* masquerading as Kreutz. Corbett is dead. Drowned in the Chelm, after being drugged, as Doctor Bannerman here will tell you in a moment when he's made his examination. And Kreutz too is dead. Otto Kreutz, mark you. At least that's my opinion. We may never look upon him again. Come, gentlemen, we needn't waste any more time here."

Sir George licked his lips and seemed to sag in front of Bathurst. "Corbett is *not* masquerading as Kreutz? And Kreutz is dead? Once again I do not understand. That's what you said, wasn't it?"

His eyes left Bathurst's and sought Goodaker's. The inspector, however, anxious for vindication, was looking at the thumb on the dead man's right hand. He raised it a little and held it up to us. He was undoubtedly right in what he was trying to show us. There, on the nail, was the purplish bruise that we had seen before on the thumbnail of Kreutz. To my astonishment, Bathurst waved it away; the impression that he gave to us was that he didn't consider the bruise to bear the slightest importance or significance.

Then I began to wonder . . . and I wondered still more when I saw him jerk his head in my direction. "Yes, I fancy Kreutz is dead, as I said to Sir George. But not so our friend 'Aquila—the Eagle'. Unless I am mistaken he will be found to be very much alive. Doctor Bannerman, I want you for just a minute. Excuse me, gentlemen." He walked to the door with me, turned, and gave me certain instructions. Then he left me and returned to the others.

"Sir George," I heard him say, "can you spare me a moment? Thank you."

CHAPTER XXV
THE FOUR ACES

THE appointed rendezvous that evening was to me an entirely surprising and unexpected one. When Bathurst had first told me of it, I had marvelled, but had maintained, at the same time, a respectful silence. The look on his face, as we had stood at the door of the mortuary, had summarily checked and choked any little inclination I might have felt towards my usual irresponsibility.

I met Bathurst just inside the two big iron gates through which you approached Sir George Bligh's house. Goodness knows where Bathurst had been since we parted at the mortuary; I hadn't seen him again for the rest of the day. To be precise—until 9.30. I looked at the time as I went through the gates. There was no sign of him for a few paces but suddenly I felt a hand on my arm and I found him walking silently at my side.

"Revolver with you, Doctor?" he asked me.

I nodded. "As you requested me. You, too?" He grinned. "You bet, Bannerman. I wouldn't face to-night's job without it, I can tell you. Don't you remember what I told you some few days ago? Strong, swift, silent and belonging to the shadows? He's all that and more, Doctor."

"Why have we come here?" I whispered.

He chuckled grimly. "The kill is here. I brought it here an hour ago. And the killer will come after it."

"But why *here*?" I persisted.

"Nice roomy house, and empty for to-night. Barring us and Co. Sir George Bligh and Lady Bligh are spending the night in town. By arrangement. Mine! Bligh seemed damned glad to go and get out of it. Don't talk too loudly, Doctor. We may not have a great deal of time to spare. Come along with me."

But I tarried a little and pondered over his words. "You said that the kill was here. Mrs. Cotterill, do you mean? She was threatened . . . I know. . . . She was to be the fifth victim."

"Good God—no, Bannerman. Why do you still harp on that. I thought I had convinced you of Mrs. Cotterill's safety days ago. What hard nuts to crack you Scots are, to be sure. According to my reading of the case, Mrs. Cotterill stands in no danger whatever from our friend the killer. Remember his leniency towards Melsheimer."

I stared. "But the warning, Bathurst—"

"S'sh," he whispered. "We're close to the house."

"Who's in the house?" I asked him.

"Miss Fredericks," he answered with ominous quietness. "The kill."

"Who else?"

"Nobody," he returned imperturbably.

"Iris—alone?" I queried, cold fear and stealthy terror clutching at my heart. "Aren't you running a grave risk leaving her like that?"

He chuckled again. "Don't be uncomplimentary, Michael. The situation is well reviewed. I've seen to that, my dear chap. The risk that I am taking is almost infinitesimal. Believe me, I have taken many greater during the course of my career. By the time friend 'Aquila' gets here, which will not be for some time yet, there will be great odds against him. You and I and Tabernacle will be here when he is forced into the open. Also Goodaker. I 'phoned them both early this evening."

"Suppose he arrives earlier than you anticipate. What then?"

"He can't, my dear Bannerman. Even if he were Roche's ubiquitous bird. I've attended to that little contingency myself."

As he spoke, an owl hooted, away in the distance, and I heard the flutter of wings of many birds in the branches of the trees around us. Back on the road behind us could be heard the faint throb of passing motor-cars, which seemed to me to link us with clean and normal things. I drew grateful comfort from the sound. After all, I argued to myself, civilization with its protecting barriers was not far behind us.

"Here we are," whispered Bathurst. "The door's open. I just left it so." The big door yielded to his push and we stood together inside the Bligh mansion. "It's a quarter to ten, Bannerman," he said softly in my ear. "I'm going to shoot the bolts here now and leave a convenient window for our friend the enemy to use, if he so choose. We can let Jack in when we hear him knock. Jolly good of Sir George to leave me a free hand, don't you think?"

He looked at me sharply. "You're nervy, Doctor. Pull yourself together. For the love of heaven, don't let Miss Fredericks see you like that. That sort of thing's infectious."

We tiptoed from the door, I behind him, along a heavily carpeted corridor, until we came to the door of a room. He opened it and I followed him across the threshold. Iris was sitting in the corner on a low couch. She looked a frail, pathetic little figure. She came to Anthony Bathurst immediately he entered, her small face uplifted to his. It was plain to see that horror held her in bondage.

She beckoned to me to come closer, and when I had done so, she slipped behind me, went quickly to the door and closed it. She was pale and silent. There was a small table at the head of the couch that she had left, and upon it I saw a longish piece of paper. My training told me from a couple of quick glances at her that she was haunted by haggard fear. Her whole body was like the exposed nerve of a carious tooth, throbbing with an exquisite paean of pain. Evil, in colossal form, was close to her—pernicious and insidious evil—and she knew it! Knew it and shivered in its thrall.

Anthony took one of her hands and patted her on the shoulder. "It's going to work out all right, Miss Fredericks. Please don't worry. You're quite safe and, if you obey my instructions implicitly, after to-night you'll be safe for always."

"I will try to, Mr. Bathurst. I have done so ever since I went away, I think. Will you please tell me what you want me to do?"

"All in good time, Miss Fredericks. When Jack comes, we'll talk things over and have our campaign all ready for later on. You aren't in the slightest danger, because we're going to look after you. In the meantime, show Doctor Bannerman what I handed you just now. It may possibly surprise him and will certainly interest him, I know." He rubbed his hands. "Vendetta, my dear Bannerman. Always vendetta. Don't you remember the sweetness of its music in my ears?"

Iris walked across to the couch by the table and picked up the long document that I mentioned just now. Her hand shook and I wondered what the hell the thing could be. Without a word she handed it to me and then resumed her former sitting position on the couch. Directly my eyes fell on the paper I knew from its form and appearance what I held.

It was a marriage-certificate. Or, rather, the copy of one. But if I were a little surprised to see this, I was amazed at the details that it gave me. It was no less than the marriage certificate of Elsie Rhodes, spinster, and Duncan Fredericks, bachelor. Duncan Fredericks, who had died under my care months previously. I looked at the date and saw that the certificate was over a year old.

"Well," demanded Bathurst. "What do you think of it now? Plain as a pike-staff—what?"

There was a ring at the bell as the words left his lips which prevented me from replying. I think I welcomed it on the whole, although it made me jump a bit and seemed, too, to chill my blood.

"That's Jack," said Iris.

Bathurst nodded. "Yes. It can't be . . ." He broke off. "Let him in, Bannerman, will you, please? All the servants have the night off and we have to run our own errands. Although my dear old friend, Sir George, doesn't know that. I took a liberty with regard to his staff that I didn't tell him about."

I looked at Bathurst and felt at the same time for my revolver. "Supposing it's not Jack? Supposing it's—"

Bathurst shook his head. "Don't worry about that. When he comes, my dear Doctor, he won't come that way, never fear. Once again, don't forget that he belongs to the shadows. He comes from, and he will go to—'his own place'."

Reassured, I crept down the hall to the front door. I kept a hand on my revolver, though, all the same, as I drew the bolts and opened the door. This done, I stood back a pace to see who was there. There was no reason, as it turned out, for my apprehension. Bathurst was right, and to my great relief, Jack slipped in and shook hands with me. Goodaker followed him, a pace or two behind. The three of us joined the others in the room from which I had just come.

"You're safe, then, Iris," said Jack, going to her anxiously. "I've been at my wit's end these last two days wondering where you were. If old Bathurst hadn't given me such specific instructions I should have deserted my post long ago and tried to find you."

"But you didn't," Bathurst rallied him, "and that's all that matters. You stayed at your post. Look at this—and you, too, Goodaker."

He handed them the copy of the marriage-certificate that I had looked at just previously. Tabernacle whistled and the inspector was hard put to it to find comment. Bathurst tapped the document significantly.

"A link in the chain, Goodaker. The marriage was a secret—known only to the parties to it. Miss Fredericks here, for instance, was as ignorant of it as anybody else. Now for our business to-night."

"One moment," I intervened, "before we decide anything. Where is Rosemary? Despite all you say and tell me, I can't altogether—"

Bathurst held up his hand to stop me. "Mrs. Cotterill is not a hundred miles from here, Doctor. I have not neglected anything, as far as I know, in the arrangements for to-night. Make your mind easy on that score."

"Righto," I conceded. "Forgive my anxiety. You were going to say, when I interrupted you . . ."

"Oh yes, our plans for to-night. The most important part of all. Listen, please, all of you."

We settled down and hung on his words. "We hold all four aces of the pack. There are four of us under this one roof—all pretty useful, I should imagine, in a rough house. Tabernacle, we'll call the ace of hearts—for obvious reasons"—he cast a whimsical glance in Jack's direction. "The doctor here, the ace of spades—considering him professionally, and Goodaker, the ace of clubs—I know what the inside of a police station's like. I had a cousin who was a special constable. I'll call myself the ace of diamonds—diamond cut diamond, eh? If we can't keep Miss Fredericks from harm, between us we ought to retire to bath-chairs and drink cocoa for the rest of our lives. For more reasons than one." He paused. I was rather shocked at this flippant mood of his, taking into consideration all the circumstances, and before I could acclimatize myself, as it were, he was off again.

"Firstly, the murderer does not know that we four are here—waiting for him. When he arrives he will receive an unpleasant surprise. That gives us advantage number one. Secondly—"

Here Jack interrupted him. "A minute, Bathurst, please. Forgive me interrupting, but there's something about this that both puzzles and worries me. Before we go any farther, may I ask what seems to me to be a most vital question?"

"Certainly, my dear chap. Ask anything you like. What is it?"

Jack leant over towards Anthony, determination written all over his eager face. "If your plans have been known only to our own intimate circle, as I understand they have been, since Iris, Rosemary, and I have been in town, how is it that the murderer knows that Iris is here to-night? How has that information leaked out?"

"Good egg," I thought to myself, "Jack's the boy. On the spot, absolutely."

Bathurst gave me a sort of sideways look which I only half caught, and offered explanation. "You've heard of Corbett's murder, haven't you, Tabernacle?"

"Only the bare facts," returned Jack. "Nothing in the way of detail."

"Corbett's dead body was taken from the river this morning, wearing a wig and what we will call the working clothes of Otto Kreutz."

Jack stared at him incredulously. "Do you mean that Corbett was disguised as Otto Kreutz?"

A.L.B. considered the question for a moment. "In regard to that, I think, there are two possibilities. Corbett was either purposely disguised as Kreutz, or the man whom we knew as Kreutz was a disguised person in the first instance, and Kreutz—as Kreutz you understand—never had a real separate existence. Follow me there, Tabernacle?"

"I think so. Well enough, at all events. Anyhow, go on—you haven't answered my question yet."

"The inspector, Doctor Bannerman, and I, saw Corbett's body in the Chelmersley mortuary this morning. But we parted company, and when I left there I had a specific object in front of me. I will let you into the secret. I have interviewed three people during the course of the afternoon . . . one of whom I definitely suspect as the killer of the four people whom we know to have been murdered in Chelmersley since the last day of August. I shook hands with those three people that I mentioned—with each one of them—and to the one whom I suspect I seemed to pass on a tiny piece of excessively vital information in a moment of inadvertence. When that moment of apparent carelessness, on my part, came, I watched to see how the information was received. Gentlemen, the trap was baited. I'm confident of it."

Jack wiped his forehead with his handkerchief. "That's much more satisfactory. It's taken a load off my mind. I was afraid that Iris herself might have given the game away in some manner without knowing it. And it fretted me."

Iris Fredericks shook her head, disclaimingly. "No, Jack. Don't worry. You need not fear that. Mr. Bathurst's orders all the way through have been far too imperative for me to think of disobeying them."

He smiled back at her gratefully. Just as she finished speaking, it seemed to me that I heard a dull sort of noise somewhere in the upper part of the house. It disturbed me. I caught my breath and looked round at the others. None of them, however, appeared to have heard it. I listened again. For a good five seconds I should think. All was quiet . . . but the chill truth struck hard at my heart and set it racing perilously against my ribs. I knew, beyond the shadow of doubt, that the killer was in the house.

At that mad pulsing moment, before I could translate my knowledge into words, the telephone bell rang. Once—twice—three times. Nobody spoke—we just looked at each other.

Chapter XXVI

WE DIVIDE OUR FORCES

I answered it. I was nearest to it. Of the men, that is. I stood at the side of Iris as I took off the receiver. When I heard the voice at the other end of the line, I clicked my mental heels to attention. It was Rosemary speaking, of all people. What she said introduced me to yet another fear.

"I want to speak to Mr. Bathurst. It's dreadfully important. Oh—is that you, Michael? It's Rosemary speaking. Please ask Anthony Bathurst to come to the 'phone at once. I must speak to him. I can't stay here another minute."

There was a kind of sob in her voice which told me that she was pretty well all in. I beckoned to Bathurst. "Hold on a sec.," I said to her. "I'll ask Bathurst to speak to you."

As he crossed the room to the 'phone, his face held a look that I had never seen there before. It was something much more than a look of annoyance. There was a suspicion of ugliness in it—what appeared to me as the ugliness that is born of thwarted effort. As he lifted the receiver, his face hardened into the image of inflexibility.

"Yes . . . Bathurst speaking. 'Who is it? . . . Mrs. Cotterill . . . yes. What is it that you want? No, I can't think of it on any account. I'm sorry. But you must . . . you really must. You *must* pull yourself together. . . . Yes, I know. . . . You may be in danger. I'm willing to grant that, but there are others whose danger is greater. Surely you know that by this time."

Then came a space of time during which he listened. During which, we—silent, each one of us—watched him, wondering all that this dramatic interruption might mean to us, and to our plans. Then we heard his voice again—authoritative, imperative, dominant.

"No. Don't do that for God's sake! If you do what you threaten you'll ruin the plans that I have made for to-night. There's so little time, now, for us to move. . . ."

His face worked convulsively. . . . I saw him bite his lip in distress . . . he was speaking again: "It's a cursed nuisance, Rosemary, but I'd a thousand times rather *that*, than what you first suggested. You *must* not come here. That would be absolutely fatal. I'll send over to you within the hour."

Replacing the receiver, he turned to us in explanation. He looked like a man who has only just survived an intense shock.

"Mrs. Cotterill—as you heard, no doubt. Panic-stricken. Lost her head completely. I would have given anything for it not to have happened. To-night of all nights. But I've promised and I suppose that I must keep my promise."

"What's the promise?" queried Iris.

"She's alone in her house and her nerve has gone. She wants help from us—companionship, if you like it better. Almost begged me to go over. I've promised that I'll send somebody over to her. I can't go myself, that's certain. I dare not leave here."

"Why not?" I queried audaciously. "We three chaps can look after Iris, can't we? Or two of us even, come to that."

He eyed me queerly. I thought of the noise that I had heard and of the horror that I was certain lurked somewhere within that house, and for some vague, nebulous reason I resolved not to tell him of these things at the moment. I felt that I was capable of taking charge on an absolutely straight, clean-cut issue such as this seemed to be, and, that when the brute emerged from the shadows, I should be perfectly well able to tackle him.

Goodaker came to my support. "Yes, Mr. Bathurst, I think the doctor's right. Surely it can be managed?"

For a moment or two Bathurst seemed undecided, irresolute. Suddenly, he appeared to make up his mind. "Very well, then, you chaps. I'll fall in with the suggestion. I'll leave this part of the show to you, Bannerman, and Tabernacle. Goodaker can come with me to Mrs. Cotterill's. Perhaps I may be able to get back to you in an hour or so. But—and I'm most insistent in regard to this—I must make an important provision. If I am going to leave you for a time, I must give Tabernacle and the doctor specific instructions as to what they are to do, and where they are to go within this house. Please come upstairs with me, gentlemen, and you, too, Miss Fredericks."

Those of us who had been seated rose to do his bidding. "Come between Jack and me, will you, Miss Fredericks? You others follow on behind. Lead the way, Tabernacle."

We made our way upstairs until we came to the bedrooms. There were four of them opening out on to one large landing. I found myself looking furtively over my shoulder. I was the last one of the file and I could not rid my brain of the noise that I thought I had heard . . . and of that brute that might lurk somewhere in those shadows.

When we came to the bedroom that directly faced the staircase, we halted. Anthony addressed us, Tabernacle and me particularly. "Miss Fredericks will sleep in this room. Until you retire for the night, Miss Fredericks, Tabernacle and Doctor Bannerman will stay with you always. For every moment until the door of that room shuts upon you. This door." He pointed to it. "When you are inside, you will lock the door and bolt it." He smiled. "And by the morning, Miss Fredericks, your troubles, will, I hope, be over."

He turned to us. Before he could say anything, however, Goodaker was in with a question. He rubbed his chin contemplatively. "You're covering the inside, Mr. Bathurst, I quite agree. But what about an attack from the outside of the house. We must not neglect the possibility, you know. The bedroom window, for instance?"

"I'm not overlooking that chance, Inspector. This is what I propose to do. Listen. We will have a sentinel here, on the door, and we will also have a sentinel on the window. We'll station him outside the house. We'll have Tabernacle on the door here and Bannerman on the outside duty. Fit, each of you?"

"I think so," I muttered. "What about you, Jack?"

"It's O.K. with me, Michael," he answered. "I understand what we're expected to do. ' You and the inspector can get along, Bathurst."

Then Iris said a surprising thing. "There's just this," her voice was appealing; "but could I go to my bedroom now? Would it upset any of your arrangements, Mr. Bathurst, if I did? I'm hopelessly tired and I feel that I really can't stay up a moment longer. The strain's too great. Yes?"

"Go to bed, by all means, Miss Fredericks, if you think it will help you. It will make no difference to our plans whatever. All that it means is that sentinel duty must start at once."

Turning, he motioned to Goodaker. "In that case, Inspector, we'll be getting along. And a murrain on most women. What have you got to say about that, Goodaker? H'm?"

"They're much of a muchness, sir, taking 'em all round. But they're not treated too well sometimes, you know, sir. I had a girl—my only child as it happens—who was badly let down by a—. But you aren't thirsting to hear about that now, sir. Good night, Doctor. Good night, Mr. Tabernacle."

Iris entered her room and we heard her shoot the bolt on the inside. "You, here, Tabernacle," said Bathurst, "and if Doctor Bannerman will accompany us, we'll get him fixed up as well."

I fell in behind the inspector and him, and we raced down the staircase, the three of us. It was evident that A.L.B. didn't intend to waste time. A matter of seconds saw us outside the Bligh house.

"This is your place, Bannerman," said Bathurst. "That's the window of the room where Miss Fredericks is. Not so very high up either, is it? A quick-footed climber would be up to it in a brace of shakes, if he meant business. Thick-growing ivy and a pipe. Look! Might have been made for him, mightn't it?"

My eyes followed his demonstrating finger. I could see all that he meant, and knew now, better than I had known, why he was placing me there. He held out his hand. "Night, Doctor. I'll be back to you as soon as I possibly can."

A minute or so later, I heard the purr of the Crossley as it made the main road. I knew what it meant. The inspector and he were away again. I wondered when we three should meet again. And such is the power of association, there came into my head as I took up my post beneath Iris's window that other line from "Macbeth", that once heard can never be forgotten: "Aroint thee, witch, the rump-fed ronyon cried."

I repeated it to myself, aloud, mechanically. Then I thought of sailors' wives with laps covered with chestnuts. Nuts, which they picked avidly from their laps with their ugly red hands, to "munch and munch and munch". Time and time again, I repeated the words of the strong consonant and saw at the same time the image of the women, nuts on laps. There was a touch of rheumy humour in the night air; so, in order to keep moderately warm, I allowed myself the rope of a few paces, either side of the actual spot that Anthony had allotted to me.

I kept my eyes and ears well open, however, and moved close to the wall of the house so that none could track me and come behind me to my hurt. I should think that about half an hour went by in this fashion; the only sound that I heard was the crunch of my own short footsteps on the crisp gravel. I was pretty well fed up, I can tell you, and the idea of "kip" distinctly soothsome; but, reviewing the entire situation, I concluded that I would rather have my job of work than Jack's, and that to him had been assigned the harder part.

By this time, witches and sailors' wives had yielded place in my mind to such thoughts as of Cawdor, Glamis and Birnam Wood. "That shall be King hereafter," I whispered to myself . . . and I tangented again to Macduff, the Caesarean operation . . . and actually to my early days at Charing Cross. I had just reached a mental picture of the operating theatre and old Gubbins, the house surgeon, bending over a poor wretch eaten up with sarcoma—one of my first "ops"—when I heard my name shouted.

"Michael! Michael! Help! Help!" The voice was Jack's, and I knew at once that there was a healthy nip of trouble knocking about somewhere close at hand. I looked quickly up at the window of the bedroom where the girl was. The kill, as Bathurst had called her, and I half shuddered at the thought. The room was still in darkness. She had the sense, I thought, not to switch on the light. Then Jack's voice came again.

"Quick, Michael. Help. There's a . . ." His voice died away in a sort of strangled gurgle and I knew that I simply must run to his help. Turning in a flash, I skirted the house to find the window that Bathurst had told me had been conveniently left open.

I had just reached the angle of the wall, when something or somebody leapt upon me from behind. I felt a crashing blow on the back of the head, saw myriads of flying stars and floating sparks . . . and knew no more.

CHAPTER XXVII
THE BRUTE FROM THE SHADOWS
(As told by Anthony Lotherington Bathurst)

THIS is the second occasion, during my career as an investigator of crime, that I have been compelled, by force of circumstance, to break into the narrative of another. But, inasmuch as I am in a much better position than Doctor Bannerman to tell of the events of that memorable night, it may help the reader if I take over, at this juncture, and carry on until the finish of this remarkable case.

Looking back at the previous chapter, I observe that the doctor has described how he heard the sounds of my car carrying the inspector and me back to the house of Mrs. Cotterill, to which we had been so urgently summoned. In that bare statement of his, however, he was wrong. I had deceived him. To do so was necessary.

I also notice that he has been at some pains to describe a look on my face, that he had seen but a little while ago, as a look of "thwarted ugliness", or at least, of something resembling that. That statement of his pleases me tremendously. It tickles my vanity. It takes me back to those exceedingly happy days I spent with the O.U.D.S., during which time I had the honour and pleasure of playing "Claudio" in "Measure for Measure" and "Synorix" in "The Cup", and I am flattered to think that the passage of time has not eradicated all my histrionic cunning.

To come, however, to that night at Sir George Bligh's. The bedroom into which Miss Fredericks had retired, had been specially chosen by me. It had one great feature that commended it to me. It had a communicating door that led to another room. Which, in turn, led to a third room which opened out on to the staircase that served the kitchens and outhouses.

Actually, I travelled a mere matter of fifty yards in the car when Bannerman heard it going away. Twenty-five yards from the house and the same twenty-five yards back again. To the kitchens and the staircase that I have just mentioned. At the top of that staircase, I met an ally by arrangement, agreed that everything was going according to plan, and then entered the bedroom that communicated with that which Iris Fredericks had entered a short time before.

The door of this latter room, you will remember, was bolted on the inside. From where I crouched, revolver in hand, I had a fairly clear view through the open communicating door, of the head of the bed and also of the window, below which, outside, stood—as far as I knew—Doctor Michael Bannerman. Through the light of a tiny table-lamp, a girl's head was visible to me on the pillow—it seemed that she slept already. Thus the half-hour sped by upstairs that Bannerman described to you in the previous chapter.

Suddenly, I heard Jack Tabernacle shout the words that the doctor has told you about. I heard also the sound of flying feet. Feet that raced down the staircase as though they were pursued by demons from the heat of hell. I heard a bumping noise, followed by Tabernacle's strangled gurgle. I knew then that the critical moment would soon be upon me.

Wriggling along the floor, to the threshold of the inner room, I looked to my revolver, raised myself on my two elbows and waited. I should think that I waited there for about five minutes. At length, precisely, too, as I had foreseen, I heard a swishing, scraping sort of sound. It came nearer and nearer and suddenly I saw the casement window of the bedroom pushed in slowly and deliberately. I could just see the figure leaning across the sill dressed in a white linen jacket, and as I looked more keenly, I was just able to distinguish the features of the man whom we had known as Otto Kreutz. Horn-rimmed glasses and moustache!

He peered at the sleeping figure in the bed, raised his arm and fired three times in rapid succession. At such short range it was impossible for him to miss, and he turned away, the light of triumphant madness in his eyes. It was at that moment that I receipted his bill. I fired at the glass of the window-pane and the sharp shock of the splintering sent him staggering backwards. He recovered, however, and before I could get to the window, he had thrown himself upwards, caught the top of the pipe and was scrambling on to the roof.

To go after him was to offer myself as a chocolate box in the way of targets, so I dashed through the bedroom, drew the bolts of the door, ran downstairs and out through the front door. From the gravel drive where I stood I could see the white-coated figure running across the Bligh roof, brandishing the revolver. According to my reckoning he should have three bullets left. I knew what he was after and watched him. For I knew other things, too, and could afford the privilege.

He came to the eastern end of the roof . . . and from there saw the Crossley—and a man standing by it, waiting for him should he decide to descend. Uttering a snarl of rage, he fired viciously across the intervening space. But his aim was out—the bullet smashed the wind-screen.

Then he turned quickly and ran across the roof in another direction. Not towards me, on my side of the house, but the other way, where the roof sloped, on the side over towards the kitchen gardens. My heart went to my mouth as I judged his reckless pace. I knew as I watched him what would inevitably happen . . . and sure enough it did. I had hardly registered the thought, when his foot slipped on a loose slate, he gave a little jump in an endeavour to recover himself, failed . . . and fell. He had been too near the edge.

He rolled a little way, clutching at air, and then crashed heavily through the glass of the Bligh green-houses to the ground. Goodaker left his place by the car, and he and I reached the body almost simultaneously.

"Did you fire, sir?" the inspector asked me, as he dashed up.

I shook my head. "No. Not then. He fell. His foot slipped when he was almost at the roof's edge. It's a matter of minutes only, I'm afraid. He's cheated the gallows, after all."

Goodaker knelt by the body. "Badly smashed, Mr. Bathurst. Broken to bits. Nasty fall—the glass, too, has cut him to pieces."

I nodded, just as the dying man opened his eyes for the last time. They glazed, almost as I looked down at him. He muttered something and I bent my head to catch his words.

"Dear old Dad," I heard him whisper faintly, "I've paid that debt for you. And for the mater. My darling . . . mother. Four eyes . . . for two teeth. That's double payment, anyhow. Every one . . . of them. They're wiped out." He sighed, his jaw dropped and his head rolled over in death.

I took the wig and glasses off just as I had removed similar appointments from the body of Corbett when it lay on the slab in the mortuary. "Recognize him, Inspector?" I asked my companion quietly.

Goodaker gasped as he gazed and looked on truth. "Good God, Mr. Bathurst," he cried, "it's young Mr. Tabernacle!"

Chapter XXVIII
JOINING THE FLATS
(Mr. Bathurst continues)

"Yes," I said, "and don't let Miss Fredericks see him. Despite the fact that she knew the truth some days ago, she's played out. She's still in the car, I suppose?"

He nodded. "Yes. I'll tell her to stay there. I think I'd better, hadn't I? What happened in the house?"

"What I had anticipated. He climbed up the pipe, after outing the doctor, and fired three shots into the plaster cast that we had put on the pillow. Right through the head. Then I fired at the glass to frighten him. I was certain that he couldn't make a getaway, and the chase began. But the best thing we can do now is to find Doctor Bannerman. He shouldn't be very far away."

I was right. He wasn't. Goodaker and I found him against the wall of the house, trussed like a fowl and with a nasty welt on the back of the head where he had been struck down from behind. The inspector and I carried him inside and jointly rendered first aid. He soon came back to consciousness and grinned at us feebly.

"Physician," I quoth unto him, "heal thyself. This is all the wrong way round, you know."

"What's it all about?" he gasped when he regained more accurate understanding. "Is Iris safe? And Jack?"

I held up my hand to him and in a few short sentences told him the truth. An appreciable period of time intervened before he spoke to us. When he did it was accompanied by a shake of the head.

"I can't believe it—it's incredible. Is the man a maniac then? Have you . . . taken him?"

I told him of the murderer's end . . . of the last few dreadful moments. Bannerman took it rather badly. That was not to be wondered at, I suppose, considering everything.

Eventually he looked across at me, and spoke two words only. They formed a question. "Mrs. Cotterill?"

I smiled at him, comfortingly.

"What about her? Is she all serene? No trouble?"

I leant down and patted the dear old scout on the shoulder. "Absolutely. None whatever. Rest assured that she's in the real original coral pink. You'll kiss her hand yet."

He looked a little puzzled. I went on. "Her 'phoning to us to-night was according to plan. I arranged it with her. Feel fit enough to come with us in the car?"

The doctor nodded. "I think so."

"Righto," I returned. "Goodaker . . . make arrangements concerning . . ." I jerked my hand in the direction of the greenhouses.

"Very good, sir. I'll 'phone through at once."

"Come round to 'The Rowfants' after breakfast . . . and I'll tell you one or two things you're bursting to know. Of how it all began . . . and how the end was staged. Come on, Bannerman, or Miss Fredericks will be frozen stiff. Good night, Goodaker."

Goodaker joined us at "The Rowfants" soon after the Ramage had cleared away the breakfast. The bow that he accorded Rosemary on his entrance was a truly gallant effort—worthy of the ill-fated Valentino himself.

"Sit down, Inspector," I said to him. "The doctor's still a bit under the weather, so I'm doing the honours for him this morning. 'The Rowfants' has a new O.C. Smoke, Inspector?"

He filled his pipe from my pouch. Then slowly and deliberately lit up.

"Comfy, each of you?" I asked them. They assured me. "Well listen to me, then, for little while, and I'll endeavour to make your crooked paths straight. First of all, we'll deal with the much vexed question of motive. My first idea of 'vendetta' proved to be the right one. Funny how first impressions are so frequently the best? Glance your eyes over that."

I handed Bannerman a typewritten statement. "That, I announced to them, "is a copy of a report in the *Morning Message*, dated May eleventh, nineteen hundred and eight. Read it."

The inspector rose and went to look over Bannerman's shoulder. This is what they read.

At the Old Bailey yesterday, John Casselton Clive, director of the London and Suburban Industrial Bank, was sentenced to fourteen years penal servitude for embezzlement and misappropriation of funds. Extradition warrants have been issued in respect of the two other directors who have absconded, Walter Fryberg and Montague Fryberg. Painful scenes were associated with the passing of the sentence by Mr. Justice Flint. Mrs. Clive, the young wife of the guilty man, fell into a stupor as her husband was taken from the dock.

"Got that?" I asked them. "Now read this one. That's an extract from the *Evening Moon*, July eleventh, nineteen hundred and fourteen."

Bannerman read it aloud:

John C. Clive, under sentence of fourteen years penal servitude, died this morning in the infirmary at Portsea Prison. The dead man was the notorious swindler connected with the London and Suburban Industrial Bank case of six years ago.

"Now this, last of all," I added. "From the obituary column of *The Times*. Bannerman read this out also:

On the 22nd inst. at Cranford Lodge, Loaningdale, Celia Elizabeth, wife of the late John Casselton Clive, aged 34 years.

I took back the papers, carefully folded them and replaced them in my pocket. "Well?" I queried of my two companions. "Have you arrived? Or are you still travelling hopefully?"

Dear old Bannerman tapped the table rather impatiently. "Explain, Bathurst, please."

"Celia Elizabeth," I repeated, "wife of the late John Casselton Clive and née, Tabernacle."

"I begin to see light," said Michael Bannerman. "Jack Tabernacle was the son of these two people."

"The only son—the only child. Only a nipper when his father was sentenced to that stretch of fourteen years. Sentenced, from many points of view, somewhat unjustly. The brothers Fryberg, whom you knew as Fredericks and Corbett respectively, absconded with something like one hundred thousand pounds, leaving the scapegoat, Clive, to face the music with a lone hand. The bank, of which the three men were acting directors, had started operations as a building society, and by reason of steady success, had gradually developed and expanded into a bank. Its principal customers and depositors, however, remained of the same class, that of the small capitalist. Suddenly, it was called upon to face a severe shock—the fraudulent failure of a very much larger and more influential society conducted on similar lines. The blow was prepared for, by the quick realization of securities, but—the Frybergs took fright and flight (with the cash) and Clive was left behind to pay the penalty. That was the only thing which he was able to pay.

"He was sentenced, as you read, died in prison, and his young wife, smashed, body, heart and soul, very soon followed him. But before she went she had trained her boy to the task that she meant him to accomplish. He took it from her as his life's work. In his mind, she sowed the seeds of revenge so thoroughly that it dominated him, and, as I said, became his one aim in life. The Frybergs went to South America, covered their tracks successfully, and evaded justice. In course of time, they took a chance and returned to this country under other names. They called themselves Walter Fredericks and Montague Corbett. They settled in Chelmersley, as you know, and became prominent members of local society." Here Goodaker interrupted me.

"How did Tabernacle recognize them as the Frybergs?"

"I thought you would ask me that. I don't know. I can only surmise. This is my suggestion. His mother had given him a photograph of each man. Also, she told him, I've no doubt, that they had gone to South America. He went out there, you will find, a few years ago, and in some way picked up the trail. Learned that they had returned to the old country, and followed them. Satisfied?"

They nodded. I went on. "As himself, he managed to effect a condition of intimacy with the family, by becoming engaged to the daughter, Iris. Paid her a great deal of attention and eventually had his suit accepted."

"That's very true," interposed Rosemary, "he was at her side for months before the actual engagement was announced. I think Iris rewarded his persistence more than anything else."

"The stage set, then, he planned the first murder. He determined to have a complete alibi for the person known as Jack Tabernacle. He 'went abroad'. As far as Melsheimer's hairdressing saloon, where he obtained the job of assistant, in the name of Otto Kreutz. You will find, I think, that he was always proficient with his hands. For his lodgings, he sought the house of Mrs. Rhodes, because, from what he had previously seen and heard, he had a shrewd idea that Duncan, the elder brother of the Fredericks' household, was mixed up pretty seriously with Elsie Rhodes, his landlady's daughter."

Here I saw Bannerman eyeing me queerly. "Here, half a minute, Bathurst. . . . I don't quite get all that. Didn't he go abroad? I had two postcards from him, from Rome. How—"

"Each of your postcards, Doctor, was posted to you on a Sunday . . . over a week-end. He flew to Rome twice during his stay with Melsheimer. Do you know who his cousin is?"

Bannerman was incredulous. "No. Who?"

"Captain Carstairs."

"*The* Carstairs?"

"Exactly. Holder of the Cape to Cairo record. I've seen him. He took Tabernacle, or Clive, if you prefer, over to Rome on two occasions." Then Goodaker chimed in.

"I see the idea. Fredericks senior was a regular customer at Melsheimer's. Always used to go in just on the stroke of closing time. Tabernacle had met him there, no doubt. But why did he wait six months to kill Fredericks?"

"I'll tell you," I said to him. "He was waiting for Melsheimer to take his holiday and leave him in sole charge of the saloon. When the German engaged him, he told him that he would be away during the last days of August."

"How do you know that, sir?"

"Easy, Inspector. At the end of February, he wrote and told you that he would have his man by that very date, August thirty-first. Don't you remember? Melsheimer's absence meant that he would have his chance."

Goodaker looked a bit shamefaced, so I rattled on to help him a bit. "He knew the habits and routine of his man thoroughly by the time August came. The result was that the way he 'predicted' the first murder to the very day was nothing like so clever as you all thought it was. Did you see through it, Doctor, when we called at the sorting-office?"

Bannerman made a sort of clucking noise that doubtless expressed denial.

"I'll explain it then. As I said just now, Fredericks dropped in to Melsheimer's on one particular evening every week. Close on 'shutting up' time. On his way home to dinner. He was proud of his hair . . . fond of the 'trim' and the 'shampoo'. Tabernacle knew when to expect him . . . his plans were made. He was doomed the first time they were alone together in the saloon. Goodaker, here, is informed by letter. But that letter, with the West Street address, written in pencil, *easily erased*, mark you, was first sent by our friend *to himself*. In that way he obtained the morning postmark. When Fredericks was actually lying dead in the saloon, he rubbed out the pencilled address, substituted the inspector's (already prepared) and delivered the letter himself at the police-station by hand."

"I see it," said Goodaker moodily, "walked in and shoved it on the desk along with all the others that had come by the ordinary post. Easy as falling downstairs."

"Of course. It stood to reason that the sorters would have noticed it had it gone through their hands."

"How did he kill Fredericks?" This from Michael Bannerman.

"As easily as he delivered that letter. Held the victim's head over a basin, attending to his hair, and cut his throat. He had the man at his mercy, you see. The position was ideal for the blood-letting. The stains, for instance, could be so easily washed away. Water and all that, absolutely to hand. After he had cleaned up the place and delivered his letter, he went back to his own house. For his car. Came back, I think, parked the car in Torrelli's yard, and dined at the restaurant. Kreutz at his best. Then the time came to dispose of the body. I told you, Goodaker, that there was a communication door between the restaurant and Melsheimer's, didn't I? I think it is used by enthusiastic patrons of the 'sport of kings', who place their commissions with Melsheimer by entering Torrelli's for the ostensible purpose of light refreshment and then going through from one place to the other. The continual traffic into Melsheimer's would have attracted the notice of the police. In Torrelli's it was a different matter.

"Tabernacle slipped through this door, dressed the body in the outdoor clothes, which, of course, Fredericks had been wearing when he entered the saloon, hoisted it on his shoulder and went back down the staircase that leads to the yard where his car was waiting to go on its journey to Taggarts Way. There was little risk. It is only during the day time that this staircase is used. You can imagine the rest."

"I think so," said the doctor. "I suppose he enticed Donald up there on some pretext."

"To Taggarts Way? Undoubtedly. Told him that he had discovered something with regard to his father's death, I expect.

The murder of the girl, Elsie Rhodes, was more difficult. He had stolen her marriage lines and used them as bait to bring her into his clutches. Like most girls of her class, she valued her marriage certificate inordinately, and she worried excessively over its loss."

"He stole it, of course," said Goodaker, "because he wanted to—"

"Leave that for a moment, Inspector," I said to him. "I'll explain that in its proper sequence. Let's take the four murders first. There's only Corbett's left, I think, now, and once again I am left to surmise. This is how I look at it. Things were getting much more difficult for him. The people of Chelmersley were on their guard. He was forced to act quickly and to take risks. The 'patrol' business, I should say, gave him the idea. He would 'get' Corbett one night when he was on patrol. He took his car, picked up the place where Corbett and Melsheimer were, lured the latter away—you know how—and then in some similar way, got the better of Corbett. Hit him from behind, I imagine—like he hit Melsheimer—drugged him, and drove away with the unconscious Corbett on the floor of the car. Before he put the body in the river, he had what he thought was a brainwave. It might suit his book admirably were 'Kreutz' to disappear. The most effective disappearance is by death. He made an attempt, therefore, to foist the identity of Kreutz on to the dead Corbett, hoping, that when the disappearance was discovered, it would so complicate matters and confuse our minds generally that we might be inclined to connect, at least, Corbett and Kreutz. That is how I think his mind functioned. He had the materials of disguise to hand and he even went to the length of trimming the dead man's moustache to make the affair more convincing. The way was now clear for the last of the Fredericks. You know how we blotted his copybook there. Well?"

Michael Bannerman rubbed his top lip. "Yes, I follow all that. But tell me, how did you fix on your man?"

I looked from him to the inspector. "Are you anxious to know too, Goodaker? Or had you arrived at the same conclusions?"

"No, Mr. Bathurst, I never had the slightest suspicion in that direction. The alibi at the time of the first murder put me off, you see."

"I'll trace the thing through then from the start. How my reasoning worked and how I had little pieces of luck that materially helped me."

I slanted a glance here at Rosemary, but she wasn't taking any. "If you want to ask me anything as I go along, don't hesitate to interrupt. My first deduction was that Walter Fredericks had been murdered in a barber's shop. I'll tell you why. There was scarcely a bloodstain on the silk muffler, from which fact I argued that it had been put on after the man's throat had been cut, and also the dead man's hair smelt of liquid soap. I wondered whether he had had his hair cut just before he was murdered. Now you know how hairs, after trimming, get left behind somewhere. In the ears, on the neck. I looked for one or more. Master Kreutz had, however, wiped them all off except *one*, which I found, by carefully wiping the neck and face of the corpse. I knew then that I was 'warm'.

"When our post-office expedition led us to a barber's shop of all places, I knew that I was 'hot'. That brings us to the first appearance of Otto Kreutz. Do you remember, Bannerman, how he produced the letter that I was so anxious to inspect? The one that he was supposed to have received the day before? Once again, he was clever. And once again, too, not quite clever enough. He showed me a different envelope and tried to beat me on the matter of the postmark date by having torn off the used stamp. And to be more secure, off other envelopes as well. For his young cousin! I contrived to drop that envelope and its enclosure so that I could see the latter. The date was July something. I knew then that Kreutz was my man. But why—and who on earth was he? It was a vendetta business, I felt moderately certain. There was 'Aquila' and the strange correspondence to Inspector Goodaker. Fredericks, too, had not been robbed of anything worth mentioning. Also he hadn't fixed any particular appointment for the evening on which he had been murdered."

"How do you know that?" flashed Rosemary at me.

"Because he hadn't telephoned home. Donald told us that it was his father's invariable habit to 'phone home if he were going out anywhere."

"Thank you, Anthony. Go on, please."

"While I was finessing with this vendetta idea with Doctor Bannerman, there came the second murder. Of the dead man's *son*—mind you! I regarded it as complete corroboration of my theory . . . which, however, sustained a shock when poor Elsie Rhodes was removed. This, I admit, brought me up with a jolt. Where was the family line here? But gradually even that straightened itself out. Elsie wasn't all that she seemed to be."

"You were inclined at first to entangle her with the mysterious Kreutz, I thought. That's so, isn't it?" This from Bannerman.

"Yes. I was, Doctor. You yourself cleared the air for me eventually, when you passed on the information that the murdered girl was an expectant mother. Could she, I said to myself, be the *wife* of any of the Fredericks? Had the murderer discovered that fact? If he had, and it was quite a possible contingency, the mother of an unborn child of this line, would link up in the chain of vendetta. Follow me?"

Bannerman nodded and I could see from their expressions that my other two auditors had, also.

"Good. Leaving the fourth murder for a brief period, the problem then resolved itself into determining the real identity of Otto Kreutz. To tell the truth, I was inclined to include our friend Tabernacle in the premier circle of suspicion from the time that he first arrived upon the scene." I waited then for the inevitable fusillade of interruptions. They came almost simultaneously. Rosemary, I think, got there by a short head. I will omit what the others asked.

"But why? How could you, with no—"

This was hers—as far as I let her get. "My first suspicion hinged on that peculiar psychological vanity that seems inseparable from the mental make-up of so many murderers. Do you remember, Goodaker, the book from which, I said, the murderer's pseudonym of 'Aquila' had been cut?"

"Very well, Mr. Bathurst. I understand that you meant the Bible."

"Full marks, Inspector. Now listen carefully while I develop my theory. What did our murderer first sign himself, Doctor?"

"The Eagle," replied Bannerman promptly.

"And his second *nom-de-guerre*?"

"'Aquila.' The Latin form of the first. The same name, you might reasonably say."

"Any alternative?"

"I don't follow you. Sorry and all that." It was apparent that Bannerman was at a loss. I tried to help him.

"Think, Doctor. The clue is in the Bible."

"I know what you mean," said Rosemary quietly. "'Aquila', the tent-maker. Husband of Priscilla. It's in the Acts, isn't it?"

I beamed on her. "Go on. You're doing splendidly."

But here the fount of her inspiration dried up. "Nothing doing?" I queried.

"Afraid not."

"He obtained his pseudonyms backwards. If I can put it like that. He was John Tabernacle Clive—calling himself at this time by the middle name of the three. Tabernacle. Tabernaculum—Latin—'a tent'. Tent—tent-maker. Tent-maker—'Aquila' of ancient fame. Aquila—an eagle. *Voilà*."

"But surely that was calling attention to himself," Goodaker objected.

"Exactly. By the same trait of psychology—a radiation of vanity—that causes a murderer to lurk in the cemetery during the burial of his victim. That makes him send anonymous letters to the 'Yard' during investigation of a clueless crime. He *exults*, you see, in his success, and in a way, he wishes the world to *sense* his exultation. It galls him to think that safety spells obscurity. He will even take a risk over it. What do you say, Bannerman?"

"I think you're right. It's another expression of a murderer's abnormality. Pretty septic too."

"Very likely. But to proceed. My suspicions, however, were useless without *proof*. I had to wait in patience. At last came my chance. After the Rhodes murder, I made up my mind to have a look round our friend's place of abode. How was I to manage it? I took a bold step. I recruited him as an ally. Let him think I was intrigued by the village pageant and sent him on an errand to Sir Austin Kemble, the Commissioner of Police. That same afternoon, I broke the law of the land, entered and took a good look round his premises."

Goodaker was keenly interested. "Any luck?"

"A very pleasing reconnaissance, Inspector. I will recount my discoveries one by one. *(a)* The marriage certificate of Duncan Fredericks and Elsie Rhodes, *(b)* An account of the Clive trial, with the reference to the Frybergs that I read to you just now. *(c)* A Bible, mutilated as far as the eighteenth chapter of the Acts of the Apostles went, in its first three verses. Let me see if I can remember them, as they should be: 'A certain Jew named Aquila, born in Pontus' . . . and *(d)*—listen with all your ears—a shoe . . . and on the sole of that shoe . . . *a small speck of squashed pink chocolate-cream.* And mark this! He was entirely unaware of this last fact . . . didn't know of its possibility even until I told him . . . and then—realizing—spoke of a *boot* that might hold the damning piece of evidence. *A boot,* of course, because it was his own habit to wear shoes always! I had my man now, for a certainty, and when he quoted the Bible to me, I knew that there wasn't the slightest shadow of a doubt."

"What was the next step?" queried Rosemary.

"Well, I marked down Walter Fredericks as a Fryberg and wondered if the brother were anywhere near at hand. I hadn't long to wait. Here was the solution of Corbett's cold feet. He knew it was vendetta right enough, but dared not say so. Also, he was completely ignorant as to who the hidden enemy was. A Clive certainly—but who—and where exactly was he lurking? Then came the complications. When Master Tabernacle endeavoured to 'fog' the issue. The warning that was sent to you, Mrs. Cotterill . . . and the inclusion in it of 'one other'. Corbett, no doubt, but why were you dragged into the meshes of the conspiracy? I tested my chain of reasoning all ways, but the links held true and fast. To threaten *you* with Corbett, was 'bluff'

9 781913 527419